CHEROKEE MISSION

KARL H. MEYER

A Dell/Banbury Book

Published by
Banbury Books, Inc.
37 West Avenue
Wayne, Pennsylvania 19087

Dell ® TM 681510, Dell Publishing Co., Inc.

ISBN: 0-440-01183-3

Printed in the United States of America

First printing—August 1982

A BRUTAL DECREE DIVIDED THE INDIAN
TRIBE . . . DESTROYED A WAY OF LIFE . . .
AND UNLEASHED A TIDE OF LAWLESSNESS . . .

Three miles beyond Spring Place, John Parker saw
smoke billowing above Tom Laurel's fields. Through
the smoke he glimpsed Tom's wife, frantically waving
for him to hurry. Parker spurred his horse to the edge
of the clearing and swung down.

"Betsy! My God!" Her hair had fallen from her
sunbonnet and strands were tangled across her damp-
ened cheeks and forehead. She'd been crying and when
she saw Parker she burst into sobs again.

He held her, vainly attempting to calm her sobbing.

"Betsy! Tell me! Where's Tom?"

Unable to collect herself enough to speak clearly,
Betsy took Parker's hand and dragged him to the far
side of the cabin. There, Tom lay writhing on the
ground, hands clutched around his shattered ribs, his
face swollen and bloody. Parker knelt and placed a
comforting hand on Tom's forehead.

"Men came," Betsy began breathlessly, "white
men. Said they wanted our horse. 'Here's a dollar,' one
man said. 'Since the government's sending you out
West, you'll need every penny you can get to live on.'
Oh, John, you should have heard him laugh when he
said that. Tom ran in the house to get his rifle. That's
when five of the men jumped him. 'Pass this on to your
redskin friends,' they kept telling him, and then they
kicked him and beat him. . . ."

Parker looked out at the burning cornfield. "Why
. . . why . . . ?"

Betsy stared blankly at the devastated land. "I refused to sell them the crop . . . for fifty-cents' worth of
whiskey."

THE AMERICAN INDIANS SERIES

Ask your bookseller for these other titles:

To Captain David Larry Hicks (USA Ret.)
who proudly and rightfully is known
among his Cherokee people as
U-tsi-di-hi

The Cherokees
1831-1834

UCKY

Mountains

NORTH CAROLINA

Appalachian

• Vahn's House

• Spring Place

New Echota

• Cedartown

SOUTH
CAROLINA

River

Savannah River

Augusta •

• Carrollton

GEORGIA

Savannah •

Chatahoochee

Atlantic

Ocean

xico

Chapter 1

New Echota, Georgia
27th July, 1827

Chief Clerk Charles Madden
Office of Indian Affairs
War Department
Washington, D.C.

Dear Mr. Madden:

Today, delegates from all sectors of the Cherokee Nation met and approved a constitution. Chief White Path, however, is a full-blood and representative of those Cherokee who feel that their Nation should refrain from modeling its government after ours, but instead, return to ancient tribal ways. Fortunately, White Path represents a very small minority.

John Ross, acting Chief of the Cherokee Nation, almost certainly will be elected principal chief when the council reconvenes next spring. Ross steadfastly remains the diplomat, and Major Ridge, his only opposition, seems more the warrior. I suspect that most of the constitution is the work of Ross.

Elias Boudinot has departed the Nation again, this time for Boston. He is seeking friends to establish a newspaper at New Echota, Georgia. The newspaper there is to be published in the Cherokee language and will likely be heavily supported by the Board of Foreign Missions; such an enterprise would support its missionary efforts in the nation.

Yr. obdt. Servant,
Wm. Cullen, Agent

Sullivan's Public House lay around the corner from the firm of Baker & Greene. It was much like any other tavern in Boston, except for the odors that seemed to hang in the air. Mingled with the rich aroma of roasting lamb and pork, the acrid smoke from dozens of pipes and the fetid mustiness of spilled ale and rum, there arose a pervading smell of printer's ink.

Nearly all of Sullivan's patrons were employed by printing houses in the district and most of them felt comfortable and at ease with the odors they wore on their clothing and hands. When the talk was not of the sultry wenches who drifted in and out of the tavern, it generally centered on the day's work as well as on the prospects of the many small printing establishments that had been springing up in the neighborhood.

"There ain't enough work now for the places we already got!"

"I hear Baker & Greene hasn't gotten a new job in for a month, Charley. True or no?"

"Not if a pig's got feathers," Charley Adams replied, wiping a ring of foam from his mouth, "that's true."

"All we've had in weeks is handbills and a couple

of tracts from some crazy fool who wants to convince the world that Columbus sailed around Africa to get here!"

The talk stopped momentarily while Polly distributed a tray of steins around the table. Deftly she dodged the ink-stained hands that reached out for her ample buttocks.

"Why all the glum talk about there not bein' enough work?" she asked, gathering up the empties and placing them on the tray. "We ain't lost no business in here lately that I've noticed."

Charley Adams looked around the crowded room, then nodded in agreement. "Seems to me you could use another wench or two around here, though. Takes forever to get a meal."

"Is that so?" Polly replied lightly, her eyes twinkling as she regarded the rotund old printer. "You sure ain't missed many!"

"I'm just makin' up for all the ones I missed durin' the war. Made up me mind if I ever had to go fight with Jackson again I'd be carryin' a good reserve with me."

Groans went up along the table. "Lord save us! Time for Charley's old war stories again!"

"Anybody care to bet we'll hear how some Cherokee redskin saved Andy Jackson's life at Horseshoe Bend?"

Laughter greeted this gibe. Jackson's victory at Horseshoe Bend was one of Charley's favorite stories and most of the listeners knew all the details by heart.

The old printer was only half listening to the teasing. Part of his thoughts were focused on the fiery battle that so long ago had changed the course of history and laid the groundwork for Jackson's tremendous power.

"That bastard," Adams muttered in the midst of

the company, but there were no comments and no rebuttals, so engrossed were the men in beer and laughter.

In just moments Polly had delivered to the table steaming bowls of boiled potatoes and carrots. "You thought enough of Old Hickory to vote for him, didn't you?" she teased, just as Charley Adams was beginning once again to launch his Jackson gripes out loud.

"Never!"

Snickers escaped from the lips of several of the printers, but the expression on Adams' face froze them into silence. "Old Charley likes to keep it in the family. That's why he voted for Uncle John."

Charley exploded with a splutter. "John Quincy Adams ain't no relation to me!"

"Hell," one of the men blustered at last, "we thought you were a loyal supporter of Jackson."

"Only when it comes to fightin' with him," Adams slammed back. "I don't trust the man for anything else. At Horseshoe Bend, Jackson wouldn't have won if it hadn't been for the Indians. Then, after the peace conference that ended that whole mess with the Creek, he turned right around, he did, and began spoutin' off about sendin' all the southern Indians west. Supporter of Jackson! That's some laugh. I didn't vote for the man in '24, and I ain't votin' for him next year. Tennessee's a good place for Andy. That's easy enough to see if you've got eyes! Where's Parker tonight?" he changed the subject.

"He's late, all right."

"Don't look for John," someone said. "Told me this morning he's goin' to a fancy reception at Greene's house."

"Whooee! Sounds like John Parker's gettin' up in the world," exclaimed Cyrus Moorehead. "How come the boss invites the likes of Parker to dinner and not the rest of us?"

"Because the rest of you ain't got a likin' for Indians, that's why," Charley jabbed.

"And Parker does?" Moorehead was surprised. "Wasn't too long ago he was sayin' he never laid eyes on an Indian."

"Parker's quiet, but he's curious; smart, too," Charley replied, dexterously rolling an extra potato onto his plate. "Anyway, tonight old man Greene's got his house full of Indians."

Adams leaned across the table and speared a slab of roast pork. "Greene gets himself real worked up over that missionary school down in Connecticut," he added. "I swear the man thinks more about savin' the souls of heathens than he does about his business right here."

John Parker carefully worked his way through the muddy streets and drifting fog. He hated this weather. He had been the oldest of four children on a barren Vermont farm, and he had done his share of chores in all weather, but he didn't have to like it. As a boy, he had trained himself to turn his mind away from physical discomfort, and he did so now. He would think about Elias Boudinot, the man he was on his way to meet. What he remembered of the Indian fascinated him and Greene had promised that Boudinot would be at the reception.

Parker had seen Boudinot before. The Cherokee had stood at the pulpit of the Bay Presbyterian Church two Sundays earlier, decked out in a frock coat, white broadcloth shirt and gleaming silk cravat. Except for his bronzed features, Boudinot had looked like a white American minister. But there was something about the fervor of his resounding speech that set him apart from the preachers who occupied the pulpit on most other Sunday mornings, a musical sound that had inspired Parker to imagine at the time that St. Paul himself must have had such a voice.

The entire congregation had been mesmerized as the Cherokee proudly discoursed on the advances made by his people. "You have all heard how Sequoyah invented an alphabet for the Cherokee language," Boudinot had begun, "and how in a matter of weeks every Cherokee could read and write. Not years, weeks!

"Many of our white neighbors who cannot read or write their own names," he went on, "find this news galling. These are the same people who are so afraid of us because we have patterned a constitution and system of government after the United States.

"As of now, we are fifteen thousand and sixty strong, a figure that includes one hundred forty-seven white men and seventy-three white women who have married into the tribe. Not long ago, we were a nomadic people who hunted to live; today our Nation lives by means of peaceful trade and agriculture. There are at this time twenty-two thousand cattle, seventy-six hundred horses, forty-six thousand swine and twenty-five hundred sheep." Boudinot recited the figures as though they had been burned into his memory. "The Cherokee boast seven hundred sixty-two looms, twenty-five hundred-odd spinning wheels, one hundred seventy-two wagons and almost three thousand ploughs. There are thirty-one gristmills and ten sawmills, sixty-two blacksmith shops and eight cotton machines. There are eighteen ferries and a number of public roads. We have eighteen schools and are planning to establish others. In one district alone, there were last winter more than one thousand volumes of good books and eleven different periodical papers, both religious and political. These are all eagerly read. I am not exaggerating when I boast that in only two generations my people have changed from a primitive to a civilized nation."

Boudinot paused as the buzz of admiration and approval spread through the congregation. He remembered how just the year before, he and his white bride, Harriet, had feared for their lives from the very people who were now so captivated by him. Shivering, he recalled the day before their marriage, when Harriet had been burned in effigy. The North was as capable of bigotry as the South, he had thought then. At least now the northerners were ready to make up for past insults.

"The time has come," Boudinot continued finally, "to climax the achievements we have gained. We now have an alphabet and a written language. Because of that, we are at the threshold of another monumental step, one that could further our education and establish better communications with our valued white neighbors. We are planning to purchase a printing press. Having it will enable us to disseminate material of interest to our Nation, to yours and to the world. We shall have the type set both in Cherokee and in English. If the kind people of this audience could feel free to bless this undertaking with their prayers and contributions . . ."

John Parker handed his hat and cloak to the servant at the door of the Greene mansion and surveyed the vestibule. His eyes were drawn first to the chandelier hanging in the middle of the room. Fine beeswax candles, he noted, not the tallow that left the air so smoky. And the expensive whale oil in the lamps around the entryway proclaimed to the world that David Greene was more than slightly affluent.

The curving marble stairway was a masterpiece of design. Parker could not remember seeing the likes of it before. He knew such luxury existed, but it had always been so far removed from the world into which he was born that he had never once dreamed of being surrounded by it. His gaze rested on one of the paintings in the entry hall. It was a pastoral view and for a moment, as he studied the sheep grazing on a lush, green meadow, he felt a twinge of homesickness.

"Ah, there you are, John!" rang his employer's voice. "I was afraid you might not come."

"No chance of that, sir," Parker replied, taking the hand Greene had thrust forth. "I've been looking forward to meeting some of the people you said would be here."

The young guest was led into the ballroom. So bright was the light cast there by the rich array of lamps and candles that the instant impression he had was that daylight had returned.

Crowding together in the huge room were people presenting a kaleidoscope of skin color and dress. There were blacks from Africa, two of whom were dressed in their native costumes of feathers, beads and furs, not to mention the trousers they had added as concessions to their hosts. Some of the guests were Indians who seemed slightly uncomfortable wearing white man's clothing. Other Indians appeared to be as much at ease in shirts and ties as the Africans in their feathers.

Greene steered Parker through knots of people who were talking in various exotic languages. Then he asked casually, "How long have you been a journeyman now, John? Two years? Three?"

"Two, sir; it'll be three in March." Parker wondered why Greene was asking. Hadn't his host invited him to meet Boudinot and some of the students from the Foreign Mission School at Cornwall? The question about work seemed out of place.

"John, Elias Boudinot of New Echota. Elias, I'd like you to meet Mr. John Parker, a journeyman with my firm."

The two men warmly shook hands. Boudinot was stocky and powerful and even up close, he compared favorably to every white man in the room. Parker was immediately impressed by the man's easy, outgoing charm and by the fact that once again he was so finely dressed.

"A printer, Mr. Parker?" Boudinot said, his eyes brightening.

"Journeyman, sir. I've been with Baker & Greene since I began my apprenticeship."

Greene beamed proudly. "Good man, too. Oops! there's Mrs. Greene. Gentlemen, you must excuse me; I need to speak with her." As their host moved off, Parker and Boudinot walked toward one of the food-laden side tables.

"Mr. Greene has told me much about you, Mr. Boudinot," Parker began, starting in on the best food he'd ever eaten. "And since I heard you preach at the Bay Church I've wanted to ask you something. Is it true that all the Cherokee people can read and write?"

Boudinot laughed heartily, his dark eyes sparkling. "Pretty hard to believe, isn't it, that a bunch of 'savages' could be so smart. Oh, I'm sorry," the Indian apologized, seeing his companion's face color. "Please don't take offense at my teasing, Mr. Parker. To answer your question, yes, nearly all the Cherokee can read and write. Haven't you ever seen our written language?"

When Parker shook his head, Boudinot put down the glass of wine he had been sipping and drew a sheaf of papers from a leather case he'd kept with him. He spread the papers out on an empty table nearby. Some of the handwritten inscriptions bore a resemblance to familiar Roman letters and there were several that reminded the young printer of Greek, which he had studied for two years before leaving school to take up his apprenticeship. The remaining large number of symbols, however, had no meaning at all.

"We have eighty-six letters in our alphabet," Boudinot explained, "not the twenty-six used in English. But each of the letters stands for one sound only and generally represents an entire syllable. Because of these designations, there is less confusion in Cherokee than there is in English, whose letter C can stand for either S or K. Most important, anyone who knows the language can read and write it as soon as he learns the alphabet."

For a few minutes, John studied the sheets in puzzled silence. Then Boudinot took a lead pencil and wrote: "S B Z H."

"This, in English, takes this many letters." Again he wrote on the paper. The message said "DO YOU KNOW ME."

Pointing to the S, he went on, "This letter is sounded DOO. This looks like a B, but is pronounced YOO; and Z is equivalent to the sound of NO, and the H is ME."

John had to agree that though the symbols were strange, the system had some obvious advantages over English. Yet his head was spinning within ten minutes.

Boudinot laughed. "Don't worry," he comforted, "Once you speak the language, the reading and writing come easily."

With those words, Boudinot launched once again into his favorite subject and talked about the progress the Cherokee had made by using their new form of government.

"Elias, you just don't stop, do you?" David Greene commented, returning to the conversation.

Boudinot grinned widely. "I want everyone to know."

"Fine, but don't monopololize Mr. Parker all evening. There are other people here who have stories of their own to tell."

Boudinot bowed a playful good-by as Greene steered Parker across the room toward Mrs. Greene, who had a group of women gathered around her. Two of the women she had been talking with were near her own age and three looked younger. Greene stayed only long enough to introduce Parker, then bustled off to meet a latecomer who had entered the ballroom.

Mrs. Greene introduced the young man around the group, but as far as Parker was concerned, they all could have vanished instantly; that is, all except one, for his eyes were fixed on the most beautiful woman he had ever seen. "And this," the hostess finished, "is Miss Agatha Lake."

"How do you do, Miss Lake." Parker was surprised that the words didn't tangle on his tongue; he was thoroughly entranced.

Agatha Lake made a polite curtsy. The gesture was as graceful as a dance and Parker stared in dumb appreciation. He noted the finely tailored gown his companion wore. It contrasted markedly with the rather plain woolen dresses worn by the women with her. Agatha Lake's blue eyes sparkled when she returned his greeting and her complexion, blooming with health, showed no trace of powder or rouge. Parker was delighted when those standing nearby drifted into other conversations. He wanted all of this lovely girl's attention for himself.

"Mr. Green said you are a printer, Mr. Parker?" Agatha asked politely.

"Yes. I've worked for Mr. Greene for nearly ten years."

"You enjoy the work, then?"

"I wouldn't know any other, except farming, Miss Lake. Actually, I've been thinking about moving on. Boston has its attractions, but I like small towns. Are you from Boston?"

"No, my home is in the South. I've been here studying to be a teacher. When I've finished, I'm going back to teach the Cherokee in one of the mission schools."

Parker hesitated. "I'm a bit surprised, Miss Lake, I have to confess it, that a girl of your breeding would consider giving up a comfortable life to work in a mission school. Most of the young women I've met who have chosen missionary work are poor and quite plain."

"I have never been one, Mr. Parker, to choose a way of life merely because it was expected of me. If we get to know one another well, you will quickly learn that."

This woman is as sure of herself as she is lovely, Parker thought. Soon, as if of one mind, they made their way to the verandah, stopping at a table by the door to take some wine out with them. The iron bench they sat on by the garden provided little comfort, but soon the wine had taken hold and where they sat held little interest. Conversation came easy and in time it settled on the farm life they remembered as children.

"One morning, I got up before my father," John recalled, "and ran out to the cornfield to snap off an ear and eat the raw corn while it was still cool from the night."

"Did you ever pick berries all day and have your mother ask why you only had one basketful?" Agatha asked, her eyes mirthful.

"My pa whaled the tar out of me once because I'd eaten more than I brought back to the house."

"What about trying to gather eggs in the winter and being afraid your fingers would be so cold you'd drop one?"

The two howled with laughter, then covered their mouths with their hands like embarrassed children. "Taking care of the chickens was work for my sisters," Parker went on, "and it's still good work for women. But if I may be frank, Miss Lake, I still can't picture you doing chores like that."

Agatha had no chance to answer. David Greene appeared again, with Elias Boudinot in tow.

"You two have been talking for over a half an hour," Greene said with a knowing smile. "Please forgive me for interrupting, but Elias needs to leave shortly and he'd like a few minutes with you, Mr. Parker."

Parker reluctantly excused himself from Agatha. "I'm confident we will see each other again, Miss Lake," he smiled, bowing over her hand.

She stared straight at him. "I'm confident of that, too, Mr. Parker."

Boudinot was waiting near the center of the garden. He wasted no time in getting to the point.

"As you know, Mr. Parker, I made this trip to secure contributions for our printing press. Well, my efforts have been successful and the press I wanted already has been ordered from Baker & Greene. I've also made arrangements to have the type cast. What I lack now is experienced printers. We've already engaged a printer from Tennessee, but at least two others will be needed. Would you consider working for us?" Boudinot ignored Parker's astonished expression and went on. "I know the salary won't compare to what you've been making at Baker & Greene," he conceded, "but there are other considerations. You'll be able to have all the land you can take care of to plant a garden or even grow some cash crops. The move won't set you back financially as much as you might think."

Thoughts of being able to get his hands into clean, sweet earth again flooded Parker's mind, rekindling memories of a way of life that had meant much more to him than money ever could. He'd be able to raise tomatoes and beans again, and corn and squash and melons, all while being a printer and doing the work he valued most.

"Yes, I think I'd like to take you up on your offer, Mr. Boudinot. But of course I'd have to clear the new arrangement with Mr. Greene first."

"I'm certain he'll approve," Boudinot smiled. "Greene is the one who suggested I ask you."

Chapter 2

The sunlight poked through the mists of Boston Harbor as the schooner caught the rising tide and moved out into Massachusetts Bay. Secure in the hold were the crates that held the cumbersome printing press and the boxes of type that were destined to carry the message of the Cherokee Nation to the world. David Greene personally had contributed substantially to the purchase of the equipment and John Parker's final days in Boston were spent learning every inch of the equipment.

Elias Boudinot, when not soliciting more funds from friendly congregations, supervised the type founders, making sure that all the characters for the Cherokee alphabet were correct. Once the type had been approved, Boudinot left Boston in order to return home and coordinate the details of setting up the operation. He wanted everything in order before the arrival of the printing press.

David Greene was accompanying Parker and the press on the trip. Greene's hope was that much of the tedious journey would be spent teaching Parker the Cherokee alphabet. But the second day out of Boston, after they passed an incoming whaler plowing deep into the water on its way to New Bedford, the ocean roughened. Parker's face suddenly went ashen.

"John? What's wrong?"

"I . . ." The young printer's words congealed into an agonized groan and he jumped from his seat. Racing from the tiny cabin, he leaned over the rail, then vomited what had been a substantial breakfast.

Greene roared with laughter. He waited until Parker returned and wiped his face with a towel he had found in a built-in chest next to the bunks. "You'll be fine by tomorrow, my boy. I've never seen a case of seasickness last more than a day."

Greene's estimate was incorrect. John Parker was sick for the entire journey to Savannah and barely able to keep down enough nourishment to stay alive. Not until the ship had docked in Savannah was he able to face the world in anything resembling his normal fashion.

"Thank God the riverboat to Augusta won't leave for another two days," he told Greene. "For a while there I was sure I was dead!"

Greene's eyes twinkled. "Isn't it a good thing printers don't have to serve an apprenticeship at sea, John? You might never have completed yours. And then where would you be?"

"Back home raising hogs and apples," Parker replied with no hesitation. "I've seen all of the blue ocean I ever want to see. The only waves that excite this printer/farmboy are the waving fields of wheat and oats."

"Maybe you'll be able to stake out a garden plot when you get to New Echota. Elias told me that everyone, including Cullen, the Indian agent, has a plot of ground to do some farming."

"Sounds good, but the more I think about it, the more I've got a feeling that there's going to be more than enough work to keep me busy just in setting up a newspaper. Mr. Boudinot might be many things, but he isn't a printer. The farming, I'm afraid, will have to wait."

"I agree," Greene chuckled. "For all his courage and expertise, our friend Boudinot is naive as a baby about what our office is going to need. I went over everything in the shop with him and I think all he thought would be necessary were the press and the type. That's when I put him in your hands."

After an uneventful trip up the Savannah River by steamer, Greene and Parker were met at the dock by John Ross, Acting Chief of the Cherokee Nation. Parker was astounded. He had been expecting to be met by a swarthy Cherokee, but John Ross appeared more the dour Scot than Indian.

Ross smiled, seeing Parker's reaction. His clear blue eyes bore no trace of Cherokee ancestry. "I'm only one-eighth Cherokee," he explained as if reading the printer's thoughts.

"It's good you told me," Parker answered appreciatively. "Most of the Indians I met in Boston were tall and muscular. You look pretty rugged yourself," he went on, encouraged by Ross' bemused expression, "but you're shorter than I expected you'd be and seem more like a Boston banker than you do an Indian chief."

Ross bore no more resemblance to an Indian in his manner or dress than he did in physical appearance. His dusty frock coat and silk cravat bore traces of a hard journey, but he would have looked perfectly ordinary among the crowds that thronged the streets of any major eastern city.

"Whatever you make of me," Ross replied laughing, "I'm glad you're here. And you know I'm pleased to see you, too, Mr. Greene. It's a pleasure to meet you."

"Thank you, Mr. Ross. Let me introduce this young man more formally. This is John Parker, the journeyman Elias engaged."

"*O-si-yo!*" Parker said as he took Ross' hand.

Ross' face beamed with pleasure, and he responded with an unbroken string of musical Cherokee.

"I'm sorry, Mr. Ross, but I'm afraid I don't know more than a dozen words of your language. I've been making some headway with your alphabet, though."

"No apologies, Mr. Parker. You've made a fine start. I'm sure the next few months will be a real education for you. Here's someone that will help you start off well." And Ross introduced both men to the driver of the freight wagon that would take the press and type to New Echota. "Little Tree has an excellent command of English, Mr. Parker. I believe you'll be able to learn a great deal from him during the next few days."

Little Tree's manner was warm and friendly and he smiled easily. "John Parker? From now you'll be Tsani. That's as close to 'John' as you can come in Cherokee."

Ross supervised the loading of the crates onto a wagon for the overland trip to New Echota, then drove his buggy ahead of the wagon for the hundred-fifty-mile trip to the new capital of the Cherokee Nation. Parker rode the hard seat alongside Little Tree, pleased that the driver seemed to welcome the idea of having someone to talk to on the long journey.

"I am," Little Tree explained, "the highest ranking muleskinner in the Cherokee Nation. My father thought I would be a fine hunter and warrior and taught me everything he knew. But an Indian doesn't make a very good living hunting deer and beaver these days, Tsani. Our hunting grounds have shrunk. My people have become more like white men, they've chosen to plant and farm."

"You haven't taken an English name like so many others have, Little Tree. Why?"

"Little Tree is English. My father wanted to call me Great Forest, but my mother said it was impossible for one tree to be a whole forest, so she named me Little Tree and said she would need many more trees if my father wanted to think that big!"

He paused as though that were the end of the story but Parker was curious and asked, "How many trees are there now?"

"Still only one. My sisters were no help. Little Tree makes a small forest instead of a great one."

Parker mused that small was not an appropriate word for Little Tree. The Indian stood a bit over six feet tall and embodied the strength of any two men Parker had ever met. Unassisted, he'd picked up each of the heavy boxes of type and put them in the wagon as easily as if they were small bundles of laundry.

The Cherokee's buckskin trousers, shirt of bright gingham and heavy woolen jacket were more in keeping with Parker's idea of Indian clothing than what John Ross was wearing. Even the muleskinner's feet coverings, high-top moccasins that appeared to be warm and comfortable, were in line with what the printer had expected.

As they traveled northwest, Little Tree kept up a running commentary on the country they were passing through. When finally they reached the ferry crossing at the Chattahoochee River, he pointed with pride. "Home! That land on the other side of the river is the Cherokee Nation."

Farther on, to the west and north, Parker saw a distinct change in the appearance of the villages they saw. The first thing he noticed was that there were few if any white men about. The settlements were smaller, too.

What struck him most, though, were changes in the attitudes of the people they met. As soon as the small procession entered a village, men and women alike came out to hail them and pay their respects to Ross. There had been no such ceremony on the other side of the Chattahoochee. Parker found it surprising that the full-blooded Cherokee held Ross in such high regard, but he kept the thought to himself, certain that in time he would learn why.

The day before the travelers arrived at New Echota, there were snowflakes whirling, then melting once they touched the ground. Ross had stopped at the home of one of the local chiefs to tell him that the printing press had arrived and that he could tell his people they could expect to have their first newspaper soon.

The elderly chief and his wife were surrounded by a family that numbered about twenty, including sons, daughters, brothers, sisters and grandchildren. Parker noticed that few of them wore much more than leather aprons to cover their private parts. The old woman wore light cotton and had the skin of a cow draped over her shoulders. Even the children, like the old chief, were barefoot and despite the cold were gathered under a thatched pavilion-style roof without benefit of walls to keep warm.

"Why aren't they inside?"

Little Tree gave a deprecating grunt in reply. "We're an outdoor people, Tsani. Many of us have adopted white ways, but there are those who live as the Cherokee have always lived. Only when it becomes unbearably cold do they take shelter inside."

"And how do you live, Little Tree?" Parker wondered.

Little Tree laughed. "I live in a four-room house with a fireplace. One of the advantages of progress. Could you tell, Tsani? Do I look that soft?"

Parker's first glimpse of New Echota the next day was a disappointment. Again his expectations had missed the mark. Where was the bustling town that was worthy of being called the seat of a nation? Boudinot's description of the capital was glowing, although he'd admitted that there was still much work to be done.

"My uncle, Major Ridge," Boudinot had said, "thinks Baltimore is the finest place he's seen and hopes that some day New Echota will rival it."

But what greeted Parker's eyes was a mere handful of houses and cabins. Little Tree saw the look of disappointment on the printer's face and explained. "New Echota used to be called New Town, but when the Council decided to make it the national capital it was renamed. We picked this place because it is nearly in the center of the Nation and easy for people to travel to for council meetings. Actually, there were more homes in New Echota before it was chosen for the capital, but because the land is so level and well suited to use as a place for a government seat, nearly all the old buildings were torn down so that new street and building arrangements could be planned."

Parker commented that two of the houses would have been at home in any New England town. Of two-story construction, each had a double verandah and a splendid chimney indicating a central fireplace. Both were neatly whitewashed with gray trim.

"That house," said Little Tree pointing to one, "is Elias Boudinot's. And the other one is the preacher's, Samuel Worcester."

In all, Parker could see half a dozen new frame

houses and several log cabins with shingled roofs. Little Tree pointed out the council house, the court-house, the log building that would house the newspa-per, and four stores. Near the center of the town, which was as level and smooth as a barn floor, was a public spring that reminded Parker of the mill pond in the Massachusetts town near his father's farm.

"It's pretty quiet now." Little Tree was almost apologetic. "But when the Council meets, there are tents as far as your eye can see and thousands of people from all over our nation. It is beautiful, Tsani, to see all the campfires and the torches people carry at night. And of course there is the singing and the dancing and the ball play. Ah! Wait until you see!"

A scant twenty by thirty feet, the home of the *Cherokee Phoenix* shouted its existence to the world. A bright white sign hung over the front porch. On it was the name of the paper, in both Cherokee and English, also the symbol of a phoenix rising from a bed of ashes.

The building had been constructed of squared-off logs and had doors at either end. Each of the long side walls had windows and the front porch featured a pair of whitewashed benches flanking the door, making a cosy place to sit.

Word of Ross' arrival with the press had already reached the town and in front of the building stood a cluster of men cheering them on the last hundred yards. Parker climbed out of the wagon seat and as he did, Greene asked, "Does this town look small enough to suit you, John?"

Parker grinned. "I'd say it's just about right, sir. And smell the air! That's something you don't dare do in Boston."

Elias Boudinot stepped forward and greeted Ross

first, then Greene and Parker. "This is Henry Wheeler," he announced, indicating a thin little man. "He's the printer from Tennessee who's in charge of the plant."

He looked around. "Where's Isaac?" he asked Wheeler.

"Don't know. He was here a minute ago. Maybe he . . ."

"Indeed," Boudinot sighed, "maybe he went over to McCoy's place again. Oh, well, let's start moving things inside. We'll get to work as soon as we feed you."

Suddenly, the air was rent by a stream of curses. "In a pig's ass we'll get to work! How in the name of bloody blue hell do you think you can print a goddamned newspaper with this?" A short, skinny, grubby-looking man who could have used a shave was stomping and storming around among the packing cases.

Boudinot and Ross exchanged startled looks.

"What's wrong?" Greene asked, a note of fear in his voice.

"What's wrong! Just about everything, that's what's wrong! How in hell are you going to print a newspaper with this junk?"

"That junk as you refer to it, sir, is a Union Press," Greene replied, maintaining his calm. "It should prove more than adequate for the job."

"Adequate ain't the point, goddamn it! Sure, this here's a press, and these boxes hold type. Here's two crates marked Massachusetts Maple Furniture, and here's the ink. But I'd still like to know how you expect to print a newspaper!"

Boudinot started to yell, too, then thought better of it and said quietly, "Just tell us what the matter is, Isaac."

"There ain't no goddamned paper to print the news on, that's what the matter is!"

With that the enraged journeyman jumped down from the wagon and stormed across the village square to pay his respects to Alexander McCoy.

Chapter 3

"Who was that?" Parked asked, stunned.

"Your fellow journeyman, Isaac Harris," Wheeler grunted in disgust. "He arrived here two days before Christmas and I've been in a constant state of embarrassment ever since."

"You're too concerned about the man's morals, Wheeler, and not enough about his ability," exlcaimed Boudinot, waving an impatient hand. "Isaac's a good printer and that's why we have him. Besides," Boudinot continued, "I wouldn't be too worried about his outside activities if I were you. He's been engaged by the Cherokee Nation, not the Board of Foreign Missions."

Ross cast a slightly disapproving glance at Boudinot, then turned to Greene. "We're deeply grateful for the assistance of the Board, of course, David, but our primary concerns are our newspaper and printing plant."

Greene spread his hands in a gesture of helplessness. "Look, how could I object to him? As a member of the Board of Foreign Missions, I am supposed to give you all the assistance I can. I've spent all my life around printers and Isaac's no better or worse than most. I'm sure Mr. Wheeler would agree with that."

Wheeler nodded reluctantly.

"And if you're worried about any reaction from the Board," Greene went on, "I should say they're infinitely more concerned about Elias."

Boudinot's eyebrows went up. "About me? Why?"

"Elias, my friend, you've spent years in our schools. You have an excellent education, far better than most. We believed that you had seen fit to embrace Christianity, but rumors have reached Boston that you still engage in ball play and other pagan religious ceremonies. I wouldn't for one minute suggest you are anything less than the perfect man to be editor of the *Phoenix,* but . . ."

There was a moment of awkward silence until Boudinot interjected, "Then let's leave the matter right there, gentlemen. Anyway," he said, brightening, "who knows? It may provide an excellent subject for an editorial some day. I'll give it some thought, David."

He turned to Wheeler and Parker. "Let's move these things inside. We'll never get anything printed while they're still on the wagon."

The three men held a hurried conference regarding the supply of paper that would be needed. "I believe I can locate what we need in Tennessee," Ross offered. "I'll get started on it right away."

The interior of the *Phoenix* already seemed crowded. There was barely walking space between the tables, workbenches, Boudinot's small desk and the rack that held the type cases and furniture racks. Parker noticed that the log building incorporated another typical Cherokee architectural feature: no provision had been made for a stove or fireplace and it was as cold indoors as it was in the street outside.

Harris returned from McCoy's before the men had finished moving the crates inside and swung to work as though he had been there every minute. He worked silently, almost pleasantly, as though his earlier show of temper had never occurred.

Greene supervised the work of uncrating the press, suggesting that they lay out the pieces for the stand and main framework, then take time off to relax. Assembling the machinery was going to take more than a full day and it would take another few to adjust it before anyone could expect to test it.

Greene spent the night with Samuel Worcester and his wife Ann and Parker stayed in the home of Elias and Harriet Boudinot. After the grueling journey from Boston and the early stages of transferring equipment into the shop, the young printer was so exhausted he hardly knew what he'd been eating and was asleep almost before he reached his bed.

No one needed to awaken Parker the next morning. Many years of early rising had imprinted an automatic mechanism inside his head, and he appeared in the kitchen before the sun had fully risen.

"Oh, you startled me, Mr. Parker." Harriet Boudinot was in the midst of preparing a batch of cornbread. "I thought you'd sleep later."

"I never could, Mrs. Boudinot. It's what comes from being raised on a farm, I guess."

'My name is Harriet, John," she replied. Smiling, she poured Parker a mug of coffee and indicated a chair at the table. "We'll be working quite closely here, and you're going to be part of the family."

Harriet Boudinot was a frail woman, best described as plain. Parker had heard about her marriage to Boudinot in Cornwall and the scandal that had resulted when the daughter of one of the town's leading citizens had married one of the so-called savages who had been studying at the school. Harriet's parents had succeeded in making the young couple wait until Elias had completed his training at Andover, but then he returned to Cornwall in a splendid carriage and claimed his bride. It was a situation the Board of Foreign Missions had not anticipated and one they did not especially care to see repeated.

"You seem happy here," Parker offered.

"Oh, yes," Harriet agreed. "The Indians are wonderful people, but I wasn't quite prepared for the reception they gave me. You see, by Cherokee custom, I married not only Elias, but his entire family. I'm more than just a sister in name to Elias' brother and sisters, I'm aunt to all their children. His parents and grandparents are mine, also, and there have been times when I've been expected to cook and keep house for twenty or thirty people. It's a tremendous job, John, but I wouldn't trade it for anything."

"You don't get homesick?"

"How could I?" she answered with a warm smile. "This is my home. Besides, Ann Worcester and I have a lot in common, and you can see that we've made this little corner of Georgia as much like a piece of New England as we can. No, I have no regrets. My hope is that you won't either."

Ross came into the *Phoenix* office a few days later and announced, "If you can spare a man to go to Tennessee, we'll have the paper we need."

Wheeler didn't hesitate a minute. "Isaac, how about you going? We can get things set up here while you're away."

"Damned if I don't like the idea," Harris grinned. "My head's so scrambled with all this here Cherokee type, there ain't no way in hell I'm ever going to learn how to set it. I'll make the trip, all right. Be good to clear my mind." Within the hour he'd saddled up and was on the Federal Highway headed north.

Even before the press had been set up, there was

another hurdle to overcome. While waiting for the arrival of the equipment, Wheeler and Harris had spent months building cases for the type. Frames to hold the cases and the furniture had been constructed, but now it was obvious to everyone that they wouldn't work.

Wheeler sighed heavily. "We built them the same way type cases have always been built," he explained. "But we never considered the fact that the eighty-six characters in the Cherokee alphabet would demand more room than an English alphabet."

"Then there's only one thing to do," Boudinot said with a philosophical shrug of his shoulders. "We build new cases."

"It's going to take over a hundred boxes in each case to hold the type, figures, points, quads, and . . ." Parker paused, then said, "you know, here I am talking about everything we'll need and even though I've tried, I still can't make head or tails of your letters or feel capable of telling one sound from another. Your language is incomprehensible to me."

Boudinot laughed. "I find it easier than Greek or Hebrew either, John. So let's go outside and do some planning."

Parker followed Boudinot onto the porch, where they proposed various layouts for the type cases. Elias had no idea how to place the compartments and left the decision to Parker.

"I have a problem with that," Parker admitted. "That's because I haven't any idea of the relative frequency of the characters."

"Frequency?"

"For example, in English an E occurs much more often than a Z and will need more space in the type case to accommodate the greater number of pieces of type. We also put the E's closer to the front of the case than a Z, to save time in setting and distributing type.

But I don't have any idea which *Tsalagi* letters are used more frequently than others."

Boudinot shrugged his shoulders. "I couldn't give you more than a guess, John." He thought a moment, then wrote down several of the characters he thought would occur with greater regularity than the others. "Do what you think best," he advised.

They spent two days rebuilding the cases. Then it was discovered they wouldn't fit the frames, which had been designed to slip in under the windows, not in front of them, in order to provide the maximum amount of light for the setting of type. They made an attempt to rebuild the frames, but they ended up being too high for the windows and darkened the interior of the shop.

"I've got the answer," Boudinot exclaimed. "We'll get Cheowa back to raise the windows."

"Who's Cheowa?" Parker asked.

"The carpenter," Boudinot replied. "The whites sometimes call him Arthur."

The only part of the set-up operation that presented no major challenge was the erection of the press itself, and that was thanks to the supervisory prowess of David Greene. Aside from the fact of its tremendous weight, the press was simplicity itself. A cast-iron base held a tray containing the hand-set type. Once the type was in place it would be inked, then overlaid with a single sheet of paper. Directly over the tray was a horizontal metal plate hanging from a grooved shaft, which passed through a spiral threaded cylinder.

Protruding from one end of the press was a huge iron lever with a wooden handle. In operation, the handle was turned a full circle, lowering the plate onto the paper and pressing it down onto the inked type. The "minor adjustments" Greene had spoken of were those necessary to keep an even impression over the full page. These proved tricky, but once taken care of initially, would cause little difficulty in maintaining satisfactory print quality.

The four-page paper would be printed one sheet at a time, one page at a time. Boudinot planned on printing five hundred copies of each issue.

Two days after the problem of the oversized type cases was discovered, a team and wagon pulled up in front of the building. Wheeler looked out the door. "Cheowa's here to move the window," he announced.

Parker went out to greet the man who had built the log building and came face to face with the most repulsive-looking Indian he had ever seen. His features were chiseled into an expression that was fixed and cruel. Extensive areas of his face and head were marked with numerous scars, as if warrior, not carpenter, were his profession.

In keeping with the old Cherokee ways, the Indian's body had been plucked completely clean of any hair except for a tufted topknot that hung to his shoulders. Eyebrows, facial hair, even pubic hair was absent. The carpenter's ears had been slit and in them he wore dangling pieces of copper, ornaments that jingled as his head moved.

Boudinot spoke with the Indian in Cherokee and then told Parker, "This is Cheowa, one of the best carpenters and builders in the Territory. Perhaps you could give him a hand moving the windows."

Parker studied the foreboding figure before him. Cheowa stood some six inches taller than Little Tree and looked strong as an ox. Cheowa showed no trace of a smile nor even spoke when Boudinot introduced them.

"Does Arthur speak English, Elias?"

Parker couldn't have picked anything to ask that

would have displeased Cheowa more. "I speak English as well as any of my people," he replied, glowering at Parker. The young printer noticed that his pronunciation was nearly flawless.

Boudinot pulled Parker aside for a moment. "I think it would be better if you called him Cheowa rather than Arthur," he suggested. "His name in our language is Tsi-ya, and the closest the English tongue can come is Cheowa. Tsi-ya means otter, and it didn't take long for the whites to start calling him Arthur. He doesn't care for it."

"Cheowa suits me fine," Parker agreed. "I wouldn't want to rub that man the wrong way." He turned back to the towering Indian. "*O-si-yo,* Cheowa!"

Despite himself, Cheowa almost smiled. Then he recovered. "For an *unakă,* you'll do," he muttered reluctantly.

During the next two days, Parker worked closely with Cheowa to remove the windows from their sashes, then the frames from the building. It was necessary to cut through the two logs immediately above the window. They were pulled out and the top one split. Cheowa and Parker replaced half the split log at the top of the window, then laid the other two pieces at the bottom of the opening and replaced the frame. Parker was amazed at the tightness of the fit; Cheowa had nothing but crude tools to work with and used no nails in the job. Instead, he bored holes at angles through two logs at a time and fitted wooden pegs into place. Finally, the chinks were plastered and the job finished.

There had been almost no conversation between the two men as they worked together. At first, Parker did his best to be friendly with Cheowa, to speak with him in English or the few words he knew of Cherokee, but he was rewarded only with a few nods of the topknotted, bald head and some unintelligible grunts. When Cheowa needed to explain something, or when he wanted Parker to do something, though, he came through in perfectly understandable English. By the end of the first day, Parker had given up on trying to initiate conversation. Cheowa had made it clear that he was doing the work on the *Phoenix* building for the Cherokee Nation only and that it was his opinion that the entire operation could do without so many whites.

The night after Cheowa finished construction and left town, Parker and Wheeler were having dinner at McCoy's tavern. "I don't mind telling you," Parker began, "if Cheowa had been the first Cherokee I'd met rather than Elias, I wouldn't have considered coming here. That Indian gives me the creeps."

Wheeler grinned. "Backwards type," he agreed. "About as savage as they come, I suppose. But he's a good carpenter. He comes from a fairly wealthy family, John, but he doesn't have any more to do with whites than necessary. He's got white blood in him, I understand, from his mother's side, but he took a Cherokee wife and lives as his people did a hundred years ago. Actually, according to Cherokee custom, he belongs to her clan now, not his mother's."

"What about his father's clan?"

"The men don't have that much standing around here. And you'll find that the women have more say in tribal affairs than their husbands do. It's a matriarchal society. Goes back to the days when a man's continued existence was doubtful; he'd go off hunting or to war and perhaps never come back. A woman needs a husband to provide for the children, so a Cherokee woman has always been free to accept any man she wished as her husband, even if she already has one. It's not unusual for a woman to have a couple of men around the place and the men live pretty free and easy, too. They

don't seem to mind having marital relations with anyone who happens to strike the fancy, and they even do
it quite openly. I find all the goings on a bit shocking.
Listen to this: divorce is as easy as marriage. If a
woman gets tired of her husband, she can divorce him
simply by putting his personal belongings outside the
home. And he can divorce her merely by picking up
his things and leaving. The children are hers, not his.
In fact, the only things a Cherokee man owns are his
clothing and his implements of war."

"What about his land, his crops?"

"The crops belong to the women. The land belongs to the Nation. You see, John, no Cherokee Indian has ever owned his land, but merely been given
exclusive right to whatever land he can cultivate and
care for. And that's where the powers in Washington
find themselves up a tree. They can't negotiate to purchase an inch of land from any individual; they have to
make a treaty with the representatives of the Nation,
who have the authority to negotiate for the entire tribe.
And ever since we've been taking once piece of ground
after another, the Cherokee have become more and
more adamant in insisting they will never yield another
foot of land. It's even been written into their constitution."

Parker wiped his plate clean with a chunk of bean
bread. "But we've bought much of their land through
individual purchases, haven't we?"

"Sure we have. But the legality of it is something
else again. You've heard of Major Ridge, haven't
you?"

"Believe I have. Isn't he the one who fought with
Andy Jackson at Horseshoe Bend?"

"One of 'em. So did John Ross, so did Sequoyah,
Hicks and a lot of others. The Ridge made a name for
himself when he killed old Doublehead, a Chicka-

maugan who negotiated a treaty to sell off some of the Cherokee land, then was stupid enough to keep the money for himself and some of his friends."

Parker listened with reluctant fascination to the story of the killing. The Ridge had caught up with Doublehead over at Hiwassee, where the Chickamaugan had been enjoying a few drinks at his favorite tavern.

"C'mon out, you bastard!" Doublehead ignored his pursuer, so the enraged Ridge jumped off his horse and came storming into the saloon.

"It's low life like you that'll be the end of us all!" Ridge thundered, and without a moment's hesitation shot his startled enemy through the head right below the ear. But Doublehead wasn't done yet. Fighting his way through the crowd of customers who were scrambling for available hiding places, he headed for a neighbor's house and dived under a pile of blankets he found heaped near a shed close by. It didn't take long for The Ridge to find the pile of quivering cloth.

"Say your prayers, you damned traitor!" Ridge shouted, firing into them. But Doublehead threw off the blankets and made it to his feet. He grabbed Ridge and they grappled for a few minutes, grunting and cursing. Then, thrusting his enemy away from him, The Ridge managed to get his tomahawk free enough to bury it in Doublehead's skull.

"That's murder, Wheeler," Parker blurted when he had heard the story. "Don't the Cherokee have any laws against what happened?" he asked.

"The killing of Doublehead wasn't murder in their eyes," Wheeler replied. "What happened was the traditional penalty for disposing of tribal land without authority. Major Ridge is a full-blood. He and others too are afraid that adopting the white man's way will destroy the integrity of the Cherokee people. The

Ridge was highly honored for his act; the people figured him for one who wouldn't tolerate any compromise. He's still not one to compromise, although he
did introduce an act before the national council out-
lawing such executions. You'll have a chance to meet
the old boy one of these days. He's speaker of the
council, and there's a good chance he'll defeat Ross
when they elect a new principal chief later on this
spring. There are a lot more Indians than you can
imagine who feel strongly against trusting the whites."

"Like Cheowa," Parker grinned.

"That's correct," Wheeler replied. "Like Cheowa."

Parker considered everything he'd heard about
Major Ridge, and as they walked back to the *Phoenix*
office, he asked Wheeler, "How does The Ridge compare with Ross as a leader?"

"Ross is a natural born diplomat, and he's got the
support of the people. The Ridge? Well, he's always
been quite something as a warrior, but I don't think the
Cherokee feel they need a warrior as a leader anymore.
They need someone like Ross. Besides, I don't trust
Major Ridge for one minute and I suspect many of the
Cherokee feel the same way. He's an opportunist, even
if he is Boudinot's uncle. Mark my words, there's trouble brewing between Ross and The Ridge."

A frequent visitor to the *Phoenix* office during the
hectic setting-up days was Samuel Worcester. The slen-
der missionary had been looking forward to the in-
stallation of the press almost as much as his close
friend Boudinot. Worcester knew that the invention of
an alphabet by Sequoyah was only the first step toward
tremendous progress by the Cherokee. The printing
press and the Cherokee type would make possible a
translation of the Bible, and he and Boudinot had been
laboring for some time to write it. He had even written

a dissertation for the first issue. Watching him poring over it, Parker was reminded of a child eager to see what he would get for his birthday.

"The *Phoenix* is more than a vehicle for the transcription of Cherokee laws," he told Parker. "It means more to the Cherokee even than the publication of their memorials to Congress or their constitution. And it even means more than the translation of Holy Scripture, for it's all these and more in one. This first issue is going to present the Lord's Prayer in Cherokee and English, their constitution, their laws, news of what's happening—all of these things are of vital concern to the Nation."

Of even more vital concern to the crew of the *Phoenix* was the necessity of dealing with all the minor difficulties that mercilessly plagued them.

"You and Wheeler can handle setting that goddamned Cherokee type!" Isaac stubbornly insisted to Parker.

Because of its phonetic charactertistics, the Cherokee columns took less space than the English and what took two columns of Cherokee required three in English. Neither Wheeler nor Parker was familiar enough with the language to set the type with ease, though.

"Efficient language you call it? Damned queer you can't keep up with me, then!" Harris sneered as his fingers flew smoothly and quickly from the type cases to his composing stick. He could set English faster than they could Cherokee.

Finally the day dawned when the first page was made up and in the tray. As the crew breathlessly awaited the first sheet to read proof, Harris pulled a can of ink from the crate, pried off the top and asked, "Where's the ink roller?" Parker and Wheeler looked helplessly at each other.

"Shit!" Harris exploded and stormed out of the door toward the tavern.

Nothing seemed to ruffle Elias Boudinot. In an hour's time he had come up with the idea of wrapping cotton balls in buckskin. Then he poured some ink from the can to a board and spread it thin by means of one of the buckskin pads. Finally, he used another buckskin ink applicator to transfer the ink to the face of the type and Wheeler carefully laid on the first sheet of paper.

Wheeler turned the handle halfway around and Parker picked it up without a break in its swing, completing the impression. The plate swung back up and Wheeler pulled the sheet from the type. He held it up for Boudinot and the others to admire.

"Gentlemen, you are looking at the first impression of Page One, Volume 1, Number 1. The *Cherokee Phoenix* is on the wing!"

Chapter 4

Office of Indian Affairs
War Department
Washington, D.C.
20th April, 1828

Agent William Cullen
c/o Postmaster
New Echota, Georgia

Dear Mr. Cullen:

There is no doubt in anyone's mind that the periodical being published by the Cherokee represents an astounding feat and an accomplishment hitherto thought impossible. But my own view—and many here agree with me—is that the eloquence displayed by Elias Boudinot in the editorial column is the work of someone other than an Indian. You would do well to discover how much influence has been exerted by the Reverend Mr. Worcester.

The inflammatory tone of Boudinot's editorials will lead to nothing but disaster in view of the agreement between the United

States and the State of Georgia dated 24th April, 1802. As you are well aware, Indian title to lands lying within the boundaries of that state are to be extinguished on peaceable and reasonable terms as soon as practicable. The Georgia delegation has for years been charging the United States government with bad faith for not acting more rapidly in the question of removal. Since the adoption of a constitution by the Cherokee last year, the gentlemen from Georgia have demanded of the President some resolution of the question and further demand to know what the United States intends to do about "the erection of a separate government within the limits of a sovereign state."

Actions taken by the Georgia legislature indicate the state's intention of taking the matter into its own hands by taking possession and control of Cherokee lands. The State of Georgia has agreed to allow individual reservations within the State, but they are not to exceed one-sixth of the total part of the territory in dispute. Should the Cherokee still refuse to negotiate, they have been warned of the unfortunate consequences likely to follow, for it is Georgia's contention that the Indian lands belong to the state. The state furthermore argues that the Cherokee are merely tenants, there by the grace of Georgia's good will.

There have been assurances that the State of Georgia will not use force to accomplish the removal of the Cherokee people unless compelled to do so. Action by the legislature this past winter, however, extends

Georgia's laws and jurisdiction over all persons, white, black or red, living within her boundaries. These laws incorporating the Cherokee are, in my opinion, invalid, yet there are few here in Washington who will speak out against them.

Consequently, you would do well to attempt to convince individual Cherokee as well as their chiefs that removal to the West is inevitable. It would be wise, too, to advise Boudinot that his editorials will ultimately do more harm than good to the Cherokee people.

Charles Madden
Chief Clerk
(for the Commissioner)

After the newspaper's first flush of success, Parker's life settled into a routine that was alternately peaceful and exhausting. David Greene had stayed only long enough to attend (and pay for) the publication party before he left to go home to Boston. Parker missed him a little, but he felt a pioneer's exhilaration at being cut off from his mentor, his background and even, to some extent, his language.

It had taken nearly a full day to correct the proofs of the first edition. Wheeler, like Harris, could not understand a word of Cherokee and had left the task of reading the Cherokee columns to Parker and Boudinot.

By the time the fourth edition had come off the press, Parker was becoming adept at working with the Cherokee symbols, although his knowledge of the language was still marginal. To help them out, Boudinot hired a young half-breed by the name of Michael

Candy as an apprentice, and he proved adaptable to the work.

By the publication of the fifth edition, Parker had earned several days' leave, so he rode with Little Tree to distribute the *Phoenix* to the northern parts of the Nation. In many cases, only one paper would be left at a village, but there was always a crowd awaiting its arrival.

Some copies of the paper were delivered to individual homes as well as to central locations.

"Take a good look at this house," Little Tree instructed as the two approached a residence in Spring Place.

Parker had never seen a mansion so splendid. His first view was of three brick chimneys towering above the orchards that surrounded acres of well-tended lawns. Decorating the lawns were profusions of spring flowers and on one side of the house, rising from the midst of the lush beds, was a wide verandah the men could see as they drew closer.

When Little Tree pulled up at the gate in the white picket fence and hollered something in Cherokee, the shout was answered immediately. A black boy about eight years old came running from between two of the columns on the verendah to get the paper.

"Who lives here?" Parker asked as the young boy ran back to the house.

"Joe Vann. One of the richest men of the Nation."

"And the boy, is he a slave? I thought that all blacks were. But I can't picture a Cherokee owning one."

"Why not? He's rich enough to own anything."

"But, slaves?"

"Tsani," Little Tree explained, "there are many black slaves living in the Nation. We've adopted from the whites what we've imagined is the best way of life. The slaves work alongside their owners and most of them are free to leave if they want. They're more like members of the family than our possessions. And just as many of our people have married whites, many have married blacks."

As they left the Vann mansion, Parker took a backward glance, remembering what Wheeler had told him about Cherokee not owning the land they lived on.

"Does Vann's land belong to all the Cherokee, Little Tree?"

"All the land belongs to all the people," he replied simply. "Just as we cannot really own the air or the sea, we cannot own land. It has been entrusted to our care."

"But let's suppose that something forces your people to move out west—there are many white men who do not think as you do, Little Tree—what happens to all the money that the Vanns have put into their home? It just doesn't make sense that anybody would build up an estate like that one if he couldn't say that what he had made was his own."

Little Tree shrugged. "It doesn't make white sense, maybe. You must listen carefully to what I say and then you will understand why it makes Cherokee sense, *Tsani*.

"*Sge sge,* this is what the old man told me," Little Tree began, lapsing into an ancient myth and mingling Cherokee and English words as he went along. "*Hila hiya,* long ago, before this world was created, all the animals and all the men lived on the Sky Rock in *Galunlati,* the place called Up Above. Man and animals lived in peace and spoke the same language. The animals asked *Asgaya Galunlati,* the Man Above, to build them a new world to live in, and he made this earth for them. Because the animals were his favorite children, he was happy to give them whatever they asked and created this world.

"At first it was all mud and water, and only *Dahunisi,* Beaver's Grandchild, was able to live here, but he found it a good place. Soon he was joined by *Tsiskagili,* Red Crawfish, who also found it good.

"But it was far from the Sky Rock, and *Dahunisi* and *Tsiskagili* were lonesome for the other animals. They sent for the great *Suli* to fly to this world to search for dry land. *Suli,* the Buzzard, flew down and circled for days looking for dry land but could not find any. He flew very close to the earth and every time he flapped his wings they touched the surface of the mud. So great was the size of *Suli* that his wing tips piled up heaps of mud, leaving valleys between. The wind from his huge wings dried out the mud, and that is how the mountains and valleys came to be, these same mountains and valleys that are our land today.

"From the dried earth sprang trees and flowers and the grass of the meadows. And the other animals came to live in peace with their brothers the plants. The plants willingly gave themselves as food to their brothers the animals, and animals offered themselves to each other as food. It was a very happy and peaceful world long ago.

"And then some of the animals wanted their brother Man to come live with them, but other animals were afraid. They said to *Asgaya Galunlati,* 'If Man comes, he will kill us to satisfy his hunger.' And *Asgaya Galunlati* told them, 'Have no fear of Man. If it should come about that you are killed before your time, you will be reincarnated as young animals to live in the forest again. And I will make Man promise that he will kill only for food and shelter, never for sport or from anger. Before each kill, the hunter will ask the animal's spirit to forgive him. That is my law to Man.

Awaniski, I have spoken." Even to this day a Cherokee hunter will not kill an animal without asking the animal's spirit to forgive him, Tsani.

"There are still those among us who can speak with the animals. They are the *anidawehi,* what you call medicine men, and they are very wise. The *anidawehi* tell us that the best way to worship Asgaya Galunlati is to live in peace and harmony with all fellow creatures, animals as well as men. The Cherokee has been given the very important task of protecting this land for all of Asgaya Galunlati's children. *Tsiwanihu to-e-u,* I speak the truth."

The two men rode in silence for several minutes and then Little Tree, his voice choking with emotion, said, "So I tell you again, Tsani, the land is not ours to give or to sell. It belongs to Asgaya Galunlati, who has merely allowed us to use it. There is nothing that can make us sell this land. In the past, many of our people thought there would be no danger in exchanging some of it for money, or for territory in the West. But we can go no further. We will never give up another inch. Asgaya Galunlati gave us the land, and by custom and by law each Cherokee is permitted exclusive use of as much as he can care for. What he builds on it, what he grows on it, is his, all but the land itself. There used to be a custom among us that anyone selling any land without consent of the national council was punishable by death. Now that custom is written into our laws."

"Well, I wouldn't pretend to know as much about the situation here as you do," Parker admitted, moved by his friend's passion for his people and his home, "but what's going to happen if Chief Ross can't get Washington to agree to force Georgia to leave you in peace? Boudinot's editorials already have stirred up many of the Georgia legislators at Milledgeville."

"Simple, Tsani," Little Tree replied more calmly. "We have the law on our side. And nobody is better able to handle the law than Chief Ross. But if the law fails us, if there is no other way, we will do something we have not done for many years. We will take up the hatchet and become warriors again."

Parker felt himself shiver slightly. He knew that Little Tree spoke with the conviction of most of his people. He also knew that if a time of war ever came, the warriors would be led by Cherokee of Cheowa's ilk.

Chapter 5

By the end of the summer, Parker had moved into a one-room cabin near the edge of New Echota and had begun a late garden. The cabin he was living in had been the property of a family that had moved to Arkansas Territory six years earlier; it had been vacant since that time.

Although Elias and Harriet had offered to let him stay with them for as long as he wished, Parker knew the arrangement was inconvenient for them. On any given day, the Boudinot home was almost as busy as a waterfront hotel in Boston. It wasn't unusual for Harriet to find herself hostess to a dozen members of Elias' family as well as to four or five missionaries who were passing through town. The Worcester home, too, was hectic.

Parker's cabin was perched near the edge of a stream. The water bubbled through the woods, colder and cleaner than any he had found from a well. He still took most meals at McCoy's, but he was learning the knack of cooking some of his own food using the few utensils he'd accumulated. The outdoor fireplace proved more than adequate for food preparation needs.

Little Tree had brought in a couple of stools and helped build a bench that served as a bed. "I guess you'll never be a *Tsalagi,* Tsani," he said. "Outdoors is a good place to sleep when the weather is good."

Parker's cabin had been built similarly to most of the old Cherokee homes. It was about twenty feet long and twelve feet wide. Rows of posts had been set closely spaced into the ground and the spaces between filled in with a wattle of limbs and vines. After that, the entire wall was plastered with mud, then both sides whitewashed. Next, the high gabled roof was covered with bark. But now, not only the bark but several of the rafters needed replacing. There was no door and only one small opening for a window.

"Not much good for a *gotsadu,* house to you," Little Tree explained. "Before, this building was used mostly for storage. If you're going to live in this," he continued, his eyes scanning the dark interior, "you'd better have more windows."

With Little Tree's help over several weeks, windows were added to each wall. There were no sashes and no glass to cover them, but Parker was confident he would have little need to close them before the weather turned cold. The results of the construction effort were some rather crude holes, but Parker preferred them to the fine craftsmanship Cheowa would have provided, since having the sourfaced Indian around would have been more than he wanted to endure.

One evening while Parker was tending his beans and tomatoes, Little Tree rode up grinning. He had a sack tucked under one arm.

"*O-si-yo,*" Parker called.

"*O-si-yo,*" Little Tree replied. "My corn is ready and yours looks like it'll never make it unless you can find the magic words to bring a late rain." Dismounting, he handed Parker the burlap bag. In it were eight ears of tender, ripe sweet corn.

"You saved my life, Little Tree. That stuff

McCoy serves tastes like something you'd feed a horse."

"Almost as bad as his whiskey," Little Tree agreed laughing.

The friends walked to the open-walled lean-to and Parker prepared the corn for roasting while they sat and smoked their pipes. The local tobacco was more palatable to Parker than most of what he'd smoked in Boston and he'd taken to keeping a pipe going almost constantly when he wasn't working.

"There's a lot of activity in town lately," Parker observed.

"Everyone is getting ready for the council meeting. And wait till you see the council house. Cheowa's crew has been working hard, and when they're finished we're going to have a meeting place that will be finer than any in the world."

Parker nodded. The new council house was a rectangular log building two stories tall with brick chimneys and fireplaces, not the traditional open conical building. There were glass windows, sawed plank floors and a curved stairway leading to upper conference chambers.

Elections had been held in most of the districts of the Cherokee Nation, and when the council met in October, a new chief would be elected. Boudinot had opened the pages of the *Phoenix* to candidates for office and Parker had been following the campaign with avid interest.

"What do you think?" he asked Little Tree. "Is your money on Ross?"

"Sure is, Tsani. Major Ridge said he's ready to leave the government in the hands of the younger men. He claims he's had his day. The only other contenders for the post are William Hicks and George Lowrey. Going Snake might make a good show of it, but he doesn't have as much support as he'll need. Besides Going Snake and George Lowrey don't have as much education as Ross."

There had been some talk by old conservatives about replacing the mixed-breeds on the National Council with full-blooded Cherokee, but Parker thought those sentiments were supported mostly by the likes of Cheowa. One letter that Boudinot had printed summed up what he considered to be the prevailing opinion:

> The welfare of our country should be the order of the day with all who have the interest of their native land at heart. Our Nation, as a political body, has reached an important crisis and bids fair to make rapid progress in the path of civilization, the arts and the sciences. . . . The Committee should be composed of men of education and good knowledge of the affairs of our Nation . . .

"The trick," said Little Tree, "is to have a man of education who is not so dependent on the white man's ways that he allows the Nation to be absorbed by them."

Parker stripped the silk from the last ear of corn and pulled its husks back up. "You still think it's going to be Ross, then?" He buried the corn deep in the hot coals.

"Probably," Little Tree replied, spitting in the dust. "With all the rumors flying around, William Hicks doesn't have a chance. McCoy's in the same fix. Besides, having Ross as chief means salvation for our people. The man is brilliant. More than that, he is steadfast, not like some who seem to sway between beliefs much like corn blowing in the wind."

William Hicks was the son of Chief Fierce Charley Hicks, who had died the year before. He had served for his father as interim chief until the council met, then became assistant chief to Ross. Parker had noticed that Boudinot seldom spoke of Hicks, and his name rarely appeared in the columns of the *Phoenix* except at the bottom of reprints of legislation.

Little Tree was silent for a long time. Parker studied his face and finally asked, "All right, tell me. What's the rumor?"

"Well," Little Tree began, "according to some I've talked to, Hicks and McCoy are both preaching removal and they've gone so far as to discuss the matter with that Indian agent, Cullen. I don't know how much truth there is in the story; I've never talked to anyone who claims the two have tried to talk them into it. But almost everyone I run into knows of someone Hicks and McCoy have talked to. Tsani, anybody who talks openly of removal to the West is committing political suicide."

He paused to refill and relight the pipe. "You've been here long enough to get to know how we are, Tsani. Do you think we'd willingly give up the land of our fathers and move west? It is as if the Cherokee are married to their lands, my friend. Other peoples may adjust easily to another home, another territory, but this mountain country holds special meaning for us. None like it exists in the West."

Parker replied, pulling the corn out of the coals, "That may be, but sometimes circumstances shove us in directions we would rather not go."

Little Tree slammed his fist into the table. "No!" he shouted. "No!"

Later, long after the succulent ears of corn had been eaten and he was alone, Parker entertained gloomy thoughts. What was he getting himself into?

Now that he was close to the scene of those battles against the Creek that Charley Adams always blathered about, he could agree with Charley that it was lovely country and that the people here were wonderful, yet the city life that been so stable, so luxurious compared to this one had vanished. Parker sighed, listening to the stream and the chattering of birds in the trees at the approach of night. Despite the calm, he felt a knot tighten in his throat. His eyes scanned the bare plaster walls of the cabin he called home. If he had been in Boston at that moment, he'd be sitting in Sullivan's Public House enjoying familiar company. But gone were the bustling sounds of the Boston waterfront, of the busy streets.

"You damned fool!" Parker cursed himself. "Why can't you make a decision and be happy with it? You always hang between where you've been and where you are!"

He doused the lamp. As his thoughts drifted into areas that held less anger, Parker saw again the face of Agatha Lake. He'd barely had a chance to say goodbye. She had promised that when she came south to teach in one of the mission schools, she would be sure to come to New Echota and see him again. And now, as the water babbled outside near his cabin door, Agatha's haunting eyes were the last thing he remembered before being lulled to sleep.

New Echota overflowed with activity while the Council was in session. As Little Tree had promised, there were tents and shelters set up in every available foot of space surrounding the council house. The acres of village greens were packed, as were the woods beyond. Torches and campfires lit up the town at night until the area around it was almost as bright as noon.

As people greeted one another, the din of the

happy voices was almost deafening at times; many
people hadn't seen each other since the last council
meeting. Along with the traditional drums and chants,
the singing was accompanied by blasts on bugles and on
trumpets as well as sweet violins and jangling banjos.
Although the serious business of government had
brought the throngs of Indians to New Echota, the
town seemed geared more for carnivals and fun than
for discussion. The council grounds were the desig-
nated place for row upon row of covered tables heaped
high with provisions for the delegates and their
families. Beef was plentiful, as were venison, pheasant,
trout, pork and mutton. And they were accompanied
by piles of breads, sweet potatoes, vegetables and
onion dishes of all kinds. Of the seven-thousand-five-
hundred-dollar annuity Ross had received for the Nation from the United States, five thousand of it had been
paid out for salaries and expenses of the delegates and
as compensation to the hunters and chefs who gathered
and prepared the mountains of food for the vast gathering.

Not all of the people ate from the common tables.
Little Tree had brought his family, including his wife,
Martha, his father, two sisters and their children, to
camp at Parker's cabin. While they were there, Little
Tree's wife took over the stove and Parker enjoyed
some of the best cornbread and beanbread he'd ever
eaten.

Once Martha made a huge bowl of gonutse, a
combination of hominy, hickory nuts and other ingredients, a concoction that Parker knew nothing in Boston
could ever match. If he hadn't been so busy enjoying
it, the young printer knew, he would have been feeling
guilty about that recent melancholy evening he had
spent dreaming about the "good old days" in the
Northeast.

Over the cookfire hung a quarter of venison that dwindled rapidly with the voracious picking of Little Tree's family. They cooked rabbits and even a suckling pig on spits that the youngest children kept turning.

There was no regularity to the meals. Parker learned that it wasn't just a quirk of Boudinot's that he ate whenever he was hungry. This was a custom of the Cherokee people. Not once did Parker hear Martha or her sister-in-law admonish the children not to eat before supper time. The little ones nibbled when they were hungry and never seemed to overeat. If it wasn't meat or beanbread that was keeping them content, it was the parched corn that had been hung by their mothers in bags by Parker's door. During the two weeks the Council was in session, Parker never once found all his guests eating at one time, nor did he ever find the lean-to without at least one Cherokee who was reaching for something to stave off hunger.

"Do all Cherokee allow themselves and their children such freedom?" Parker asked Martha.

Martha kept her eye affectionately on Little Bear a moment longer. He had been rummaging through a pile of clothing in the rear of the room.

"Let me tell you this," she offered, turning to Parker and smiling warmly. "In a few months' time, Little Tree and I will be having another child. We fully intend our next baby to grow as free and unencumbered by demands as the rest of our children have been. Just as our government does not require our obedience, so do the Cherokee people not require obedience from their young people. In that way, they will learn. In that way, they will grow wise and strong. I would have it no other way."

Parker was impressed with this proud Cherokee woman. In her seemed to be combined a grace and conviction not so frequently found in the white women that he knew.

"But what if an Indian becomes a troublemaker? What if he hurts someone?"

"If there is personal harm done," Martha explained as she gathered additional ingredients for a mush she was preparing, "he is punished by the victim's family, often by death. If his behavior offends the community, we merely shun the offending party until he decides to pack up and leave. It's as simple as that."

As simple as that, Parker thought, speculating how difficult it would be for such a simple people ever to survive continued exposure to the devious white men who were threatening to close in on them.

McCoy did a thriving business at this tavern and there was no doubt in anyone's mind that he was dispensing free whiskey to anyone who had an ear to listen to him stump for his own election. But there was surprisingly little drunkenness in the town, only occasionally a Cherokee had so much to drink that he disrupted the holiday spirit.

Isaac Harris, though, was another matter. For the first time since he'd come to New Echota, he managed to get himself so drunk he missed work for several days. Boudinot was furious and on the day Harris finally showed up, the usually lighthearted Elias exploded.

"Isaac. We've put up with your temper and your loose living for almost a year. I can't run this newspaper if I have to worry about whether you can stay sober or not!"

"Nobody gives a damn, Elias," Harris whined, "least of all, me. Jus' leave me 'lone."

But Boudinot was steaming mad.

"Don't worry about it, Elias," Parker advised, trying to calm him down. "We've got several columns made up ahead and Michael and I can handle Isaac's work for this issue."

Boudinot agreed to let the matter drop. "But just this time, you drunken fool!" he snarled, shaking his white-knuckled fist at Isaac, who had climbed onto a table and collapsed. The raging Indian swung to face Parker.

"I've got so much to do with the Council in session, John, I simply cannot take the time to worry about whether Isaac is going to recover or not. But I promise you—and him too—either he's going to get along with everybody here and live up to his responsibilities or I'm going to fire him. I won't take much more."

"Maybe Ross will be able to suggest something," Parker offered.

"Maybe he will," Boudinot sneered, storming out of the shop.

"What do you think?" Candy asked, as they surveyed the prostrate form of Harris, now snoring loudly.

Parker looked at Harris and grinned sheepishly. "I think we'd better get to work."

By the time the Council had adjourned, Ross had been elected principal chief, George Lowrey had replaced a disgruntled William Hicks as assistant chief and The Ridge had been chosen to fill the newly created post of adviser to the chief. Alexander McCoy, formerly Clerk of the Council, was ousted by the Ridge's son John.

In Washington, Charles Madden had just received a furious letter to the Commissioner from Governor Forsyth of Georgia. In it, the governor restated a long list of grievances involving the Cherokee. "First it was the missionary schools spreading education in the Nation. Then a written language of their own and their own recorded laws. Then a supreme court and their own judicial system. Then a constitution. Then a national newspaper." Where was it all going to end, he demanded. Now that that firebrand Ross has officially been elected to the highest Cherokee office, it was clear that it was the missionaries who were behind the changeover. Hadn't they been preaching to the Cherokee to take a hard stand against removal to the West?

Ross, according to Forsyth, was no more than a tool in the hands of Samuel Worcester. Worcester, he claimed, was the power figure behind Boudinot's pen. The United States had dragged its feet long enough in this matter of removing Indians from Georgia's sacred soil. Thank God Andrew Jackson had been elected president, wrote Forsyth. He, at least, would do something positive about the rotten mess that threatened the tranquility of the State of Georgia. Three administrations had supported the concept of removal. Now, at last, something would be done.

As spokesman for the Cherokee Nation, Elias Boudinot had taken his stand in the first issue of the *Cherokee Phoenix*. "We will invariably state the will of the majority of our people on the subject of the present controversy with Georgia and the present removal policy of the United States."

It was a firm stand and Boudinot had no need to restate it, particularly after the policy was once again confirmed by the Council. He did, however, continue to print letters from his readers. One, from a group of citizens in the Valley Town district, represented the feelings of the majority of the Nation.

"The lands we possess are the gift of our Creator," they wrote. "Moreover, they are recognized by the United States and guaranteed to us forever . . . within these limits we consider ourselves at home and have no doubt to the goodness of our title. . . . Our Creator has not given us the land beyond the Mississippi, but has given it to other people; and why should we wish to enter upon their possessions?" The *Phoenix,* additional evidence of Cherokee self-confidence and pride, aroused sympathy throughout the world, but in neighboring Alabama and Georgia, stirred bitter suspicion and fear of increasing Indian solidarity. With the publication of their newspaper, the Cherokee had proven that not only were they as brave as any white man, but as intelligent as well.

As he typeset the words that expressed the Indians' national concerns, Parker was reminded of something Little Tree had told him. "Your preachers talk of a place to live after the Raven Mockers swoop down like fire, their arms outstretched like wings to rob a dying man of life. We do not know of this place you call heaven. We believe that the souls of the dead are carried on a three-day journey back to the stars they come from, where Asgaya Galunlati has prepared a place for them to sleep forever in peace. But this place is way off to the West, Tsani. It is known as the Darkening Land. That is another reason why our people want no part of moving, why we will never go willingly."

Whatever lay ahead, Parker told himself, there was going to be trouble. But was it his trouble?

Chapter 6

Indian Agent Cullen drummed his fingers impatiently on the table as he reread the letter from Madden. Hardly a week went by that he did not receive something from the man, either another directive or another memorandum, and every piece of correspondence ordered him to encourage the Cherokee to withdraw from the land they loved.

The Choctaw and Chickasaw had already been pressured into moving, and horror stories that filtered back had made many Cherokee even more resolute in standing their ground. Besides, they had lived in the mountains for centuries and were not about to be uprooted to lands their legends had conditioned them to mistrust. Already they had been compelled to cede much of their land. On what land did remain, game had become increasingly scarce, forcing many of their people to seek early refuge in the extraordinarily lovely wooded land along the Arkansas River.

Cullen had been through that area two years earlier. There had been no white settlers there then and that fact had seduced many Cherokee into removing themselves voluntarily.

Cullen sighed, then leaned back in his chair and put his feet up.

Besides, he remembered, the Cherokee had been promised that the move to the Arkansas was the last one they would ever be asked to make.

Later, Chief John Jolly and about three hundred followers made their way to the Arkansas. But these emigrants were not nomads looking for new hunting lands; they were people already half adapted to the white man's civilization who believed they'd better move west while the getting was good. Their travel was more difficult than that of their predecessors, for along with them they carried the trappings of wealth, but their illusions were fewer.

Although Jolly's group was looking for land to settle on and develop, what they found was not the promised land; and the Cherokee in the East, who had refused to migrate, knew that.

The stories that came back to them were filled with detailed descriptions of the problems that the migrants had encountered. Initially, clashes with the resident Osage Indians hadn't bothered the West Cherokee a bit. They knew themselves to be skillful warriors and were afraid of no one. But these clashes, along with the problem of encroaching white settlers and the accompanying threats of violence and harassment, were subjecting the migrating Indians to virtually all the pressures from which they had hoped to escape.

Cullen thought of the delegation who grimly had petitioned in Washington for some equitable solution to be worked out. The Indians had stood proudly and eloquently before men who unfortunately were not of comparable integrity. The treaty that came out of those meetings in Cullen's opinion was a disgrace. It had occasioned another move and promised a permanent home where there could never be one because white settlers had already established property lines *beyond* the point where the Cherokees had been asked to move.

"Ridiculous," Cullen muttered. The students had become more proficient than their teachers. The Cherokee had closely followed the intent of the United States judicial system. They had been straightforward, honest and loyal to its precepts. That couldn't be said of the laws of Georgia.

Georgia recently had extended her jurisdiction over the Cherokee through legislation and had even gone so far as to declare that no Indian could testify at a trial in which a white principal was involved. Cullen angrily gritted his teeth. Georgia was using its powers for foul purposes; at least that was his opinion. Any white Georgian was now free to steal what he wanted from a Cherokee and present his side of the case if it ever came to court, but the Cherokee wasn't permitted to testify in his own behalf.

"Wisdom, justice, moderation." The motto of the sovereign State of Georgia was completely hypocritical as far as Cullen was concerned.

The stifling laws of Georgia were designed to put pressure on the Cherokee so they would be forced to leave their lands, the very lands they had made infinitely more inhabitable, infinitely more fertile by their presence there. Conditions had reached the inexcusable point where there was justice for one class of people but not for another, where thievery of stores, crops and cattle had been legally condoned. In the matter of Indian removal the law had been perverted.

These thoughts were not new to Cullen. And there were those who, though sympathetic to the Indian cause, did not completely absolve them from responsibility for their situation.

"My friend," a cousin of Cullen's had announced to him one night over dinner, "you are a blind man if

you can see these Indians only as victims. You know
the history. Most Indian tribes were so involved with
their trade wars, so eager to gain more power, that
they obliterated other nations that would have helped
them stand firm against white settlers.

"And later, during the French and Indian War, did
your precious Cherokee ally themselves with the
French, who were interested primarily in trade and not
the Indian land, or did the fools line up with the
English, who had banded together against the Indians
of the interior as well as the French, and who later un-
questionably became set on acquiring property? Well?"

Cullen had conceded these points that night. He
had even added one or two of his own. In several mon-
umentally foolish decisions after the war, both the Iro-
quois and the Cherokee had allowed the mountain
barrier to be opened to white men crossing Kentucky
and Tennessee. Through the gap in that barrier poured
endless caravans of settlers. By the time the Indians
had become aware of what was happening and tried to
unite, it was too late. For too long, they had been dedi-
cated to policies reflecting only self-interest. They had
dug their own grave and already they were feeling
more and more isolated on lands where there was
frighteningly less room to either hide or to maneuver.

Major Ridge himself had speeded up the inevitable by advocating that the Cherokee fight side by side
with the Americans against the Creek. Even after that
pledge of trust and allegiance, the spoils of victory had
been confiscated by whites alone, and Jackson, the
great American hero of the war, had turned his back
on those who'd helped him most.

Cullen allowed himself the luxury of a deep sigh.
Despite the Indians' foolhardiness in the past, they had
proved themselves to be a people deserving of the best
the United States could allow them. And it wasn't that

they had demanded much, only the right to exist in fact
as a nation. The Indians' fairly recent dependence on
the United States had arisen from their conversion to
the white man's ways of agriculture, trade and
business. Before this conversion, the Cherokee had
been able to live isolated lives as hunters. Now they
were trapped both by their own adaptability and desire
for progress and by the government's double-talking
treatment of them. One treaty with the Cherokee
guaranteed them their own land forever; another with
Georgia promised them the same land whenever the
Cherokee were ready to give it up.

Those contradictory promises pulled the Cherokee—and Cullen—in both directions at the same time.
His job was a delicate one, all right. He admired the
Cherokee, and he believed they were being treated unfairly, but his job as Indian agent left him little choice.
It was his responsibility to see that all laws relating to
the Indians were enforced.

Wearily, Cullen pulled his watch from his pocket
and frowned. Major Ridge was to meet him in a few
minutes. And a meeting with The Ridge was going to
be about as fruitful as the meetings with John Ross
had been. Stubborn, proud, defiant, Ridge was a warrior, and the old boy, Cullen imagined, must really
chafe under white man's rule. But if events kept on
pointing in the same direction, The Ridge might have
himself another war to fight after all.

Cullen knew the first thing the Indian would do
would be to present a list of petty grievances. And then
he'd ask what President Jackson was going to do about
remembering his old fighting buddies who had fought
side by side with him in the war against the Creek.
There was no way in hell he could explain to The
Ridge that Jackson didn't give a damn about saving his
old friends when he had a claim to about a hundred

thousand acres of their land and wouldn't be able to sell it until the Indian question had been resolved.

A buggy pulled up outside and Cullen glanced out the window. The Ridge was climbing down and despite his years was an impressive figure. White hair framed a scowling bronze face. The Ridge's huge bulk was clothed in part by his customary frock coat, broadcloth shirt, silk cravat and high beaver hat. A moment passed before he reached the door.

Cullen gave Madden's letter one last review.

"Are you in there, friend?" Loud knocking accompanied the Ridge's query.

"I'm here," Cullen murmured, already weary from thought and speculation. "I'm here," he piped up. "C'mon in so we can start knocking our heads together again."

Chapter 7

The *Phoenix's* first year of life had been stormy. Boudinot's fiery editorials had been avidly read throughout the Cherokee Nation, in Boston and around the world. Reactions varied.

In Switzerland, England and France, the paper was read with satisfaction by many who had made generous contributions to the once barbaric, now civilized Cherokee.

In Boston, the American Board of Foreign Missions advised Samuel Worcester to continue to "do what you think best," even though there were members among their ranks who believed he had become too involved in the politics of the Cherokee people. They had received complaints from the Governor of Georgia and the Chief Clerk of the Office of Indian Affairs in Washington; because of these complaints, they were afraid to back him too far.

In Washington, the *Cherokee Phoenix* was studied by influential congressmen and senators. For some, the newspaper was offering opportunity for real understanding of the history of the Indian treaties; for others, it provided full information on the ideas of the "enemy."

Throughout the state of Georgia, each issue

created increased resistance and contempt. Each legal, social, economic and educational advance made by the Cherokee people was seen by the Georgians as provocation. The presumption was that the more the Cherokee became civilized, the more likely it was that they would be able to maintain an independent nation within Georgia's borders. To the Georgians, that possibility was intolerable.

The Indians who had moved to new lands read the *Phoenix* and felt a surge of pride in their own accomplishments. The eastern Cherokee, too, though decided upon a final stand in eastern lands, approved of the paper.

From one end of the nation to the other, proud Cherokee awaited each week's offering. In each issue, Boudinot mixed the written laws of the nation with foreign news culled from dozens of journals obtained on exchange. There were few advertisements to offset costs of operation, but nevertheless, Boudinot packed the columns with articles he considered essential to the personal welfare of his readers. In addition to reports on the actions of the National Council and National Committee, readers enjoyed a variety of lighter material that included "Recipes for Insuring Health," "Female Delicacy," "Tight Lacing and Thin Clothing," "Improved Methods for Storing Venison and Beef," and one of his favorite topics, "The Evils of Alcohol."

Contributions from readers were encouraged. The little building was swamped with mail from hundreds of people wanting to display their new-found ability to read and write. Although there had been postal service in the Territory for more than ten years, New Echota had never had its own post office. It soon became necessary to open one there, though, and Samuel Worcester was appointed first postmaster by the federal government. Mail was now delivered directly to New

Echota rather than to Rossville or Spring Place. On days when it arrived, Worcester wondered if he would ever again have the time to complete his Cherokee translation of the Holy Scriptures.

Although Boudinot had proclaimed the columns of the *Phoenix* would be open to all who had an interest in the Cherokee Nation, he also had reserved the right to edit the material as he saw fit. When a letter protesting the zealous activity of the Moravian and Presbyterian missionaries was received, Boudinot refused to print it.

"But Elias," Worcester protested, "they have a right to state their position. We may not agree with them, but they still have—"

"All mail coming into this office is expected to have been sent postpaid," Boudinot interrupted testily. "Theirs was received with postage due. Do you honestly think I'm going to pay the postage to print letters I don't agree with?"

Several weeks later, Boudinot did print the letter, but not until he had received a visit from the Methodist missionaries and listened to their side of the controversy; and not until after he had listened to the convincing arguments of John Ross, who was a member of the Methodist Church; and not until after the missionaries had paid the postage due.

There were other problems to be dealt with. Isaac Harris had grown more troublesome as time went by and finally not even Ross could calm Boudinot down. Harris had been on a particularly loud, spectacular drinking spree.

"He's gone too far!" Elias stormed. "He's troublesome. He refused to make any attempt at learning the syllabary. He won't even lift a finger to help set type or correct it. And worst of all, his swearing is intolerable."

"Many whites are profane, Elias. Certainly you know that by now."

"But not so profane that their curses would put a stevedore to shame. Some men can swear under their breath, but not Isaac. When he lets loose you can hear him all over town. I'm telling you, John," Boudinot declared, "I'm going to resign as editor unless Harris goes."

Ross studied his friend's determined face. "I'll look into it," he promised. And Boudinot knew he would.

Both Ann Worcester and Harriet Boudinot confirmed to Ross that it was embarrassing to entertain ladies in their homes because of the foul language they could hear from clear across the square. Ross took the matter up with the Committee when they met several days later; they sided with Boudinot and fired Harris. Triumphantly, Boudinot handed Harris the paper containing the verdict.

Harris examined the sheet of paper. It had been written in both Cherokee and English and informed him concisely that his services had been terminated.

"I'll be goddamned if I'm leaving!" Isaac shouted, ripping the sheet into shreds and throwing the pieces into Boudinot's face. "I was brought down here to print this damned paper, and you can't throw me out. I don't care what kind of fancy mucketymuck you are!"

"Isaac, if you don't leave, there's going to be trouble." Boudinot was angry but in control.

"I ain't goin'!"

John Ross appeared in the doorway. His five foot five frame was drawn up to its full height, though he was still not quite so tall as Harris. "Your services have been terminated by the National Committee, Mr. Harris. You're no longer needed here in New Echota."

"In a pig's ass! An' who's going to make me

leave? You and Elias can't. Even together, you ain't men enough, goddamn it!"

"But I am. Get out."

All heads turned toward the doorway, where Assistant Chief George Lowrey stood calmly in homespun shirt, a turban wrapped around his head. Lowrey was a giant of a man, at least six feet three inches tall. His fixed stare betrayed none of the impatience that his words revealed. And his appearance was all the more formidable because of copper ornaments dangling from slits in his ears and a shiny copper plate that pierced his nose.

Harris didn't have time for another round of protest. Lowrey stepped inside the building, grabbed him by the hair with one hand and clamped down with all his might. The other hand caught the printer by the genitals, and before Harris could let out a howl, Lowrey had pitched him headfirst through the door and into the dusty street.

Worcester and Parker watched astonished while Harris struggled painfully to his feet and made his way to McCoy's tavern. "Effective, George," Ross commented, "but not very diplomatic."

"Diplomacy," Lowrey said as he straightened his shirt, "consists of talking the other man's language."

It was the middle of summer when Harriet Boudinot came into the shop looking for Parker.

"I'd like you to come for supper tonight, John. There'll be a special treat."

"Of course, I'll come over, Harriet. Any time you cook for me, the result is a special treat!" Parker said pleasantly.

"Why not take off a little early, John?" Wheeler offered—his name had replaced Harris' on the masthead. "We're far enough ahead with this week's issue that a couple of hours won't make any difference."

"Thanks," Parker replied. "I'll feel better if I have a chance to get a bath before dinner."

He cut across the commons to his cabin. Hurriedly stripping off his clothes, he plunged into the cool creek water, savoring the chill after a hot day inside the stuffy print shop. The bar of lye soap made short work of the inky residue on his hands and ten minutes later he was dried and pulling on a fresh shirt and trousers.

"Might as well do it up right," he said aloud, putting on a tie and jacket as well. "Being invited out to dinner is the most excitement I've had around here in a long time."

Little Tree rode up just as Parker was combing his hair back. "*O-si-yo,* Tsani."

"Hello, Little Tree. I hope you weren't expecting to have supper with me. I've been invited to the Boudinots, but you're welcome to anything I have here."

"Thought I'd come see if you want to go watch the ball play at Spring Place."

"When?"

"Four days from now. That's the day after the paper is sent out, so I can join my team."

"Who are you playing?"

"New Echota. Friendly little game. A couple of fools got themselves liquored up at McCoy's and said they could beat us with rocks tied to their legs."

"Well, that remains to be seen. I'd hate to see my home town play Spring Place, though."

"Why?"

"Because if you're on the Spring Place team you'll get whipped. Besides, how would it look if I were to cheer for you?"

"Cheer or not, New Echota is going to lose. But

I'll give you a word of advice, Tsani. Bet on Spring Place. We've got one of the best players in the Nation."

"And who is this superman who's going to take on George Lowrey and his team?"

"Cheowa." Little Tree allowed time for that information to sink in, then said smugly, "Now, you still want to bet on New Echota? I'll cover anything you put up."

Parker considered the offer. "Two chickens?"

Little Tree laughed derisively.

"One of my yearling pigs?"

"Make it the pig and three chickens and you've got yourself a bet, Tsani!"

"You're a con man," Parker said, chuckling as he pulled his bow tie into place. "But you're on!"

Little Tree got back on his horse looking pleased. "I can taste the pork roast now, Tsani," he teased. "Delicious! And Martha will cook up one of the chickens with plenty of onions and fine green peppers. We might even invite you to share it with us if you cheer for me."

"Get out of here!" Parker shouted in fun to the retreating figure. Then he headed for the Boudinots.

Harriet welcomed him eagerly as usual, and as he entered the house he received an additional greeting.

"Hello, Mr. Parker. It's good to see you again."

"Miss Lake . . . I don't know what to say."

Chapter 8

For still another moment, Parker was stunned. Agatha Lake was as beautiful as he remembered her from David Greene's reception. It had been almost two years since that night, and despite Agatha's promise to come south and teach, he had long since convinced himself he would never see her again.

"Well, don't fall over, for heaven's sake! Harriet's ready to set the table and Elias is threatening to eat the bare plates."

"Don't you worry, Miss Lake," Parker stated, recovering his composure. "It's just that seeing you was such a surprise. For a while today I imagined that someone else might be having dinner with us, but I guessed it would be Harriet's parents, not you!"

Harriet had done herself proud. The table had been set with the imported bone china and lead crystal The Ridge had given her and Elias as a wedding present. Parker knew Harriet considered that her special set; she used it only when she was entertaining guests who were far from ordinary.

Before dinner, Elias offered grace and concluded with, "Above all, Great Father, we are thankful that you have seen fit to send us Agatha, who will help our people grow in wisdom and in knowledge. Amen."

It had taken the engaging young woman six weeks to make the journey from New England, yet she showed no signs of strain from the arduous trip. She seemed to Parker as sparkling and fresh as if she'd spent days resting.

Harriet had prepared a feast of roast chicken and fresh vegetables that would have pleased even royalty and Parker suspected that even John Ross was never entertained more lavishly. The Lake family must be considerably influential, he thought, to have inspired the Boudinots to treat their daughter in such grand style.

"Agatha is going to set up a school here in New Echota," Harriet announced. "The town is growing so fast we already have twelve children for her."

"And there will be more," Elias added. "My uncle has even offered to provide a wagon to bring several children in from Spring Place every day. The teacher over there has her hands full with thirty-one of them."

As Boudinot spoke, Agatha's face was radiant. Parker noticed her glow of enthusiasm immediately but wondered if this delicate, lovely woman were truly capable of handling so many lively children.

"What will be your schoolhouse?" he asked.

"Just look at all the public buildings here that are only used for short periods during the day," Agatha replied. "I'm going to ask Chief Ross if we can use the courthouse until a school is built."

"It is large enough," Parker agreed.

"And whenever court is in session," Elias suggested, "Agatha can conduct her classes outdoors or even here."

After supper, they sat on the porch, discussing the large numbers of schools that were being established all over the nation. "Education for our people is the most important consideration we can attend to," Elias asserted. "John Ross and The Ridge knew that right from the beginning.

"Here's a story for you. When my cousin John first went to school, he was so independent the teacher threatened to send him home. The Ridge's reaction was to rush over to the school with a little Creek girl he'd been raising since the war. He told the teacher that if John weren't going to settle down and behave, then the girl could take his place. And if they didn't want a Creek in the school, one of his slaves would attend. That's how important we feel the schools are to the Nation."

"The first school at Dahlonega is typical," Agatha commented. "They hoped to have fifteen students and before the year was over, there were more than fifty." For a moment, she looked a bit terrified at the thought of so many flocking into her school.

"You'd be able to teach," Elias said simply, reading her thoughts, "no matter how many showed up."

"Besides," Parker teased, "you're a missionary. You could always pray for help." Agatha nodded laughing.

"When will school open?" Parker asked, hoping it would be soon so he could see her again.

"Right after the Green Corn Dance," Agatha replied. "Where will the district ceremony be performed this year, Elias?"

"Spring Place. New Echota had it last year."

Seeing the mystified look on Parker's face, Agatha flashed him a smile and explained. "A different town hosts the ceremony every year in each district, John. That way, everyone has an opportunity to take an active part in one of the Cherokees' most important ceremonies."

Parker remembered that Little Tree had told him no Cherokee would pull an ear of corn before the

Green Corn Dance, and that the first ear of corn in a field to sprout tassels was marked for ritual purposes. He'd observed the Green Corn Dance the previous year but didn't know that it moved from town to town.

"You seem to have learned more about Cherokee customs already than I have, Miss Lake, and I've been living here for almost two years now."

There was a sudden silence during which Elias and Harriet exchanged a conspiratorial glance.

"I've had good training, Mr. Parker," Agatha said.

"It's getting dark," Elias interjected, stifling a yawn. Harriet took the hint and they retired to the house.

"And now that you've been in New Echota this long," Agatha began, once they were alone, "what do you think of the Cherokee people?"

"They're not what I expected, I'll certainly admit that," Parker answered. "I guess I really didn't know what to expect. Even now, though I feel more at ease, there are so many contrasts.

"Look at men like Elias and Major Ridge. They're people I might have met anywhere. And so is Chief Ross. Chief Lowrey is something else again. And there are so many who have good educations but still hang onto the old ways. For example, there's a carpenter—everyone calls him Arthur but he prefers his Cherokee name Cheowa—he's been through years of schooling, I understand, and speaks English as proficiently as you or I. But Cheowa runs around half-naked and he hates whites."

"Do you find that so strange? There are many like this Cheowa, I'm sure, who don't really agree that progress has been that good for the people."

Parker grunted. "I think Wheeler was right when he said Cheowa was a backward type. Of all the people

I've met here, that man is without a doubt the most primitive. If you ever meet him, give him a wide berth. I don't trust him. And more than likely he's the one the National Committee will call on to build your school."

The thought of an elegant young lady like Agatha Lake living in the midst of all the naked men and women who would be in town for the Council meetings inspired a moment of panic in Parker.

"Miss Lake, are you certain you know what you've gotten yourself into? Do you really have any idea of the conditions here? Not only children, but even adults show no hesitation in appearing without any clothes. I couldn't believe my eyes last year when they held the Green Corn Dance. All the Indians stripped off whatever clothes they were wearing and went to the creek for that Going to Water ceremony, the one they call *Atawastiyi*. There they allow themselves to be scratched by the medicine man, who uses sticks that have rattlesnake teeth on them. Then they all dip themselves in the water; even those who call themselves Christians did it."

"Do you think I ought to be shocked?" Agatha replied, a note of indignation in her voice. "That ceremony you described is one of the oldest and most respected traditions of the Cherokee people. They've been doing it for centuries. In fact," she continued, her voice now calm, as though teaching one of her young charges, "there are several forms of that ceremony. Each one represents a ritual cleansing of the spirit and no Cherokee would think of undertaking anything of importance without purifying himself first. You might be interested to know that it is because the Cherokees see a similarity between Going to Water and baptism that so many have become Christians. And as far as displaying oneself is concerned, what's wrong with that? There is nothing sinful about having a body, even though many strict churchmen would have us believe there is."

"C'mon Miss Lake, be honest. Would you do something like that? How would you feel about being in a crowd of people stripped naked and plunging into a creek?"

It was too late to retract that question; but to Parker's surprise Agatha took no offense. Instead she laughed easily. "I might consider it," she replied, "if the occasion seemed important enough. You seem to think I've been sheltered from the realities of the world, Mr. Parker. I think you're going to be surprised to see how wrong you are. There are too many people who want the Cherokee to become white Christians. I believe it's more important that they become fine Cherokee who are able to stand up proudly to anyone."

"You've really developed a feeling for these people, haven't you, Miss Lake?"

"Of course," she answered, smiling slyly. "That's because I'm one of them."

Parker stared in shock for a moment. "Why did you let me go on and on like that?" he complained, reddening at the thought of how foolish he must look to her.

"I'm sorry," Agatha apologized, "but I wanted you to speak freely and was afraid you wouldn't if you knew."

"Have you heard of the troubles the Nation is encountering with the state of Georgia?" Parker asked, still zigzagging back and forth between feeling miffed and wanting Agatha to like him. "There's trouble brewing in this paradise you speak so highly of."

"I've tried to keep abreast of it while I've been at school," Agatha responded. "Anyway," she continued with an edge of ice in her voice, "since you're so aware, how do you feel about the question of removal?"

"Mixed. In spirit, I'm sympathetic to the Indians' right to keep what I see at their land, along with everything they've done to improve it. But to be honest, I don't know how much longer they're going to be able to hold out, particularly since President Jackson isn't going to lift a finger to help them."

"And if it comes to a showdown," Agatha asked, "what will you do then?"

"I don't know," Parker answered, his tone softer now. "Honestly, I don't." Agatha's question was one that had crossed his mind many times, one he'd even discussed with Indian Agent Cullen.

"I've become fond of the Cherokee people," he continued slowly. He was exploring his thoughts while he was speaking. "I think they're being pushed around unfairly. But is it really my business? I ask myself that a lot. And most of the time when I do, I answer that it's not my business, but theirs. But even though I know I'm a printer and not a fighter, that I'm an American citizen, not an Indian, something bothers me about the ease with which I seem to be able to turn away. So you see, there I am right in the middle. What I am sure of right now—perhaps the only thing—is that if the time ever comes when a serious attempt is made to force the Cherokee from this land, I have no idea which direction I will move in."

"Although I would have preferred to hear a stronger commitment to the Cherokee from you, Mr. Parker, I do appreciate your frankness." Agatha smiled and Parker warmed instantly. "For my part," she went on, "I, as you may well imagine, am committed to the belief that my people will never be removed, that the

law is on our side and as long as we have people like
John Ross to carry our appeals to the Supreme Court
in Washington, we have nothing to fear. In any event,
my new friend, whatever happens to the Nation happens
to me. My people are my future."

Ridiculous, Parker thought. Agatha was naive.
Her thinking was packed with idealistic, romantic fan-
tasies, yet the conviction in her voice, her pride in her
people were virtues he admired. He was just about to
say so when a soft rapping sound was heard from
within the house.

"Agatha, you have to get an early start," Harriet
called softly. "You'll need a good night's sleep."

Parker felt a lump in his throat. Everything
seemed to have gone wrong that night. Agatha was
probably feeling she was well rid of him.

"I hope I haven't offended you, Miss Lake," he
said as they stood to say good-by.

"Heavens no!" she exclaimed as if they had been
discussing subjects as light as music or theater all evening. "The only thing that offends me is your very stiff
formality in addressing me as Miss Lake. Am I so
unapproachable you can't call me Aggie?"

A wave of relief surged through Parker.

"I'd like that," he said reaching out to take her
hand, "and I'm looking forward to the day you come
back to open the school."

"You won't have to wait that long, John. I'm going home for a few weeks and I'll send for you before I
come back to start teaching. I'd like you to meet my
family." She leaned forward and kissed him lightly on
the cheek. Then, before he could react to her gesture
the way he would have liked, she was in the house.

In his cabin later that night, Parker felt lighter and
happier than he had since Boston. Somehow, with the

gentleness of Agatha's kiss still imprinted on his cheek, all confusions of loyalty involving the Cherokee Nation faded. A more personal future concerned him then, and to Parker it looked beautiful!

Chapter 9

On the afternoon before the ball game, Parker rode with Cullen to Spring Place. As they neared the village, they passed Elias Boudinot, who was wearing nothing but a leather loincloth.

"He's in training," Parker explained. "Every morning and evening since the challenge was accepted by Spring Place, Boudinot has been up at dawn, running a good ten miles before coming to the office. Then after leaving in the evening, he spends another hour running and exercising." Boudinot smiled and waved as Parker and Cullen rode past.

"You know why the Indians take ball play so seriously?"

Parker shook his head no.

"According to tradition, the team that wins the game also wins health and good fortune for his village. Also, it's what keeps them fit for war. Their name for the sport is *Anetsa,* which means Little Brother to War. Good ol' Sam Worcester has a fit every time Elias gets into a game. Says it's undoing the work of years of theological training. Sam has lived with these people and stood up for them, but he just can't understand them. Maybe after he's lived with 'em as long as I have he won't get so upset about their traditions."

Cullen slowed the horses to a gentle trot. "Sam seems to think that once the Indians are exposed to white man's religion, they're going to give up everything they've lived with all their lives. He's wrong, John. Dead wrong. The Cherokee have always been warriors and always will be. But now that they have no wars to fight, they've got to blow off steam somehow, so they do it in their ball games. *Anetsa* has been around as long as the Indians have. Don't know of a tribe anywhere in America or Canada that doesn't play some form of it to maintain their combat skills.

"There was a time when tribes settled some of their differences with ball play, but the contests never were satisfactory substitutes for war. The losers could always call for a rematch. One of the old-timers told me about one game that was played with the Creek when he was just a sprat. There were about a hundred players on each side. The game lasted for two days and nights with no time out to eat or rest. The Cherokee lost and they were so damned mad about it they sent a war party to square things up."

"Sore losers."

"That's right. They'll gamble on anything, and they're always out to win. But you'll find one thing true about the Cherokee when it comes to their games. They may be sore losers, but they don't cheat to win."

"Maybe Sam objects less to the game than to the gambling that goes with it," Parker chuckled.

Cullen laughed heartily and wiped the perspiration from his bald head. "You'll see every pine tree in the Nation turn pink before these Indians stop gambling, my friend. Don't be surprised if a couple of them bet their horses on the outcome of this ball game. It's happened before."

Hundreds of people had descended upon the

meadow near Spring Place and there were tents and lean-tos set up for shelter.

"Notice," Cullen pointed out, "how the teams stay away from one another till the day of the game. Neither team wants any part of the other's magic."

"Why are those older boys patrolling the ball field so carefully?" Parker asked.

"So no one walks on it before the game," was the answer. "Each team also wants to make sure that no one from the opposite side throws a slow-moving turtle or a twisting snake onto the field to slow them down."

There was a commotion near the field. All the patrol boys had lined up to prevent a hare from crossing. The hare, confused and extremely frightened by the many shouts and waving arms directed at it, fled into the nearby woods.

"You see how seriously the Indians take their ball play?" Cullen commented. "Rabbits are not considered good luck around the ball field. They lose their wits too easily and that could make a team lose the game."

Parker recalled one night a few days before. Cullen had been seated with Little Tree and his family for supper when Boudinot ran up, not even breathing hard.

"Consorting with the enemy?" Boudinot taunted Parker. "Why aren't you supporting the New Echota team?"

"He's supporting you very well," Little Tree put in. "He's even going to donate a pig and three chickens to me when it's over."

"If you win," Boudinot said smugly.

"We'll win," Little Tree replied as his children cheered. "Now if we were playing a good team, say the one from Head of Coosa, I might not be so sure. But

New Echota? It'll be easier than playing a bunch of old women."

Boudinot winked at Parker. "You ready to lose another pig and three chickens, Little Tree?"

"I accepted John's bet because he doesn't have much to lose. From you, Elias, I would expect a more substantial wager. Say two pigs?"

"I can always use two more pigs," Elias agreed. "Spring Place will be feeling the pangs of hunger by the time New Echota wins all your food."

The children roared, delighted with Boudinot's playful mocking.

Now it was late in the afternoon. Cullen and Parker watched as each team's shaman gathered all his players and began the religious ceremonies that always preceded the ball play. Each team was represented by about twenty-five players, women as well as men.

"Kind of rough for the ladies, isn't it?" Parker commented.

"Rough for everybody, but they love it. You seem to forget that Cherokee women often went out with the men on war parties. They aren't the delicate creatures you find back home, Parker." Thinking of Agatha, Parker smiled.

After the ritual prayers by the medicine men, the players went to various small buildings in the town where families kept their sacred fires burning from one year to the next. These small huts provided shelter during extremely bitter cold but otherwise were used only to keep the fire and for the purification ceremony.

The players, stripped of whatever clothing they wore, entered the ast. There they would spend the night in silence. They had fasted for two days and would now drink a bitter potion that would induce heavy perspiration.

Before sunrise the following morning, the players

were called from the *asi* to where everyone had gathered in silence at the side of the river. The players, still naked, stood quietly while the medicine men moved among them, scratching their legs with fishbone scratchers. Parker knew that the rattlesnake-tooth scratchers were used only for special religious observances or as a penalty for a religious violation of some kind.

Once all the ball players had been scratched, they walked into the water. As the *anidawehi* chanted from the bank, they plunged themselves under the water seven times and stood to face the rising sun. At a signal from the medicine men, they climbed out of the water and were painted with charcoal that the medicine men had obtained from trees struck by lightning. Some of the players were rubbing their legs with turtle meat in order to gain stamina for the game.

Another chant from the *anidawehi,* and the crowds let out a cheer. Some of the players put on their clothes, while others headed for the ball field as naked as they had spent the night.

Holding two racquets made of hickory saplings and sinew, the players marched onto the field, each player standing opposite one from the opposing team. The playing field was about a hundred and twenty yards long and seventy-five yards wide. At either end were the goal posts which were set about ten feet apart and topped with a crossbar eight feet off the ground. The number of guards at the goals depended on the total number of players, with never fewer than two nor more than five. For this contest, both teams had agreed on three guards. These players were required to stay within an area that was marked out on the ground with red paint and were permitted the use of hands as well as racquets during play.

In the middle of the field a six-foot circle had

been cleared and George Lowrey and Cheowa faced each other in it, their leather-netted racquets scraping the ground, waiting for one of the drivers to toss in the ball.

Parker looked out at the players. "Cullen," he shouted, "the women don't have racquets!"

"That's because it's too dangerous to let women have clubs in a game like this. All the women are allowed to do is grab the ball with their hands and run with it or throw it. The men aren't allowed to touch the ball with their hands."

Each team had two men called drivers, who carried long hickory switches and whose function was to make sure that the rules weren't broken. Cullen explained that the rules varied from game to game as the players agreed. "This is a friendly contest, so they've ruled out hitting another player on the head with the racquet, and they can't hit or block anyone who doesn't have the ball in his possession. Of course, if a player is in position to catch a ball or pick it up, it's the same as if he already had it, so you're likely to see a few bones cracked."

An old man who had played in former years walked onto the field holding a small buckskin ball. After admonishing the players to be fair and not to quarrel, he threw it. A cheer went up as the ball was tossed into play and Lowrey deftly swept it up and passed it across to Boudinot. Parker noticed that Lowrey's racquet kept on swinging after the ball was in the air, and Cheowa ducked his head just as the racquet whizzed past.

"I thought you said they weren't allowed to hit another player on the head," Parker mentioned.

"I don't know what you saw," Cullen replied, craning his neck to keep the action in sight, "but I saw Chief Lowrey pass the ball to Boudinot. Cheowa just happened to have his head in the way of George's swing, that's all. Can't penalize a man for following through, you know."

Boudinot ran with the ball about ten yards, then passed it to another player down the field just before one of the women on the Spring Place team smashed into him and knocked him out of bounds. He was back on his feet before they stopped rolling and offered her a hand up as they went back to the play.

The ball was carried almost to the goal posts, and then the New Echota player swung his racquet as though trying to drive a wedge into an oak log. The ball hit one of the Spring Place guards in the face and knocked him over backwards. Another of the guards caught the ball with his racquet and threw it far down the field toward the right sideline, where Lowrey was waiting.

By this time the first guard was on his feet, shaking his head dizzily, blood streaming from his nose. He grinned at his teammates as he wiped it off with the back of his hand, then ignored what was only a minor discomfort.

The action swung from one end of the field to the other and when the ball finally went sailing under the uprights to score the first point for New Echota, the crowd went wild.

"What do you think you're doing?" Parker yelled. One of Little Tree's small boys had walked up to him and wordlessly stomped on his foot before running off into the crowd.

"He pictured you already taking his daddy's pig and chickens," Cullen explained, shaking with laughter. "Imagine what he's going to do to you if New Echota wins the game."

One of the Spring Place spectators had picked up a piece of a pine branch and swung it at the man next to him, cracking a couple of ribs. Parker joined two other men to help break up the fight. They held down the angry spectator, who screamed curses at the top of his voice as they dragged him far off the edge of the playing field to cool off and securely tied him to a tree with rawhide thongs.

"What was that all about?" Cullen asked as Parker moved back to his side.

"He bet a horse that Spring Place would make the first point. Didn't mind losing the horse, just got mad as hell when the guy wouldn't bet the horse on who got the next point."

A roar went up at the far side of the field. A pile of players was on the ground flailing away with their racquets, fists and feet. The drivers from both teams were beating at the combatants with their hickory switches and one or two at a time the players pulled back. On the bottom of the heap, Cheowa and Little Tree valiantly jabbed and swung their racquets to fend off anyone who was trying to scoop the ball out from under Cheowa's back.

One of the drivers picked up the ball, then gave Cheowa two lusty whacks across the chest with his hickory switch for keeping it out of play. Cheowa grinned derisively as the switch left two bleeding gashes across his broad chest, each one of which matched the size of the cut that had been opened behind his ear.

By noon the score stood at seven for Spring Place and eight for New Echota. Parker and Cullen, like most of the crowd, munched on cornbread and cold cooked meat they had brought along; no one wanted to interrupt the game to look for a fancier meal.

For two hours there were no points scored. One spectator was badly wounded when another took special offense at an insult and there were two players from the New Echota team wounded so critically they couldn't continue play. Spring Place had only lost one player, but one of the goal guards was still in the game despite a broken arm and a gash that had striped his leg with blood.

"If someone doesn't score soon," Parker observed, "everyone, including the spectators, will be too frustrated to stick this thing out!"

Suddenly, as if fate had heard the words, in the space of less than twenty minutes, New Echota scored another point. Depending on whom they were rooting for, the crowds either jeered or screamed their approval. Then, a moment later, the tables were turned. Spring Place came back with three fast points and the game was over.

One of McCoy's kinsmen claimed that Spring Place had fouled repeatedly. Boudinot and Lowrey had to restrain him from attempting to kill every member of the Spring Place team. People were scampering from one place to another collecting bets and Parker wasn't surprised to see a bruised and bleeding but pleased Little Tree walking toward him.

"You should have listened to me, Tsani. I told you to put your money on our team. Your pig is going to taste good."

Cheowa appeared a moment after Little Tree. Parker stared at the carpenter's battered flesh and realized suddenly where he had acquired all his scars. At least six wounds were bleeding. Two fingers looked broken but the hand was so swollen and bruised it was hard to tell.

"Is this the *unaka* who bet his pig and chickens?" Cheowa asked.

"He's the one," Little Tree admitted reluctantly.

"Thanks for the presents, Parker," the unsmiling Cheowa said.

Little Tree shook his head sadly. "I bet him the three chickens that I'd make more points than he would."

"Stupid bet," Cheowa said, moving off to join the other players as they bathed their wounds in the river.

"He's right," Parker teased his friend. "Stupid bet."

Despite losing two pigs and the sight in one eye for a few days, Boudinot was happy about the outcome of the ball game.

"They were good men to play," he said. "The next time we have a contest, I'll get my pigs back."

"I'll take a bet on that," Little Tree said, putting an arm around Boudinot's shoulder and walking with him to the river to bathe.

There was a great feast that evening. Weaving themselves among those who coordinated the festivities were the children. Still playing the games of their grandfathers, they laughed exuberantly.

Under one shelter, Parker watched Little Tree's son Little Bear as he listened intently to his grandfather's instructions. The old man was teaching the boy the skill of playing hoop-and-pole. Bending together over their handwork, they wove the stiff grasses that could eventually form the hoop.

"Now cut sticks, Little Bear," his grandfather instructed him. In only a few moments, the young boy had gathered several for inspection. Anxiously he waited until his grandfather spoke.

"They are fine, my young one, as strong and as straight as you will be in not too many years."

Little Bear smiled, relieved he had done well. Then, rolling the hoop, he practiced throwing the long sticks through the opening.

Parker couldn't stop staring at the old man and boy, they were obviously so concerned for one another.

In not too long a time, an arm dropped around his shoulder. "It is a beautiful sight, isn't it," Little Tree said, his eyes filling with tears. "May my family always be this happy."

Chapter 10

As she had promised, Aggie sent for Parker about a week later. He thought it typical of her as a person of means that she didn't send word to have him come, but instead, sent a driver in charge of a fine spring buggy. The driver was black and looked to be in his fifties. He wore an elaborate brass-buttoned red and white uniform that bore the same crest as the ornate brass plate on the seat of the buggy, a crest displaying the name LAKE as well as the equivalent Cherokee word VDALI. Aside from speaking a few sullen words to let Parker know that the Lakes were expecting him, the driver had so little to say that after the first five miles, Parker abandoned his attempts to talk with the man.

Having traveled with Little Tree several times when they were distributing the *Phoenix,* Parker recognized some of the wealthier homes they passed on their way to Lakehurst, the Lakes' huge farm. Boudinot had told Parker that David Lake had one of the most prosperous farms in the country and that he raised tobacco, cotton and pecans as cash crops. "A fine gentleman," the Indian had concluded. "One of our first subscribers, too. David Lake even made a contribution to pay for most of the labor to build the shop. Fine gentleman."

As the buggy turned off the highway and bounced down a lane through a stand of pecans, Parker saw in the distance a house that rivaled even the mansion of Rich Joe Vann. They came closer and he saw that it was in fact larger than the Vann homestead.

The structure was two stories tall. Spotless white trim set off the red bricks and the pillared verandah ran the length of the house; there was a balcony on the second floor. The wide, curving drive leading to the front was lined with dogwood trees and rose bushes. Two black slaves and an Indian girl were picking peaches in the orchard to the east of the house and were so involved with their chores they didn't look up as the buggy clattered up the drive.

Parker was beginning to feel uncomfortable in such surroundings. The discomfort increased as a uniformed servant appeared on the porch to greet him. "Miz Aggie is in the library, sir," he said, guiding Parker into a vestibule that more than equaled Greene's in Boston. Where David Greene's home had been lavishly finished in marble, Lakehurst seemed warmer with its hardwood gleaming with polished varnish.

Two portraits flanked the broad, curving stairway. One revealed a stern-faced man who could have been either a statesman or an old English trader. The other was of a pleasantly smiling woman dressed in laces that had been fashionable a hundred years before.

In the center of the vestibule was a huge handmade rug woven with a pattern similar to the many he had seen in Cherokee homes. So striking was it that Parker imagined the vestibule might have been designed around it. The brilliant red, white and yellow pattern, Parker knew, symbolized success, peace, security and joy and the stylized thunderbolt was a representation of the protector of the Cherokee people.

What made the rug appear very much in place were the vases of roses on the small tables, identical to the shades in the rug, which were repeated throughout the vestibule.

Parker tipped his head back to study the circular window high above the doorway. Both it and the half-moon lights on either side were of beveled glass. Making its way through the bevels, the sunlight broke into multi-hued bands and flooded the room.

David Greene would be envious, Parker thought. How could Aggie Lake leave surroundings like this and live in New Echota?

"John!" Agatha called as he entered the library. "It's good to have you here." She took his hand and led him toward a stunning woman who was seated on the sofa by the window at the far end of the room. "John, I would like you to meet my mother, Annabelle Lake. Mother, this is the man I've told you about, John Parker."

Mrs. Lake smiled pleasantly, putting down the needlepoint she had been occupied with. Her eyes were the same blue as her daughter's and flashed with just as much sparkle and warmth. A few wrinkles marked what would otherwise have been a perfect complexion and Mrs. Lake's hair had begun to gray, but there was no doubt where Agatha had gotten her beauty.

"Welcome, Mr. Parker," Mrs. Lake said simply, raising a hand.

Parker suffered a moment of panic. Should he shake the hand or plant a kiss on it? In his attempt to make the appropriate gesture, he tried a polite bow, and felt ridiculous. He concluded he must have looked ridiculous, too, for Agatha remarked, "See, Mother? I told you he was stiff and formal."

"Oh, my heavens, Mr. Parker, sit down and relax," Mrs. Lake laughed easily. "We don't bite."

He chose one of the overstuffed leather wing chairs facing the sofa and eased himself into it. "Would you care for tea or coffee?" Mrs. Lake asked. "I know I can't wait to sip something refreshing whenever I have to make the trip to New Town."

"Mother," Agatha insisted with a note of exasperation in her voice, "it's been called New Echota for several years now."

"It will always be New Town to me. There have been too many changes lately, my dear. I simply can't keep up with all of them." She looked again at Parker, who realized she was waiting for a reply to her question.

"Tea would be fine, Mrs. Lake."

She leaned forward to pick up a silver bell and delicately shook it. Almost immediately a Cherokee girl about twelve or thirteen years old appeared in the doorway.

"Susan, please bring us tea." The girl nodded and disappeared.

"I've heard so much about you, Mr. Parker," Mrs. Lake smiled. "You'd think you were the only person Aggie had met in the three years she was away. You're a printer?"

They talked about his work in Boston and at the *Phoenix* until the girl appeared with a tray. From observing Susan's nervousness, Parker decided she'd been told to make a good impression on him and was pleased that he'd commanded such attention.

"Aggie tells me you've even learned the Cherokee language, Mr. Parker."

"I wish I could say I have, Mrs. Lake, but at least I'm beginning to feel a little more comfortable with it. Having to set type in Cherokee has been a help, too. Do you speak the language?"

She laughed. "How could I help it? I've spent all

my life here. Everyone in our family can read Cherokee, with the exception of a few of the older slaves who've never learned to read or write English, either. My husband is a long-time friend of George Guess—you probably know him by his Indian name, Sequoyah—and was one of the few people who didn't think he was crazy to work so hard to develop the syllabary for the Cherokee."

"Well, he's certainly proved himself anything but crazy," Parker replied. "And judging from the letters we've had from him, he's hoping that someday there will be a newspaper in the West, too."

"He deserves his dream," Mrs. Lake asserted. "About a year before George went to Arkansas, he spent a month with us." She picked up a filigreed candlestick and handed it to Parker. "This is what he can do," she continued while Parker admired the delicate silver work. "Our friend is a fine silversmith. Most of the time he was here we hardly ever saw him. He kept to himself in his room or stayed out in the orchard, scribbling and scrawling. Working on the syllabary was a passion with him, despite his awareness that nobody else thought he was pursuing anything worthwhile. What he had accomplished at the end of his twelve-year-long struggle was the solution to a linguistic problem that had confounded even professional etymologists."

"But during the process," Agatha interrupted, "he became so absorbed in his work that he neglected his farm and family. Eventually, his wife threw him out."

"I never met Sally Guess," Mrs. Lake sniffed, "but it's my understanding she was a shrew. After she threw George out, he started working in a little cabin near their home. Rumor says that Sally and her neighbors convinced themselves he was up to some kind of witchcraft. So while Sally lured him from his solitary refuge, the neighbors set fire to his cabin. Everything George had done up to that point was completely destroyed. That's when he came here. David gave him every possible encouragement and not long afterward, he enrolled to go west with Ahuludegi."

"Known as John Jolly by whites," Aggie promptly explained.

"Anyway," Mrs. Lake went on, "before he left, George proved to the world how easy it was for Cherokee to read and write in their native tongue."

Voices and sounds filtered in from the rear of the house. "Your father's back, Aggie," Mrs. Lake informed everyone. "That man has yet to make a quiet entrance," she said tenderly. "I'd better see that he's presentable."

"Poor Father." Agatha sighed half in fun, half seriously. "He spends all day working in the fields and then comes home to Mother's fussing about his appearance."

"I hope she isn't doing it on my account," Parker protested.

"Oh, she's not. Mother complains about Sally Guess being a hard woman to get along with, but there are times when she's almost as difficult herself. Right now it looks like she's on her best behavior. I warned her she'd better be."

Parker was amused. "My mother was like that, too," he recalled. "Pa would come in from the barn and it was 'Wipe your feet, wash your hands, put on a clean shirt before you sit down at my table.' "

"Do you miss being in Massachusetts, John?"

"I did for a while after I came here, but not any more. I've got a comfortable little cabin, some pigs and chickens and a fine garden, and I've made so many good friends like Little Tree that Massachusetts seems to be worlds away. No, I'm not homesick any more.

Particularly," he added shyly, "now that you're here."

"I hope that nothing changes your feelings for me, John."

"What could, Aggie?"

The two stared deeply at one another. Then, at the sound of approaching footsteps, Agatha turned. "Father," she said as they drew near, "this is John Parker. John, my father David Lake."

As he looked up, John Parker found himself face to face with a swarthy Cherokee who towered a full head above him. Except for the smiling face and his clothing, the Indian could have been Cheowa.

Chapter 11

For Parker, the next several weeks were agonizing. His head swam unendingly with visions of Aggie. He set type and pulled the long lever on the huge press without conscious thought. On at least two occasions Wheeler had to shake his shoulder to get response to a question.

"John, get hold of yourself, boy. I know it isn't every young man who has a girl that's both rich and pretty, but your head's so high in the clouds your mind doesn't know what your hands are doing. The mistakes you're making are going to break us! When's that young woman moving here for good so we can have our star printer back again?"

Even after Aggie came back to New Echota and moved in with Elias and Harriet, Parker was preoccupied with her. The fact that the girl he cared so much about was Cherokee disturbed him. Maybe it was prejudice from his childhood that wasn't so easy to wash away. Worse, perhaps it was his lack of true commitment to a cause that he had chosen to work for at least on the surface. Whatever the reason, he felt wrenched in two directions.

Agatha tuned in easily to Parker's confusion. One

night during an after-dinner walk, she questioned him about it.

"John, ever since the night you were at my home you've seemed distant at times. There are moments when we're speaking with one another that you can hardly look at me."

"Aggie, that's—"

"Don't deny it, John," Agatha interrupted. "You can barely look me in the eye right now! What is it? Tell me! Are you holding back because I'm Cherokee?"

The noise expelled from Parker's throat was half a sigh, half a sob. It was going to be a relief to talk about what he'd been feeling, but he knew the pain he might cause himself and Agatha because of that need. . . .

"Stop thinking so hard, John!" Agatha ordered. "Just talk!"

"It's your father, Aggie. Seeing him reminded me how proud the Cherokee people are, and how," John hesitated, ". . . and how unlikely the bravest among them would be to admit that their best opportunity for survival lies in the West. Now don't freeze up on me, Aggie," Parker interjected, seeing her reaction.

"What do you expect me to do?" Agatha asked, her voice choked with frustration. "I want you to care for me, but I won't try to hid from you who I am or how I feel. What I will try to do one last time is explain to you why I believe so strongly that my people belong right here." Agatha took several deep breaths to collect herself.

"My family," she began finally, "represents a conglomeration of contrasts. My great-grandfather on my father's side did some pretty fancy dealing with several English traders and began laying out what was to become one of the largest estates in the Nation, larger and finer than anything David Vann had created, I can tell you that.

"My father and his brother fought at Horseshoe Bend with Jackson and my uncle didn't come back. I'm one of six children. You'd better sit down for this introduction, things get a little complicated. My oldest brother married and moved some distance from here to live with his wife's family. The next oldest is Catherine. Her husband, Going Horse, supervises most of the work done on the farm. I am the third child. Then come the twins, Leonard and Susannah, who are both at school in the East. The youngest of us is Jimmy. If you remember the time you came to our house, Jimmy was the one whose ambitions led him no further than pulling the tail of our loyal, patient house cat."

"I remember," Parker replied. "Especially I remember that at the dinner table you all looked so different from one another, you and your mother and your sister all with spectacular blue eyes and all the women but Catherine dressed in modern clothing; she was lovely in calico. And there were yards of buckskin at that table. What a handsome patchwork your family was that night."

"The one thing we completely agreed on," Agatha responded seriously, "is what I keep telling you about. Whether mixed-bloods or full-bloods, we are Cherokee and we will not leave our homes and our lands."

Agatha's words clashed with the echo of Cullen from days before. "There's no way to get around removal, Parker. All Ross can do is delay it awhile. Sooner or later, by whatever means, these people are going to have to leave here and go west. I wish I could convince them of it; maybe some of them will listen to you."

* * *

Though he didn't state them clearly, Elias Boudinot was having second thoughts. As usual, he reported the news in the columns of the *Phoenix* as it happened, but lately almost every issue carried grim warnings alongside the exhortations to stand fast with the Council.

"Almighty God and the just laws of the United States are on our side," he reported in one issue, yet on the back page reprinted recent laws passed by the Georgia Legislature making it illegal for any white man to live and work in the Cherokee lands unless he registered first as an agent for the government of Georgia.

Cullen advised Parker to ignore the new laws. "Georgia doesn't have any legal authority over the Cherokee Nation yet, and Ross has taken the matter up with the Supreme Court in Washington. In the meantime my job is to see that no whites come thieving through here without permission from the National Committee and at the same time to bang my head against a wall trying to get Ross and Major Ridge to understand their cause is hopeless. God," he said, his voice harsh, "I get weary of it all sometimes."

Aggie started her school with fourteen children, ages ranging from six to ten.

Across the square from the *Phoenix*, the courthouse rang with the childrens' songs and laughter. If they had done well in their studies, Aggie let them go a little early. When she did, they raced for the stream, stripping off their clothes and plunging into the inviting water.

Once a week the children were taken on a picnic. It was always on the day Parker had finished up printing the *Phoenix* for a week and could get off early. As Agatha guided the children across the commons and into the woods to pick berries or gather nuts, he accompanied her.

"There are so many things for the children to learn," she murmured as they sat back against a tree and watched them.

"Maybe, but right now I'm thinking about all the things they're teaching me."

"Like what?"

"Old legends about how the animals used to run things and the way to shoot an arrow. You know what Fierce Bear did a couple of weeks ago?"

Agatha shook her head, looking at the round little Fierce Bear climbing a tree to see if he could find a beehive.

"He bet me he could throw a spear farther than I could, and straighter, too. That child isn't any more than eight years old and he's challenging me to war contests, for Pete's sake. Winning some of them, too, I must confess."

Agatha laughed. "Fierce Bear is the only one in the school who regularly gets himself punished. See all the scars on his legs? The *anidawehi* have worn out several rattlesnake scratchers on him already. He's always in trouble."

"Why doesn't his father do something about his behavior?"

Agatha looked at him as if he'd suggested hanging the boy. "You must know by know, John, that no Cherokee except the *anidawehi* ever punishes a child."

Parker nodded uncertainly, thinking there ought to be an exception made in Fierce Bear's case. "Anyway," he went on, "the children have taught me other things. When I was a youngster, I was scared to death of lightning, and for the longest time, I couldn't figure out why I've never seen a Cherokee child afraid of it. Then the children told me that lightning and thunder are messengers of Asgaya Galunlati and that they were responsible for bringing fire to your people."

"Of course," Agatha agreed. "And that's the reason that only the anidawehi are allowed to touch a tree that has been struck by lightning. I thought everyone knew that."

"Dumb John isn't up on all those Indian legends yet," Parker grinned. "But seriously, Aggie, I wonder if I'll ever really understand your people."

"Maybe you're trying too hard. Come on," she coaxed, getting to her feet. "The children want to go swimming and I don't know how deep the water is here. We'd better keep an eye on them."

Parker watched as without another word Agatha stripped off her blouse and skirt.

"You're incredibly beautiful," he said, carefully monitoring his reaction to her nakedness.

"Well," she returned, racing into the water after her pupils and ignoring his compliment, "aren't you coming in?"

Parker had often seen Cherokee girls gathering berries or working in the fields wearing little or nothing, but it came as a surprise to see Aggie Lake transform so quickly from the exquisitely dressed daughter of a wealthy farmer to a simple, unashamed native. Yet in a moment he, too, was stripped and diving in, heedless of the taunts of the children, who swam like fish and left him far behind.

Fierce Bear ducked one of the girls and distracted Parker for a moment. When he turned back to Aggie, there was no sign of her.

Panicking, he splashed toward the place near the reeds where he'd last seen her. His mind was full of every conceivable tragedy that might have happened to her. As he stood searching, waist high in water, he pictured explaining to Aggie's parents that she had drowned. . . .

"Aggie!" Parker called her name over and over and over, completely unprepared for the pair of hands he felt grabbing his ankle and pulled him under. Still convulsed with worry—and now surprise—he came up sputtering and only inches away from Aggie's laughing face.

"You're too serious, John," she chided, eyes twinkling, "and not much of a swimmer, are you? Do you think you can find breath enough to catch me?" She waved a playful good-by and dived beneath the surface.

With the giggles of the children ringing behind, Parker went after her. Aggie was almost within his grasp when deftly she swam away again. Finally he caught her.

"You had the advantage but let me catch up, didn't you?"

Agatha smiled her answer, her glistening black hair framing her lovely face as she and Parker floated and drifted like dancers, with the gentle current. Gracefully, Agatha slipped her hands behind Parker's head, and he held her gently. For several long moments they said nothing, sharing, instead, the sounds of whirling leaves and happy children.

"Aggie," Parker said impulsively, "I love you."

Agatha pulled his head toward hers for a kiss, savoring it as much as he did. Then suddenly she withdrew and in a less convincing attempt at playfulness, quickly splashed water in his face and swam quickly off.

"I love you, too, John," she called out to him, "but showing each other properly will have to wait until the children aren't around."

The afternoon passed too quickly and that evening after he climbed under the thatched shelter outside his cabin and tried to sleep, Parker thought ceaselessly of Aggie.

"*O-si-yo!*"

There had been no sound of anyone approaching, but the interruption was passionately welcomed.

"Aggie!"

She stepped toward him silently and once again dropped her clothing to the ground.

"The children aren't around now, John."

Two months later Parker was again at Lakehurst. During dinner, he was uncomfortably twisting around in his mind how to ask David Lake for permission to marry his daughter, when one of the slaves came running from the kitchen.

"What is it, Amos?" Lake demanded, noticing at once the terrified look on the old man's face.

"The surveyors are here!"

Lake and Going Horse exchanged worried glances, then headed outdoors. There, along with Parker, who had joined them, they witnessed the dismaying sight of a four-man surveying crew of white men pounding stakes and measuring their way across the wide lawns in front of the mansion.

Lake demanded to know why they were there.

"Git outa our way, Indian," the hefty leader shouted. "We gotta get this land recorded fer the lottery."

"Lottery? What are you talking about?"

"Shit, you're as stupid as we thought! Jist as soon as all you Indians git the hell off of Georgia land, we're gonna have a lottery for the property."

"This is my property!" Lake thundered. "And nobody's going anywhere but you!" The Cherokee took a step forward, but felt Parker's hand restraining him.

"Mr. Lake, look."

Several hundred yards down the lane a detail of eight Georgia militiamen sat astride their horses, their rifles held ready across their knees. They were a ragtag bunch, that was obvious, and there was no doubt in anyone's mind they would just as soon shoot as sit their mounts.

"Thet's right, Pops, get a hold on that heathen temper," spat the surveyor, "and don't worry. My friends there—ain't none of 'em gonna come in here afore you're gone. We're jist gettin' ready, that's all. An' we've got lots more men to back up the group you see right here. So, my friend," the perspiring spokesman ordered, "kindly move yer red ass outa my way. We got work to do!"

Lake didn't budge. "Sir," he spat. "If you and your men do not remove yourselves from my land right now, I personally will ride to the home of my friend Andrew Jackson and request assistance. There are treaties our Nation has made with your federal government that prohibit what you are doing here! Now, get out!" Lake stood like stone, waiting for a reply.

Stalling for time to think, the loutish Georgia man extracted the grimy rag he had tucked in his belt and wiped his face on it. By the time he spoke again, he had calmed himself, not knowing exactly the status of this fierce looking Indian's connection. Despite what he'd heard about Georgia's increasing power in the Indian removal matter, the power of the federal government was still nothing to sneeze at. No sirree! So not knowing whether the man that stood so confidently facing him could back up his threats, the surveyor waved his men off.

"You win, Indian," he sneered, ". . . this time!"

For the next few hours, David Lake looked too distressed to be approached about the possibility of a marriage. Parker, in fact, felt during late afternoon that he was intruding and made his excuses for leaving early.

"Your father and I will talk another time, Aggie," he promised gently. Her lack of protest indicated he had been wise in deciding to leave.

The trip back to New Echota was uneventful until late afternoon, when he reached a spot three miles beyond Spring Place. There, he noticed smoke billowing above Tom Laurel's fields. When he galloped toward the Laurel home, Parker saw Tom's wife frantically waving for him to hurry to her. He spurred his horse to the edge of the clearing near the Laurel cabin and swung down.

"Betsy! My God!" Her hair had fallen from the sunbonnet she was wearing and strands of it were tangled across her forehead and cheeks. She'd been crying and was still so clogged with tears she could hardly speak.

Parker held the sobbing woman, trying to soothe her enough to learn what had happened. Finally he slapped her.

"Betsy! Tell me! Where's Tom?" Still unable to collect herself enough to speak clearly, Betsy took Parker's hand and dragged him to the far side of the cabin. There, Tom Laurel lay writhing on the ground. Parker knelt and placed a comforting hand on his forehead. Next he checked as well as he knew how for internal injuries and possible fractures. It was anyone's guess how many ribs had been broken and Tom's swollen, bloody face itself warranted attention.

"Men came," Betsy began breathlessly, "—white men. Said they wanted our horse. 'Here's a dollar,' one man said. 'You'll probably need every penny you can get for out west where you're going.' Oh, John, you should have heard him laugh when he said that. Tom ran in the house to get his rifle. That's when five of the men jumped him. 'Pass this on to your redskin friends,' they kept telling him, and then they kicked him and beat him till the man holding the horses made them stop and they rode off."

Parker looked out at the burning cornfield. It had been one of the finest in the entire Spring Place area. "Why did they do that?" he cried.

Betsy stared blankly at the devastated land. "I refused to sell them the crop for fifty cents' worth of whiskey."

Nausea welled up inside Parker. "Betsy," he whispered, "I'm sorry." Then, forcing the feeling away, he ordered, "Go get some water and some cloths. We'll see if we can make Tom more comfortable until I can get the doctor here for him."

Betsy walked to the spring near their cabin as Tom struggled painfully to speak. "Betsy is a good woman, Tsani, a good woman."

"Just lie still, Tom, please. I'm going to get you some help."

"Help no good now, Tsani. Raven Mocker coming."

"Don't be silly, you old buzzard. Why would the Raven Mocker want a skinny Indian like you?"

The eye that Tom had fought to keep open fell closed. Half delirious, he kept on bragging about his wife. "Betsy fight like panther! Kick two men in balls, tried to bite ear off another. They would have killed her if the leader hadn't made them leave."

Betsy came back with the water and cloths and she and Parker cleaned Tom up as best they could. Then Parker said, "I'm riding for the doctor, now, Tom. Don't give Betsy any trouble after I leave, and none of that talk about dying or it'll be your ear she'll be biting off!"

Boudinot and Worcester listened gravely while Parker told them about the surveyors and the beating of Tom Laurel. "I left word with Dr. Sloan's cook that he should head right out to the Laurel place, but she said it would be a while because the doctor was already out taking care of someone else those rednecks had beaten up."

"Cullen is already on his way to send word to get federal troops here," Boudinot said. "It's amazing how fast the news spreads, isn't it, Sam?"

Worcester nodded sadly. "And I'm afraid that the discovery is going to do more damage than anything else, Elias."

"What discovery?" Parker asked.

"You haven't heard? Gold, my friend, that's what we're talking about. A whole mess of it has been discovered near Dahlonega. Now nothing will stop the Georgians from taking our land. First it was our farms they wanted, and our crops, not to mention whatever other improvements we've been able to make here. But now that gold's been found, watch out! You see if they don't make it illegal for a Cherokee to take gold from his own land."

". . . and do nothing about punishing Georgians taking Cherokee gold from Cherokee land."

Trouble developed rapidly as soon as the serious search for the precious substance began. And as expected, soon the Cherokee Nation found itself on a collision course with Georgia. Bands of marauding whites calling themselves the Pony Club swooped down on isolated farms, robbing the Indians and unmercifully harassing them.

At Dahlonega and Auraria, mining camps sprang up almost overnight. Camping areas crowded with drunks, prostitutes, brawlers and thieves made murder an everyday occurrence. In response to pleas from Cullen and the other Indian agents working in the Nation, Madden and the commissioner made arrangements for protection of sorts. They convinced the Georgia delegation in Washington that if Georgia allowed foul treatment of the Indians to continue, there would be a public outcry heard from all over the United States, so loud, so persuasive that even the president and congress would be unable to prevent outraged whites from taking up arms and siding with the Cherokee.

Georgia responded to Madden's warning by sending the Georgia Guard to clean up the mess in the camps. The Guard rode in roughshod, scattering the Indian miners and driving them off. One aged Cherokee was ridden down when he ignored the captain's order to open a gate and allow his troops to pass. Another was so overcome with grief at what he was witnessing that he hanged himself from a tree outside his home.

In a matter of days, the cavalry had put an end to the mining camps by burning the shacks and destroying shovels, picks, and anything else that had been left behind. Although the Guard was effective in checking Cherokee mining, for the most part it turned its back on the forays of the Pony Club, which was interested in nothing less than making life unbearable for the Indians.

"The lands west of the Mississippi are the only place the Cherokee will find peace and quiet," the commander of the Guard, Colonel Sanford, was overheard to say.

Boudinot printed a notice in the *Phoenix* that was calculated to rile Sanford:

CHEROKEE WOMEN, BEWARE

It is said that the Georgia Guard have received orders, from the Governor we suppose, to inflict corporal punishment on such females as hereafter be guilty of insulting them . . . According to our understanding of insult, we think, first, it is undignified for a female to exercise it under any circumstances; and second, it is equally undignified for any gentleman to inflict corporal punishment on a female who may be guilty of such a crime.

The notice brought a prompt and venomous rebuttal from Sanford. He dismissed the "foul aspersions cast upon the Guard and upon those conducting the operations. Emanating as they do from that most polluted of all receptacles, the *Phoenix*," he asserted, "they would have passed me as does the idle wind but for their dissemination abroad. They are false, sir, as false as the canting and hypocritical fanatic who indites them."

A more violent reaction was displayed by Colonel Charles Nelson, the local field commander of the Guard. Nelson stormed into the *Phoenix* office, shoved Parker aside and grabbed Boudinot by his coat sleeve, pulling him to his feet. "You slimy little snake-eater," he spat, "I ought to arrest you and let you rot in the penitentiary!"

"On what charges? They ought to be interesting!" the Indian snapped back, extricating himself from Nelson's hold.

"These!" the Guard commander replied, grabbing a handful of Boudinot's articles and editorials and slamming them down on the desk. "In this one, right here, you slander the President of the United States by calling him a 'false and faithless father.' And this! Here you claim that the fine troops of the Georgia Guard encourage lawlessness. Boudinot, if I thought for one minute you had enough brains to write stuff like this, I'd put you in irons and haul you off to Milledgeville."

"Your doubting I could write these columns is an example of the Georgia Guard's prejudice against and ignorance of the Cherokee, Colonel Nelson," Boudinot replied, trying to control his temper. "And of course I wrote these columns. What's more, I intend to keep writing the truth of what is happening in the Cherokee Nation."

Nelson picked up Boudinot's inkwell and tossed it through the open window, then turned on Worcester. "I don't care what this big-mouth Indian maintains. I'm not so dense I don't know you're behind all the troubles here."

"Are preaching, teaching and baptizing such offenses, Colonel?" Worcester asked calmly. "Your men seem to think it's a crime comparable to murder."

"My men are God-fearing Christians!"

"Even those over at Tensewaytee? The ones who were there during a baptism at the river? Oh, they were such God-fearing Christians then that they waited until the ceremony was over and rode straight into the congregation while the people were still in the water. Imagine, Colonel! Your God-fearing Christian soldiers said they had been so moved by the ceremony that they wanted their horses baptized, too! A nine-year old child was ridden down by one of those soldiers, Colonel, and she nearly drowned. The day is coming when—"

"Worcester, you listen to me!" Nelson thundered. "The State of Georgia has done everything possible to encourage your good works among the Cherokee. The day is coming, you say. You can believe it is. That day is March 12, and if all of you so-called missionaries haven't quit your political machinations and gotten licenses to work here, you're going to find yourselves subject to four years' confinement in the penitentiary."

"And to obtain the license?" Worcester taunted, knowing well what the answer would be.

"Take the oath of allegiance to the State of Georgia."

"That is impossible, Colonel. We've already taken an oath of allegiance to God, and even you, God-fearing Christian that you are, must realize in your heart that such an allegiance is infinitely more important than one made to Georgia." Worcester turned his back and busied himself with paperwork. Parker and Boudinot did the same.

"March 12, you hear me?" Nelson sputtered as he stormed outdoors and across the square to the courthouse. Seeing where Nelson was headed, Parker ran out behind him, concern for Aggie's safety flooding his thoughts.

Nelson and his troopers waited politely for fifteen minutes until the school children had been dismissed. Then the Colonel removed his hat and spoke to Agatha.

"Ma'am, don't you know it's against the laws of the State of Georgia to teach blacks?"

"I'm well aware of that, Colonel," she replied. "But thank heaven this is not Georgia. This is the Cherokee Nation. Our people are far too civilized to make such laws."

"You are mistaken, ma'am; this *is* Georgia," the colonel replied coldly.

"That, Colonel," Agatha countered, "is for the Supreme Court to decide."

Parker watched as Nelson scowled and motioned

for his men to mount up. As they rode out of town, Parker put his arm around Aggie to comfort her.

"John, I'm not worried for myself," she said, her eyes brimming with tears. "It's the children—can't you see? I just know that the two black children who come to class won't be back. I saw them peering at us from around the side of the courthouse while that awful man was talking to me."

Several days later, Parker was on his way back to work after a mediocre lunch at McCoy's. He heard a shriek and wheeled around.

Cheowa was swinging Aggie around on the steps of the courthouse. Not giving a thought to Cheowa's massive size, Parker raced to the steps and whacked the Indian with the full weight of his doubled fists. The three fell in a heap, and Cheowa's hand snaked toward his knife as they rolled down the four steps to the street.

"Cheowa, no!" Aggie commanded, recovering. Immediately the Indian pulled back, but not before he and Parker were on their feet glaring at one another.

"He thinks you're hurting me," Aggie told Cheowa. Then she laughed and for a moment even Cheowa brightened.

"What was he doing with you, Aggie?" Parker asked, beginning to wonder if he had made a complete fool out of himself.

"Good heavens, John, we were just saying hello. We haven't seen each other in months. John," Agatha explained slowly, trying to restrain another laugh, "this is my older brother, the one I told you about who moved away. Cheowa, this is John."

Both men grunted their greetings. "We've met," they said simultaneously.

Chapter 12

A chilly January morning dawned over the river that wound past The Ridge's splendid home. Cheowa and Little Tree emerged silently from the *asi*, where they had spent the night drinking sacred potions and fasting in silence. The frost was shaken from the grass as their bare feet were joined by those of more than sixty other volunteers who had spent the night preparing for the purification ceremony. Within the space of twenty minutes, the naked Cherokee had assembled at the water's edge, oblivious to the chill in the winter air. A cloud of steam rose as their breaths mingled, the only sounds the chants of the *anidawehi,* who moved among them with rattlesnake scratchers. When each man had been scratched until blood was drawn, he walked into the water, shattering the thin ice that had formed near the shore during the night. Seven times the Indians immersed themselves and seven times rose to face the rising sun. Once more on the bank, the *anidawehi* completed the solemn Going to Water ceremony and then the men were led by The Ridge to the wide lawns that surrounded his home.

Some of the Indians put on the trousers they wore every day but most of them slipped into buckskin breechclouts; only a few wore buckskin shirts. There were as many bare feet as there were in moccasins. Totally absent was any white man's clothing.

The Cherokee women who had accompanied some of the men had prepared a simple meal for them. While the others ate, The Ridge disappeared into the house, then returned moments later. In one hand was the well-kept major's uniform that had been a gift from Andrew Jackson.

"Once I wore this uniform with great pride," The Ridge announced, holding the garment high, "and you have all seen me wear it at council meetings. It has been said that men knew me from many miles away because of this costume. And that's exactly what it is, a costume." He paused and regarded the army uniform at arm's length.

"Today," The Ridge went on, "the last thing I would do is wear anything Chicken Snake Jackson has given me!" Tossing the uniform on the ground, he stomped on the material and wiped his moccasins on it. As he did, a cheer exploded from the crowd.

The Ridge's son John gravely handed over a buffalo head, which his father pulled down tightly over his bushy white hair. Clad with the immense headdress, The Ridge with John's help, began applying gaudy red paint to his rounded torso.

"Where'd that come from?" Little Tree asked while the crowd roared its approval.

"Just some of the junk Elias has had stored in Worcester's house for a museum someday. Nobody knows what all is in that attic." The Ridge completed his preparations and again the crowd roared its approval. Then he called for food.

While The Ridge ate, the others began smearing themselves with war paint. Cheowa had braided feathers into his topknot and his face was a jagged pattern of red, white and black. His brother-in-law Going

Horse had prepared for the occasion by shaving his head, leaving a topknot that was somewhat on the short side but still recognizable as the mark of a Cherokee warrior. Around his shoulders he wore a deerskin robe.

Each of the more than sixty warriors was armed with a rifle, a knife and a tomahawk. Those who had them carried pistols, although Little Tree was concerned that the weapons were too old to fire well.

When finally the men were ready and The Ridge was satisfied that they were a fierce enough looking band, he reminded them of the instructions they had been given during the week.

"When Chief Ross went to the Council to ask permission to use any means necessary to drive out the white invaders who have settled on our lands, the Council appointed me to select the volunteers. It is a source of great pleasure to me to know that our Nation has no lack of warriors, including those who are old or disabled."

He glanced at his son, who had suffered from poor health since an early childhood illness. John Ridge, as all who were assembled on the lawn knew, was a statesman rather than a warrior, although he would gladly have joined the band.

"And I have been plagued by the women," The Ridge continued, looking fondly toward them where they sat by themselves. One young woman shook an angry fist, which the Ridge acknowledged with a smile.

"It is true I didn't choose them," he continued, "not because they lack courage or skill or pride, but simply because they have been too eager to take matters into their own hands. Each of you here has demonstrated the virtue of being capable of obeying orders without question. We can have no independent warriors, men or women, on this action!"

"Most of the whites who trespassed on our lands have taken up residence in the homes of those of our people who went west years ago. They have no right to anything here and need to be shown that the Cherokee will not tolerate confiscation of their property. Wherever we find them, we will drive these intruders out but there will be no bloodshed; the Council has insisted on this. We will merely demonstrate to the white men that they are unwelcome here."

"Are you telling us that we aren't making war?" Cheowa asked angrily. "That's why I volunteered for this action."

The Ridge smiled benevolently. "The Council has not declared war. But if any of you chiefs want it, that, as usual, is your affair. Just remember, if you go against the majority, the Council cannot back you. All we are going to do now is give the whites a little taste of their own medicine and," he said, eyes twinkling, "make them shit in their pants."

Little Tree grinned at Cheowa. "This is going to be a more of a real party than you think."

"It would be a better party if we could take it to your friend Parker," the surly Indian replied.

"You're too hard on the man, Cheowa."

"I don't trust white men, not even the ones who seem to be on our side. You watch, when there is even worse trouble, your friend Parker will be one of the first *unaka* to run out on us. And he will disappoint not only our people, but my sister as well."

"You're wrong, Cheowa," Going Horse spoke up. "Tsani will make a good addition to the family. He's a fighter."

"Some fighter! If Aggie hadn't stopped me at the courthouse, I would have fed his guts to the buzzards. What makes you think that Parker is any different from any other white man who's wormed his way into the Nation? He's brought nothing but his clothes and is here to get everything he can. He has a hut, a scraggly little garden, some chickens that aren't fit for my father's slaves. And," Cheowa said even more angrily, "he's been taking my sister to bed almost every night."

"That's her business," Going Horse reminded him.

"It's my affair when that two-faced *unaka* talks of marriage."

"Oh, drop it! Tsani Parker is my friend, Cheowa," Little Tree scolded. "He is like a brother to me."

Cheowa studied the defiance in Little Tree's eyes. "And you," he said solemnly, "are *my* friend. But just as surely as we stand here now, I promise you that Parker will have to prove himself to me one day."

An hour later the shrieking, hollering band swept down on a lonely cabin. Cheowa pounded on the door with his rifle butt.

"Come out!"

"Like hell!" came an angry but quavering voice from inside.

"We can come in and get you if that's what you'd prefer," Cheowa snarled. "We count to five, then come in . . . ONE!"

The latch pulled back and the door opened slightly. A frightened face peered through the crack. Than just as quickly as the door had opened, it shut. Cheowa slammed his shoulder against it.

"Out!"

There was silence.

"Out!" Cheowa shouted again. And when the door didn't open, he bellowed, "TWO!" and turning to face the painted warriors surrounding the cabin, held two fingers aloft.

"Three-four-five!" one of the warriors whooped prematurely, firing his rifle into the air.

Two men tumbled out of the cabin, and The Ridge thundered, "It's about time, you swine. Gather your personal belongings and load them onto your wagon. Then head off toward Alabama or wherever it was you came from."

It took the two men less than five minutes to throw everything they had into the wagon. As they harnessed their team, Little Tree and Going Horse set fire to the cabin.

The wagon bounced down the dusty road toward the Alabama line with hooting warriors bearing down behind it, firing their guns high over the heads of the terrified intruders and their skittish horses. Before day's end, the band had traveled far southward through Vann's Valley, driving out trespassers and burning cabins and houses behind them. There was only one man who put up any resistance, and Cheowa and Little Tree soon hacked his door to splinters. Before the squatter was even out of the house, Going Horse had driven off his team of horses and personally dragged the man a half mile down the road. Then he turned him loose.

Days before, after The Ridge had been seen drilling a troop of recruits, the Guardsmen had alerted the sheriff at Carrollton that there might be trouble in the area. When word of the early-morning raid reached Carrollton, the sheriff instructed his men to head off the war party at Cedartown. By the time the troops arrived there, however, four cabins had already burned to the ground.

Five of the raiding Cherokee had found a keg of whiskey that had been left behind by the squatters. Ignoring orders from The Ridge, they had attempted to salvage it from the flames before it burned, too. Once

rescued, the keg was tapped, and by the time the sheriff's men got there, the Cherokee were uproariously
drunk.

"Whee-oo!" one of the deputies shouted. "This is
gonna be as easy as picking up pine cones."

Seeing what a mess they were in, one of the rev-
elers, named Chewoyee, attempted to grab his tomahawk, stumbled and fell. Another Cherokee was able
to scramble off into the woods as the small posse
fought to subdue the remaining four Indians.

With the four prisoners bound to their mounts
and the extra horse in tow, the posse headed for Carrollton. On the way, Chewoyee slipped out of the
saddle once and was lifted back. Before the group had
traveled another mile he fell again, and this time an
irate deputy lunged at the prostrate Indian and kicked
him in the ribs.

Chewoyee grunted in pain from the blow to his
kidney. Rolling onto his side, he urinated.

"That red son-of-a-bitch pissed on me!" the deputy shouted, seeing the yellow liquid trickling down his
boots. He delivered another kick, this time to Chewoyee's face. There was a sickening crack as the Indian's jaw broke. Then two more deputies joined in.
After the attackers had exhausted themselves, Chewoyee was left to die on the road.

"Any other red bastard who thinks he can piss on
a white man and get away with it will die just like this
one!" the deputy hissed, trying to rid his hands of
blood and dust. "Now, let's ride."

As the party neared Carrollton, the road nar-
rowed through a pass that was thickly wooded. Before
the unprepared deputies could stop them, two more of
the prisoners managed to free themselves and escape
on foot.

The sheriff shook his head sadly as he watched

the small band bring in only one prisoner and four riderless horses. "I see a few got away from you, Sam," he sneered. "Maybe they managed it while you were napping or had yer brain turned off for repair."

"Well, damnit, sheriff, we done the best we could," the deputy in charge whined.

A stream of tobacco juice shot from the sheriff's mouth into the spittoon near his desk. "Well then, Sam," he replied slowly, "I'll jist have to remember how shit-poor yer best is."

Chapter 13

"You have to come down from the clouds. The trouble we're having with Georgia isn't a child's game."

"I don't know the answer, John. But I do know I have faith in the Council."

Agatha deftly chopped another onion and sprinkled it over the top of the stew meat. She had moved into a large addition to the Boudinot home that Elias, John and several others had built for her. Now, as a plate of corn bread sat on the table, still hot and steaming, she stirred up a second batch, pleased that John enjoyed her cooking enough to ask for some to take home.

The printer shuddered. Aggie's faith in Ross and the Council was staggering. And though her beliefs were typical of most loyal Cherokee, he couldn't help asking, "How can you think the Council is going to do anything but lead the Nation to war? Sending The Ridge out to harass whites isn't what I call diplomacy."

"And you think they were wrong in driving out squatters who had no right to be on our land?"

"I don't argue with what they did," Parker responded, "just the way they went about it. Aggie, ever since The Ridge took that gang out, every white man living on Cherokee land is jumpy. Every day we get reports of shooting sprees in two or three places. Maybe you don't realize it, but it's getting close around here to all-out war. And if you read what's being written in other papers, you'll realize that the country is getting pretty nervous, sitting around waiting for it to break out. If war does come, you know as well as I do that nobody's going to win."

Agatha stirred the stew and tasted it, then sat back with a sigh. "John, can't you see that the law is with us? Chief Ross has many friends in Washington—"

"—and enough enemies in Georgia that he's had to post an armed guard around his home. Aggie, think! Ross, The Ridge, George Lowrey, John Ridge, they've all got guards posted. Sam Worcester and two other missionaries are in prison because they wouldn't take an oath of allegiance to Georgia. Cherokee are being arrested for mining their own gold and for harassing the whites who try to drive them out of their own gold mines. Men who don't drink are being filled with liquor, then tossed into jail for drunkenness or for disturbing the peace and resisting arrest. Aggie, little by little the Cherokee people are being torn apart, weakened—"

"But we're still alive, John. We're still powerful. Even passage of the Indian Removal Act hasn't had any effect on us. And President Jackson has invited Chief Ross to discuss the problem with him at his home in Nashville."

"Aggie, do you think for one minute Jackson has any intention of upholding the provision of a bill that says that 'nothing in this act shall be considered as authorizing the violation of any existing treaty between the United States and any of the existing tribes'? I've memorized that part of it, Aggie. But so what? Jackson doesn't actually have to say he doesn't care about the Indians, he shows us. Instead of sending the annuities for old land purchases directly to Ross, he changed things. Just to make sure Ross can't get his hands on a lump sum for the National Treasury, now everyone has to go to the Agency office in Tellico. Little Tree told me yesterday that Betsy Laurel had to travel over a hundred miles to get her share, and do you know how much she wound up with?"

Agatha shook her head.

"Forty-two cents, that's how much. Forty-two cents!"

Stunned, Agatha said, "I know Father had to go, too, but he wouldn't make a two-day trip for something like that."

"As the head of a family, Aggie, your father can pick up everything the family has coming. Oh, they've got a good system going. Can't refuse to make the payments because there would be an outcry in Congress. But if somebody doesn't come to claim the money within three months, it goes into a fund to assist with the removal. Cullen acknowledges that it's unfair, but he can't do anything about the way Washington is handling it now."

"I know Mr. Cullen thinks we're going to give up our land, John. But we never will."

"Aggie, it's got to happen some day!" Parker wheeled around, turned his back to her. "Nobody knows how long it's going to take, but it's going to happen," he said between clenched teeth. "Listen to me, Aggie." He turned again, looking into her eyes, his voice softer. "I don't want you to be here when they finally send troops in to force you out."

She looked intently at him, searching his face for what he wasn't telling her. "John, there's something

I've been wondering about for a long time. What are you going to do if it happens?"

"What I'd like to do, Aggie," he evaded her question, "is spend the rest of my life here. I want to marry you and have children with you. But I don't know if I can stand to see you harmed in any way. I'm worried, almost sure you would be hurt if you stayed here. Aggie, will you come with me if I go?"

"You've made up your mind to do that?"

"Not definitely. But leaving is definitely something I've considered. It's hopeless to think the entire Nation isn't going to have to move to the lands west of the Mississippi, I know it. And it baffles me when you don't face up to what's really happening."

Aggie avoided Parker's eyes. Slowly, she stirred the stew and tasted it again. It was ready, and she ladled out two bowlfuls and placed them on the table. Sitting down on the bench, she stared into the food in front of her and sighed. "What would become of the children in my class if I left? Where would they find another teacher?" Agatha hesitated, then looked up at Parker, her eyes filmed with tears. "No, John," she said resolutely, "as much as I love you, I love my people more. I could never leave. Can't you understand? This is my home."

Parker and Wheeler stood on the steps of the newspaper office and watched the troops of the Georgia Guard as they dismounted. Cullen leaned back on one of the benches behind them.

"You think they're going to make any trouble?" Wheeler asked.

"No way of knowing," Cullen said wearily. "Everyone knows it's against the law to hold political assemblies in Georgia now. Personally, I think it was foolish to hold the July council meeting here."

"That's what Elias said, too," Parker reported.

"Colonel Nelson said he's stationed his troops here just to make sure there's no uprising."

Wheeler shook his head and started back inside. "Nobody seems to understand, Cullen, that the only effect this harassment is having is making these people firmer in their resolution to stick it out."

"You don't know how much I admire the Indians for their courage, Wheeler. But sure as God made little green apples, it's going to cost in the end."

After the meeting, Boudinot printed the results of the Council's decisions. The first order of business had been dispensed with almost as soon as it was announced. Jackson's invitation was declined. No representatives would be sent to meet with him. Part of the resolution read, "We have no desire to see the President on the business of entering into a treaty for exchange of lands. Inclination to remove from this land has no abiding place in our hearts and when we move we shall move by the course of nature to sleep under the ground which the Great Spirit gave to our ancestors and which now covers them in their undisturbed repose."

The Council further decided to take their case to the United States Supreme Court and authorized Ross to hire attorneys to make the presentation. Where the money to pay them would come from remained to be seen; Jackson had diverted considerable funds from the National Treasury.

The final action taken was the drafting of another memorial, this time to all the American people. The document summarized the treaties that had been made, each of them guaranteeing that no further claims would be made to Indian lands, each guaranteeing that the land in question belonged to the Cherokee as long as they chose to live on it.

> We wish to remain in the land of our fathers. If compelled to leave the country, we see nothing but ruin ahead of us. The land that has been selected to be given us in exchange for the land of our fathers is unfamiliar to us. It is peopled by hostile tribes who regard us as intruders and have made life difficult for those who have chosen to move there and take up a new life. The land is badly supplied with food and water and is generally unsuited to agriculture. But most importantly, it is not the land of our birth nor of our affections. In view of these disadvantages, shall we be compelled by a civilized and Christian people with whom we have lived in perfect peace for the last forty years and for whom we have willingly bled in war to bid a final adieu to our homes, our farms, our streams and our beautiful forests? We appeal to the great American people to remember the great law of love, 'Do unto others as you would that others do unto you.' Let them remember that of all the nations of the earth, they are under the greatest obligation to obey this law.

Again, Worcester was arrested, this time after Jackson had relieved him of his position as postmaster. Arrested with him were Wheeler and nine missionaries.

"We warned you either to leave Cherokee country or take the oath of allegiance to Georgia," the head of the militia taunted. "You so-called religious folk come in here and give yer time to the redskins rather than givin' it to yer own people. Well, Worcester," the man railed as he chained his prisoners in line behind a wagon, "if yer jail time four months ago didn't teach you good, this time shore will. Men," he continued, turning to his troops, "let's give these here God-fearin' boys—are you full of religion, too, Wheeler?—encouragement to move a bit faster."

The whips and clubs at first merely prodded the helpless men. Then when those too old or too feeble to move much faster slowed the pace, the prisoners were beaten and cursed.

"I'm not going to take that oath!" Worcester swore under his breath. Next to him, Wheeler wept shamelessly, his tears clearing channels through the sweat and mud that caked his face.

"We've got to!" he said hoarsely. "We've got to take it and we should have known long before this!"

It was thirty-five miles a day to the county jail at Lawrenceville. The day after the men were charged and found guilty of violating Georgia's law, nine men, including Wheeler, took the oath and were released.

"That damn fool!" Wheeler said to Parker about Worcester when he'd at last gotten back to New Echota. "He thinks by refusing to give in he'll become a symbol of what is unjust and unconstitutional, but they sentenced the poor bastard to four years at hard labor. More than likely he'll be dead inside of two! What good are convictions if you're not alive to have any?"

"Why do you think they arrested you and not me?" Parker inquired.

"Oh, I don't know," Wheeler replied. "I was probably handier. It didn't matter which one of us they got, anyway. I think those Georgia lawmen wanted everyone to know that it isn't only the missionaries who will be in trouble for not taking the oath; soon it will be any white man."

The *Phoenix* was having problems with the new postmaster. William Tarvin was no stranger to the Cherokee Nation, having been licensed as a trader among the people for many years. Now Tarvin had set up his post office in a new building at New Echota and was more concerned with selling whiskey and rum than in delivering the mail.

In an editorial, Boudinot protested this violation of the law, and Tarvin retaliated by refusing to release mail destined for the newspaper.

"Sorry, Mr. Boudinot, but I can't let you have it."

"Mr. Tarvin, the package you're holding contains ink for our press and it's clearly marked."

"I've told you, no. There's been too many packages coming here that ain't got the right amount of postage on 'em. Now, maybe you don't know how much time it takes to read all the regulations I've gotta live with, but I'm gonna have to make sure everything's in accordance with 'em. That package you say you need happens to be short on postage."

"How much is due? I'll pay it."

"Sixty cents, but the money ain't the point. That package is marked prepaid. That means the sender's got to pay the postage, not the receivin' party. What I've got to do, accordin' to regulations, is send yer ink back to where it come from an' have the sender pay the extra money due. Then the package can be delivered. Now, if you'd be so kind as to stand clear, Mr. Boudinot," Tarvin smirked patronizingly, "I've got a couple of customers at the bar."

Using relays of fast horses, Little Tree had brought down a supply of ink from Tennessee by the time Tarvin found the regulation that permitted the receiving party to pay any postage due. It was a good thing, too. By that time the package of ink had been sent back to Savannah.

The night he returned from his hasty four-day trip, Little Tree stayed in Parker's lean-to. The printer had a lot of questions for him. "Do you think Major Ridge will get up another war party?" Parker probed.

"Probably not, Tsani. The Council said it wouldn't serve any more purpose. The point has been made and now it's best to let things ride."

"I'll bet you had a ball," Parker grinned slyly.

"What makes you think I was there, Tsani?"

"And what makes you think I'm a fool, Little Tree? Why else would you have Eddie Birch deliver the papers for three weeks?"

"I was assigned other duties by the Council."

"And I'm a horse. You must have been a wild bunch, all right, you old devil. And so well painted up that not more than eight or nine of you were ever recognized."

"You're right, Tsani. It did sound exciting. Wish I could have been there. Let me know if The Ridge ever gets up another party like that, will you? I'd like to give it a try."

"Okay, okay, I'll drop it. Maybe you could tell me something else, though. Why does Cheowa still hate the sight of me? I know it isn't just because of Aggie. He didn't like me from the day he first laid eyes on me."

Little Tree pulled a twig from the fire and lit his pipe. Then he handed the flame to Parker. "You're white, Tsani. You don't have to be much more than that for Cheowa to want to take an axe to you. Cheowa hates whites the way some whites hate Indians. He believes we'd be a stronger people if we hadn't allowed whites to weaken us. He's one of those old-timers who thinks our ancestors didn't pay enough attention to the great national sport."

"Ball play?"

"No. War. Back in the old days, the Cherokee killed white men for sport. Cheowa thinks they didn't kill enough of them. Lots of Cherokee feel that way. Especially now. Whites we've lived with for years, been good friends with, makes no difference."

Parker extracted the last puff of smoke from his pipe. "Well, I guess I'd better keep my eyes open, then."

"Oh, you've got nothing to worry about, Tsani. As long as Little Tree's alive, you stay alive and well."

"Well then, I'd better feed you some more and keep you strong," Parker teased. "I wouldn't want you to starve to death and leave me unprotected. After all, we're good friends!"

"Friends, hell! If anything ever happened to you, where would my children get their pigs and chickens? Tsani, what do you want to bet . . ."

Chapter 14

Boudinot submitted his resignation as editor of the *Phoenix* in August of 1832. In a letter to John Ross, which he printed on August 11, he stated that the salary of $300 a year was not enough to make ends meet. Boudinot also believed that the newspaper had "done all that it was supposed to do in defending Cherokee rights and in presenting Indian grievances to United States people." Furthermore, he added, his health was being impaired by the necessity of spending so many hours indoors, a habit that no Cherokee could long endure.

Finally, Boudinot came to the primary reason for leaving the helm of the historic publication:

> I could not consent to be the conductor of the paper without having the privilege and the right of discussing important matters. From what I have seen and heard, my usefulness would be paralyzed were I to assume that privilege. I am already considered an enemy to the interest of my beloved country and people . . . Yet no matter what anyone may think of me, it is without question my duty to tell them the whole truth. For this

reason, I cannot share with anyone the belief that we will be reinstated in our rights. In truth, I believe we have no such hope . . ."

Parker's hands shook as he set the type. He sensed the agony that must have been a part of Boudinot's decision. From the moment he heard about his friend's resignation, he had known it stemmed from Chief Ross's censorship. After Boudinot had printed a few letters that openly advocated removal, Ross came down hard on him.

"All you can achieve by presenting differing opinions is further division in the Nation, Elias."

"The division exists, John, whether we like it or not."

"Elias, the love of our country demands unity of sentiment among the people, also unity of action. That kind of attitude is essential for the good of everyone."

"But the good of everyone is not what it was five years ago."

Ross sighed wearily. "Elias, are you saying that you openly advocate removal? That you, of all people, feel we must turn our backs on justice, on the laws of this Nation as well as of the United States?"

"John, you know I love my country and my people. No one, yourself included, could love them more. Don't think I'm taking sides with Georgia and the United States. Yes, the white man gave me an excellent education, a wife and even an income through the missionaries. But the white man's society and government have betrayed the Nation I love. They've tricked us with broken treaties and promises. They've degraded us with humiliating laws and they've corrupted us with vices that were unheard of before these lands ever saw a white man."

Boudinot gazed out the window and watched the

children from Agatha Lake's school playing on the commons. Shaking his head, he added, "The truth is ugly John. I just can't sit back and watch my people, people like those children out there, crushed under the hopeless odds against them. Yes, I think removal is the only solution to our problems now. Not that I like it any better than you or anyone else does. But as long as we stay here, we're going to watch one oppressive act after another erode us as though we were mud on the river bank. I've come to see, especially, that I can no longer use the *Phoenix* as an instrument of deception. I would rather see the paper die than have it be false to my people."

"Then your decision is final, Elias?"

"I'm sorry, John. It is. I have done what I could. I've served my country, I hope with fidelity."

In the final issue he edited, Boudinot printed not only his resignation, but also Chief Ross' reply. Though accepting Boudinot's resignation, Ross expressed other opinions about discontinuing the *Phoenix*: "The paper must be published. The pecuniary embarrassments of the Nation by no means ought to warrant its discontinuation. If, regrettably, you do not wish to continue as its editor, as soon as possible a suitable replacement will be found."

The next issue was brought out by a person whose attitudes Ross found more to his liking than Boudinot's—Ross' brother-in-law Elijah Hicks. It was known to everyone familiar with Hicks that the man was a staunch supporter of Ross. What Chief Ross thought about any topic, especially his contempt for the Nation's enemies, was eagerly echoed.

"Hicks is no dummy," Little Tree assured Parker. "His daddy was Fierce Charley, principal chief before Ross was elected. He's got a lot of followers around the Nation because of his connections."

But Parker, like anybody else who analyzed what he read in the columns of the *Phoenix*, could see that despite the political standing of Elijah Hicks, he was no newspaperman. And it was obvious that his main preoccupation was to use the paper as a propaganda sheet.

One of Hicks' editorials discussed the construction of the lottery wheels at the penitentiary in Milledgeville, where Sam Worcester was being held.

> The Cherokee honor is about to be run through a sporting wheel. The attempt to use a lottery to seize our lands is one of the most shameless moral crimes that has ever been initiated during Christian times. It is not only the national rights of the Cherokee that are now being endangered.
>
> The lottery can never pass to Georgia a legal title to land. It can only be an example of forcible entry and illegal possession that will imperil American institutions and plunge the governments of Georgia and the United States into deeper and darker chaos.

Hicks was wrong about the lottery being a moral crime in the eyes of Christendom. Certain members of the churches actually supported the project. While the district Methodist minister looked on, the Reverend J. B. Payne of Milledgeville, in his frock coat and collar, gave the first spin of the wheel that would determine the lucky winners of 160 acres of Cherokee farm or forest land. In the case of land that was suspected of bearing gold, the winners would receive a mere forty acres.

As might have been expected, the lottery was as honest as it was moral. During the first few spins of the wheel, one of the state commissioners was discovered to have preselected some of the winning cards to make sure his friends and relatives received the Indian land. Although all numbers went back into the barrel and the commissioner went to jail, the Cherokee people were far from grateful. If their land was to be taken, they didn't care who got it.

Chapter 15

There was no longer any question about it. The Cherokee Nation, once united, was now divided into two factions. Gradually, the divisions were becoming known as the National Party, which supported John Ross, and the Treaty Party, which favored making a treaty for removal to the West. Under the leadership of John Ridge, Major Ridge, Elias Boudinot and Boudinot's brother Stand Watie, the Treaty Party made a case among the people for getting the best deal possible for their property.

There was no hostility between Ross and Ridge, for each knew the other was working in his own way for the best interests of the Nation. Although John Ridge himself had headed a delegation to Washington to confer with President Jackson and War Secretary Cass, he admitted in public that Ross, as principal chief, would ultimately have to be the spokesman for the Cherokee Nation. And while young Ridge was exhorting his countrymen to enroll for removal to the Arkansas lands, he continued his attempts to convert Ross to his view. "Sir," he wrote to Ross on one occasion, "I have the right to address you as the Chief of the Cherokee Nation, upon whom rests, under Heaven, the highest responsibility: the well-being of the whole people. You have given every evidence of your capabilities. What remains is that you realize the impossibility of our remaining a Nation under these critical and demeaning conditions we are exposed to. It is still my hope that the Council under your leadership will agree to relocation of our people."

"I'm taking a trip," Little Tree told Parker. "Watch out for my wife and kids for a few weeks, okay?"

"Red paint again?"

"Not this time, Tsani. We've been hearing so much about the wonderful lands Chicken Snake Jackson wants to send us to that Cheowa and I are going to go look them over ourselves."

Parker nodded. "They might not be so bad as you think."

"And they might not be so good as John Ridge thinks, either."

Cheowa and Little Tree set out before daylight. The roads were blanketed with snow. River travel was uncertain at best at that time of year, so until they arrived at Paducah, the men stuck to the trails that followed the Tennessee River. There they transferred to a steamer and followed the Ohio and Mississippi rivers south to Montgomery's Point. At Montgomery's Point they took another boat up the Arkansas River. They were not at all pleased with the land they saw.

"Swamp. Nothing but swamp and lowland that might never drain after the spring thaws," Cheowa snorted.

"Do not concern yourselves, gentlemen," interjected a white passenger who stood near them at the rail. "The Cherokee lands don't start until the other side of Little Rock."

Cheowa scowled at the interruption, annoyed with

himself for using English rather than Cherokee, but Little Tree was at ease. "You're familiar with the country, sir?"

"That I am," the man returned, smiling to reveal a pair of gold teeth. "Henry Warburton," he added, offering his hand.

"Little Tree. And this is my friend Arthur Lake."

Cheowa nodded but didn't shake hands. Warburton seemed not to notice.

"You fellows from Tennessee, maybe?"

"Georgia."

Warburton's face fell as if on cue. "Georgia? Really? Damned shame what they're doing to you people back there, damned shame. It just ain't right, that's how I feel. It ain't right."

"You keep up with the happenings in the Cherokee Nation?" Little Tree asked.

"You bet. The way I see things, there's going to be a lot more of your people coming out this way in the next couple of years. Damned shame those lying bastards in Washington can't keep their word. Well, let me give you a little piece of advice if you're looking for good land to settle on. Don't stop here in Arkansas. Keep going all the way to Fort Gibson."

Cheowa's face darkened. "Because the land is no good, or because you don't want any Indians around?"

Warburton matched Cheowa's scowl. "Mr. Lake, I like Indians well enough to add another one to my house almost every year. My wife is a full-blood Choctaw."

Cheowa mumbled an apology, and Warburton continued, "I don't think it'll be more than four, five years before the same thing is going to start all over again here. I moved up here from Mississippi twelve years ago with my wife. And I've been watching what's going on. Don't like it, but there ain't a thing I can do.

Time was when the Indian Territory between the Arkansas and White Rivers didn't have more'n maybe fifty whites. But inch by inch they're getting ready. Just as soon as Arkansas gains statehood, you see if they don't do the same thing they're doing in Georgia. There's plenty of folks around Little Rock making a careful study of every law Georgia passes. That way they'll know what's the most effective method for drivin' you people out of Arkansas when the time comes."

The next day the boat suddenly ran aground on a shifting shoal. According to the crew, it would probably be four or five days before they could fix the damage to the stern wheel and be on their way again.

"Wouldn't you know," Warburton grumbled. "There's no such thing as a smooth trip anymore. Well, heck," he said, shifting to a brighter mood, "it's only a day's ride from here to Little Rock. I've got friends hereabouts. Why don't I borrow us some horses? We can make it to my home by sundown tomorrow. Stay as long as you like, gents; we got plenty of victuals."

Warburton's home was hardly more than a large shanty. "But the hospitality is so warm, Cheowa," Little Tree commented when the two were alone, "that you have to agree that no Cherokee family could have treated us any better."

Though the guests feasted on abundant portions of corn porridge and venison, though they were given the best spot of the three-walled lean-to in which to sleep, Cheowa did not share his friend's enthusiasm. And as they left early the next morning, Little Tree asked, "What's eating you, Cheowa?"

"Warburton. You're too easily taken in, my friend. That man is no better than any *unaka*."

"Nothing pleases you," Little Tree responded angrily. "You think nothing of insulting a man who opens his home to you and gives you information he hopes will help our people. Why are you being so hard?"

"I talked with Warburton's wife last night," Cheowa answered, suppressing a smirking grin. "She told me he treats her well, that he's a good husband. She also said that they had been pretty poor for years, but he's just come into a pile of money."

"What's wrong with that?"

"I'll tell you what's wrong with it! Your sweet Henry Warburton has just been given a contract to sell provisions to the removal agents when our people start coming west. His wife figures that by the time the removal is completed, the two of them will be rich. You see, Warburton's been getting barrels made special for flour and beans and lard. Thicker staves, heavier bottoms. Each barrel is going to come up about ten pounds short, and his first delivery is supposed to be for about three hundred barrels of flour and beans, fifty barrels of lard and two hundred barrels of salt pork. That's two and a half tons, Little Tree! Fifty-five hundred pounds of provisions your friend will be skimming off the top and he'll be doubling prices when he sells the stuff!"

Little Tree rode in silence, his lips almost white from pressing them together so tightly. After a while Cheowa added, "Oh, and good friend Warburton's off tomorrow on another trip to New Orleans. It seems he'll be stocking up on pants, jackets and shoes, too. And he's got a couple of neighbors loading their barns with whiskey."

"But that takes money," Little Tree said disbelievingly.

"That's no trouble if you've got plenty of white neighbors to stake you for a share of the profits. Warburton is a good friend to the red man, all right. Just like any *unaka*, he's going to cry real tears—after he can't make any more money robbing us. Anyway, I'm glad Warburton has a wife with a mouth like a running faucet. It's good to know the truth."

Chief John Jolly warmly welcomed his visitors. But he didn't waste any words letting them know that the rest of the Nation wasn't going to be welcomed with open arms.

"The United States hasn't paid the annuity it promised for two years now. Our people have had to sell their claims for the belongings they left behind in order to buy food. Much of the land here won't even support goats, and it takes many years to change land from what Asgaya Galunlati gave us to farmland that gives us food to eat and pastures for our livestock."

"Word has come to us," Cheowa probed, "that there are hostile tribes here."

"Unfortunately, you've heard right." Jolly shrugged helplessly. "The Osage feel we are intruding on their land. Even land they are not using they make us fight for. We understand how they feel, but there is nothing we can do about it. Try to understand. Sam Houston came to us—and remember, in other years he was a hero second only to Jackson. Anyway, he came to us at Hianassee Island and assured us that this move west was the only way we could escape the clashes with the whites that would soon be swamping us.

"We aren't nomads or hunters anymore, we are farmers, just as the white man has taught us to be, and we needed land to survive. Well, we found land right on the Arkansas but we didn't expect the trouble that would come with it.

"Even though the Indians didn't come in droves to the west, the whites did. And one day, one week— who knows when it was?—we looked up from our land and saw that they were pressing in on us from all sides.

They were choosing the best farmland, literally breathing down our necks. Add those problems to the ones we have with the Osage and you'll well understand why we want no more Indians to come here, even if they are our own people."

Before either Cheowa or Little Tree could interrupt, Jolly added, "Perhaps I'd better be even more specific than that. If a treaty is made giving up the old country, make no mistake about it, John Ross will not be the leader of the Western Nation. We have our own laws here. And we intend to keep as our leaders those who braved the journey west with us."

After their conversation, Cheowa managed to locate one of his wife's cousins, Donald Jacobs. Jacobs seemed to be living better than most of the Cherokee in the western lands. And not only did he explain his success, he offered to share it with Cheowa.

"I've got a good business going, and as long as Mexico doesn't want to let go of Texas, there's no end to how much money we could make. The Raven is trying to make an independent republic out of Texas, but it isn't easy."

Cheowa grunted. "The Raven! A white by the name of Sam Houston who ran away from home and was adopted by John Jolly. Houston left his Indian home and went back to Tennessee to go into politics. He got drunk. His wife left him. Then he came crawling back to his Indian home and married a Cherokee."

Donald Jacobs nodded his agreement. "He'll probably make a mess of things down in Texas, too, and then come running back to us again. But John Jolly still considers the man a son and any time he shows up there's a celebration—and that's no matter how drunk he is when he gets here. But Houston's just a small part of the reason for the way a couple of us are making a living. What galls the *unaka* down in Texas even more than the Mexicans is the Apache. Now there's a bunch of warriors for you. And that's where we come in."

"Fighting with the Apache?"

"No, making it possible for the Apache to fight the *unaka*. We've got a trader up in Kansas who sells us rifles and ammunition. All we have to do is stay away from the cavalry and sell them to the Apache. So far, no one's been able to find out how the Apache are getting their arms. Most think they're buying them from traders in Louisiana."

"Doesn't that get a little risky?" Little Tree asked. "From what I've heard, the United States metes out pretty stiff penalties to people who sell guns to Indians out here."

"Who cares about risk?" Jacobs laughed. "There isn't a cavalry troop yet that's been able to figure out where those rifles are coming from."

A week of traveling through the Indian Territory supplied Little Tree and Cheowa with plenty of information to take back to New Echota. "Some suggested we look at the possibility of going as far as British Columbia across the Great Mountains," Little Tree said, addressing the handful of listeners who had collected in the council house. "Still others say they have been welcomed in Mexico and many already have gone there. Sequoyah reports he is doing well in Mexico and thinks it is the best place. Again, there are many who think that if the Raven manages to create a republic of Texas. we would be welcome there, and he has indeed told Chief John Jolly that Texas would welcome any number of Cherokee."

John Ridge listened and then offered news of his own. "Chief Ross had a couple of meetings with Jackson while you were away. First, Jackson offered two and a half million dollars for all our lands in Georgia, Alabama and Tennessee, plus an equal amount of acreage in the West. He also guaranteed that any lands there would be inviolable and that he would pledge the United States to defend those borders. But Ross didn't even reply to that offer so Jackson came back with an offer of three million dollars."

Elias Boudinot shook his head. "The offer wasn't a bad one, really, but Chief Ross practically threw it back in his face, said it was an insult. The gold mines alone are worth that, he said, also if Jackson wouldn't protect us in the East, how were we to believe that he would protect us in the West? I guess it doesn't matter now. The problem is going to be discussed before a special meeting of the Council next month."

John Ridge allowed himself a rare show of temper. Normally he held it in close check. "For forty years, we have been making treaties with the United States and every one of them ends with words stating that the white man will want no more of our land and that we can live in peace forever. Then a few years later there is a new treaty, and then another new one, and the promises are made again and again and again that we will be protected. Why should we believe now that a white promise is any good? Are we fools? It won't be much longer before white men will want to uproot us from the western lands they promised now, I'm convinced of that, and we, along with other great tribes who have been so shamefully treated, will continue to pledge the same loyalty and service to the United States we have always given. Yet even feeling as I do, I'm furious with Ross for rejecting Jackson's three million dollar offer. That noble stuff he preaches won't keep a roof over our heads when our lands and homes are taken."

* * *

Parker was off work the next day, so he rode up to Little Tree's home near Spring Place with a brace of chickens tied to his saddle. The children squealed eagerly when they saw him. As he handed the chickens to one of the girls, she untied their legs and turned them loose.

Little Tree laughed when he saw the chickens scratching near Parker's feet. "They like the smell of you, Tsani."

"Why not? They know who owns them."

"How many times have they made the trip between our places?"

"Who knows?" Parker chuckled, pulling his pipe from his pocket. Little Tree offered him a sack of tobacco. "I'm not even sure anymore whether those chickens started out in my flock. Won't be much longer until all we'll have to do is give 'em a shove and they'll find their own way."

"Here's another bit of news, Parker my friend. Those two chickens will be joined by four more of yours before they go back home again."

"Little Tree, you're impossible. Why don't you have Martha fix those birds for supper? That way we can start all over again with younger stock."

"Little Bear," Little Tree concurred, "clean Tsani's old buzzards. We'll eat them tonight."

Little Bear and one of his sisters raced after the old hens, then set to work killing and cleaning them. Parker leaned back against the trunk of a sycamore that shaded the house. "I hear you didn't find a whole lot on your trip west that impressed you, Little Tree."

Little Tree recited a summary of what he and Cheowa had reported. "Most of it isn't too bad, but it isn't home, Tsani. I don't think the *Tsalagi* are going to get a fair deal anywhere anymore."

"How do you feel about leaving?"

"This is home. You see that marker over there by the edge of the orchard? That's where my daddy is buried and that's where I'm going to be buried some day. At least, that's where I hope to be buried. Personally, I'm beginning to think maybe Chief Ross is wrong, that maybe we shouldn't stay here, but I feel like a coward and a traitor when those ideas start running through my head. You know what I mean?"

Parker nodded. "It isn't an easy spot for you, I know."

"The hardest part is knowing that Jackson is actually making progress in breaking us apart. Divide and conquer, that's what he's doing. John Ross went to Washington and he got nowhere. His brother went to Washington and Jackson did listen to him—for about five minutes. Then he realized that Andrew Ross was acting on his own and didn't have the backing of anybody. What did Jackson do? He sent Andrew back telling him to get a few more responsible people together and he'd make a deal with them. So Andrew comes back, runs around like a chicken with its head cut off and accomplishes nothing except giving Jackson some comfort knowing that the Nation is being split into ineffective factions. John Ridge goes to Washington and tries to make a deal with Jackson, not considering at all what Ross is fighting for. And his father even takes time out to sit and have his portrait painted. All of them, Tsani, were in Washington at the same time and all of them were ducking behind doors to keep from running into each other."

"You mean Jackson isn't just trying to confuse us? He's really trying to make deals with more than one delegation?"

"That's right, Tsani. He even had someone draw up a treaty with Andrew Ross, but it was rejected unanimously by the Senate as soon as it hit the floor. Jackson's promising everybody something different, and when they finally get together and compare notes, there's chaos. Chief Ross made a final proposal the last time he met with Cass. He even offered to give up a portion of the eastern lands if the United States guaranteed us protection from Georgia on the rest of it. Couldn't do that, Cass said, that'd be interfering with the authority of a sovereign state. Then Ross proposed something the National Council had tossed out as bait. We would become citizens of the various states that are claiming our land. If we did that, Ross wanted to know, would we be allowed to keep our homes and enjoy the rights all American citizens did?"

"That's quite a bold departure for a people who were proud and independent. What was Cass' answer?"

"In words that were no better than 'Shove it!', Cass answered that nothing would satisfy the government except total removal to the West. Nothing."

Martha came from the kitchen, wiping her hands on her gingham apron. "My goodness, you two talk like a couple of old graybeards! Come inside and eat. We'll have the trout now and the chickens will be roasted by evening."

"Oh," Little Tree added, "I almost forgot. I picked up some newspapers along the way for you. Thought you might like to see one without *Tsalagi* again."

Parker grinned. "It's been six months since we've had any newspapers from outside except the ones Chief Ross and The Ridge bring with them when they come back from Washington. We just don't get any more of them through the mails."

He glanced over the handful of papers Little Tree had handed him and noted that the front page of the *Arkansas Gazette* from Little Rock had nearly two columns devoted to the problem of removal. He gave the papers to Little Bear and asked, "Slip these into my saddle bags, will you? That way I won't forget them." To Little Tree he said, "Hicks probably won't make much use of the articles, but at least I can take them into the office."

"Hicks sure isn't the writer Elias is," Little Tree remarked.

"Hicks isn't a writer of any kind," Parker replied emphatically. "He can't spell worth a damn either, but since he's the editor, Wheeler and I find that when the word 'robbery' is spelled with one B, we'd better only have one B in the thing."

"I miss the old days when Elias was running the paper. Now instead of reading about what The Ridge is up to, we get detailed instructions about how to grow beans. Tsani, if there's one thing a *Tsalagi* knows, it's how to grow beans."

"Maybe, but you've got to remember that Hicks is Chief Ross' brother-in-law. How many other people would take the job with no money coming in to pay for things?"

"I paid my two dollars a year," Little Tree said proudly, "even if I do deliver those newspapers all over this part of the Nation."

"Two dollars? You're cheating us! It's supposed to cost you two fifty."

"Is that so! Well, I made a bet with Elias that I could get more paid subscribers in a week than he could, and he gave me my subscription at *Tsalagi* price without my even trying."

Martha put a platter of corn bread on the table along with a pot of honey. "Did I tell you? Sam Worcester is out of prison."

Little Tree jerked his head toward Parker. "When did he get out?"

"About a week ago. He preached last Sunday, but only a handful of people showed up."

"What happened?" Little Tree asked disbelievingly. "Sam always draws big crowds."

"Well, you know how Elias always translates for him—I don't know why he doesn't just get up there and preach in *Tsalagi*; Lord knows he speaks it well enough—well, the rumor is that a lot of people were afraid that if they came to hear Worcester, Elias would try to talk them into going to the new lands out west. Also, there are rumors going around that Sam was let out of prison because he made a bargain with the governor that he'd try to get everyone to move this year."

"I heard those rumors," Parker put in, his mouth stuffed with corn bread. "There's no truth to them. What is true is that all those fuddy-duddy hypocrites in New England have switched gears. On his way to the governorship of Massachussetts, Everett made a complete about-face. Everyone knew how for years he had supported Ross. Well, now he's advocating removal. When the going gets tough, even the big chiefs run for cover. Anyway, pretty soon after Everett made his statement, the Mission Board ordered Worcester to move his mission west."

Little Tree blinked several times, squeezing back tears. "John Ridge, Major Ridge, Elias Boudinot and Stand Watie have all enrolled to go. Now Worcester has. Who's going to be next, Tsani?"

Before Parker could answer, Martha announced, "Here comes the trout!" The men looked up as she headed toward the table with a skillet sizzling with fish. Forgetting his shock about Worcester, Little Tree smiled and made a place for her.

Suddenly Martha stiffened. The cast-iron skillet clattered to the wooden floor. "Look, Little Tree!" Parker and Little Tree sprang to their feet, following her frozen stare out the window to where a wagon had pulled up not far from the front door. Two men were examining the house, looking intently back and forth between it and a slip of paper one man was holding in his hand. Little Tree went outside with Parker at his heels.

"What can I do for you?" he asked.

"You living here?" was the curt response.

"Of course, I live here. This is my home."

"Not anymore, Indian. I won this place in the lottery a couple months back. So it seems," he contemptuously asserted, "that you've been livin' in my house. It also seems t' me you owe me twenty dollars' rent."

"You're insane. I'm supposed to pay you for the privilege of living in my own home?"

"Don't make it hard on yourself, Indian," the man warned him. "I'm a reasonable man. Jist pay me the twenty dollars' back rent an' we'll fix up a lease. If you want to stick around for a while, it'll be a hundred dollars a year, in advance; that oughta be about right."

"Get off my land!" Little Tree thundered. Parker moved to stand beside his friend.

"The only place I'll go is to the sheriff. You're trespassin'!" spat the intruder. "You want to fight this out in court? Think about it, Indian. I'll be back in an hour."

Angrily, the men climbed back into the wagon and drove off.

Martha stood as defiantly as Little Tree. "Do you think they'll be back, Tsani?" she asked, trying to contain her fear.

"I do," he answered reluctantly. "Some Georgia bullies even threw Brother Clauder out of the mission station last month. Then they turned the chapel into a tavern to take care of the thirsty mobs that are coming."

"You don't think I have a chance, do you, Tsani?"

Parker hesitated, then sadly shook his head. "If he does charge you with trespassing you could be arrested, and what chance would you have in court? You can't testify against a white man. Can't you see, Little Tree? What's happening now is what I've been worried about for years. And now I don't think there's any way you can stop them."

An hour later the men returned. This time they had twenty-three of their relatives with them. Without a word, each person in the group began unloading furniture and personal belongings.

"I changed my mind, Indian," Little Tree was told when he ran out to defend his property. "Decided I don't want to rent the place after all. I'm movin' in on what's legally mine, right now. You got about ten minutes to clear your trash outa here afore we do it for you."

"Don't you put a hand on me or my family!" Little Tree commanded. "And get off my property!"

The man took a menacing step forward. As he did, the men behind him moved in closer, too. Parker and Little Tree knew they couldn't begin to resist the small army. Although they stood firm, inside they were trembling. Before they knew what was happening, two men came around from behind the first, who by now had drawn a club from his belt. They grabbed Little Tree and twisted his arms behind him. As he winced in pain, they pushed him to the ground. Three more intruders moved to stand between Parker and his fallen friend.

"Don't you go talking sassy to us again, redskin. Jist don't you dare!"

The men standing over Little Tree kicked him in the neck. Martha, who till this time had remained inside the house, ran out and shrieked, "Don't hurt my husband. We'll leave! We'll leave right now!" Little Tree's father followed, slowly, his eyes filled with unshed tears.

Somehow Parker and the children and other women managed to collect most of the belongings. As each piece was brought out, the Georgians threw it on a wagon of Little Tree's they had brought to the front of the house.

"Don't forget this," one Georgian woman said harshly, tossing something into the dust. It was the chickens for that night's dinner, still on the spit. "We don't want you to say we took anything that didn't belong to us."

Parker helped Little Tree to his feet. Both men, as well as the rest of Little Tree's family, were crying. Slowly some climbed aboard the wagon, others walking beside it, painfully resisting the temptation to look for one last time at the home they loved.

Later that evening, after Parker had settled everyone as comfortably as possible in his own cabin in New Echota, he pleaded with Aggie once more.

"No, Johnny. You beg and you lecture, but I can't leave my people." She hesitated, then stared at him. "Are you going to leave?"

Parker looked down, then once again straight at this woman he loved so deeply.

"I think so," he admitted, his voice subdued. "When Little Tree and Cheowa went to examine the lands in the west, they brought back a newspaper from Little Rock. There was an ad for a printer and I applied for the job. Tonight before I came over here I went to the *Phoenix* office. The reply to the letter I wrote was on my desk. The job is mine if I want it."

"I don't know what else to say, John," Agatha

whispered, "so I guess what I'm saying"—she hesitated—"is good-by."

"Please, Aggie," John begged, "don't do something you'll regret. Come with me."

"I wish everything good for you, Johnny, you know I do, but I can't go. I can't," she answered, her voice giving way. "I won't leave my people."

"I didn't think Aggie would go with you," Little Tree said later. "She's a strong, singleminded woman. As it turns out, Martha and I agree with you, not her. We're seeing Cullen in the morning and enrolling to go west."

"Aggie will probably call us cowards," Parker spoke gravely. "But I think we're anything but cowards, Little Tree. I believe staying here until the last minute, perhaps dying for our choice, is foolish."

"Do you know where you're going?" Little Tree asked.

"To Little Rock. There's a job waiting for me if I want it. I don't know where I'm going to stay yet, but maybe there'll be a nice family who likes to bet . . . They'll have plenty of chickens . . ." Parker's voice broke and instead of trying to continue he half-smiled. Grasping Little Tree's shoulder, he squeezed it hard.

After the packing and the good-bys the next morning, Parker headed west through the square in town. He hadn't gone more than halfway across when a figure stepped squarely out in front of him from the shadow of an old laurel tree.

"What is it, Cheowa?" Parker asked stiffly. "I should think you'd be pretty pleased to see me leave."

"Don't think I'm going to stop you, Parker. I just want you to know that what you're doing now is what I expected you to do all along. All the trouble we're having is because of selfish, cowardly *unaka* like you. You take jobs on our land. You take our women—" Cheowa paused meaningfully.

"Let's not waste time with that again," Parker interjected. "I've heard it before."

"Don't you tell me what I can say or what I can't say!" Cheowa ordered. "Just like all the others, you turn and run like a rabbit when things don't go well. Parker, you said you are at home with the Cherokee, but turning and running isn't a Cherokee way."

"What about all those Cherokee who've signed up for removal?"

"Weaklings! Scum we can do without, just like we can do without you. Now go, and think about this while you're running away: if you try even once more to convince my sister that she's better off with trash like you than with her own people, you're going to wake up some morning and find your little tool cut off and stuffed in your pocket—or down your throat!"

Chapter 16

Fort Cass, N. Car.
23rd November, 1833

Chief Clerk Charles Madden
Office of Indian Affairs
War Department
Washington, D.C.

Dear Mr. Madden:

Work is progressing satisfactorily, though slowly, on the construction of the stockades at Old Town on the Hiwassee River. Although construction of these pens, or barracks, is hardly different from those that have been built at other Indian agencies, the amount and variety of timber available here lends itself to a strength and quality that is unparalleled in my many years of experience with the office.

The troops have an endless supply of hickory and it is this they use in preference to the pine that is common elsewhere. Approximately two weeks were spent felling timber and stockpiling it near the stockade. Next, several days were spent splitting the timber and shaping it into pointed staves. These are being planted upright and braced well, the result being an exceptionally sturdy and well-built wall. The finished form is oblong in shape, and each of the pens within the stockade should be able to house between thirty and forty Indians. I estimate that twenty-eight such pens will be adequate to contain those who have enrolled for emigration during the coming year.

I have given my solemn promise that families will not be separated from the time they report to the stockade until they arrive in Arkansas or Indian Territories; I believe there will be less resistance to emigration with such a guarantee.

Immediately upon the completion of construction, the troops and the hired sawyers shall go to Gunter's Landing in Alabama and begin construction on the next in the series of stockades. Others shall be built as necessary when we succeed in enrolling sufficient numbers. Thus far, approximately one thousand have enrolled for emigration early in the spring. The numbers would be larger except for the persistent efforts of Chief Ross. He strives ceaselessly to find a legal means to stop the inevitable.

Of the Indians who have enrolled, the majority are ne'er-do-wells, loafers and parasites. They would prefer to eat the provisions that have been stockpiled here and at various places along the way rather than try to support themselves. Many of these Indians are camped near the site of the stockade even now, prior to its completion, and wait to enter the gates (which have not yet been built!) for the food we have promised them. These people were expecting to leave before the onset of the winter and consequently planted no crops to see them through the lean months ahead.

A natural phenomenon occurred during the early morning hours of 13th November that I'm convinced encouraged more people to enroll for removal. I myself was witness to the event, as were others throughout

Alabama, Tennessee, Georgia and the Carolinas. For approximately two hours, meteors streaked across the sky, swooping near the earth and leaving trails of brilliant hues. Some of the more spectacular meteors illuminated the face of the earth as if it were daytime. One survivor of the Battle of New Orleans told me he could almost imagine that the war had started again, such was the quality of the lights.

While anyone possessing even an elementary knowledge of astronomy would know that a meteor shower is a natural event, I sense that many Indians superstitiously see in it a sign that their gods are angry with them and consequently they are more willing to emigrate.

I am attempting to comply with your directive by carefully listing the names of those who enroll, but few of the Indians speak English and I have found it impossible to hire the services of any Cherokee to assist with the registration. John Ridge has promised to find a clerk who can read and write English and Cherokee as soon as he returns from Washington.

Your authorization to permit Indians of means to remain unmolested in their homes until such time as they emigrate will undoubtedly hasten enrollment. It was because of this guarantee that Major Ridge, John Ridge, Elias Boudinot and Stand Watie came forward as an example to the rest of the people. Colonel Sanford of the Georgia Guard has promised every assistance in keeping lottery winners from evicting those who have registered.

Yr. Obdt. Servant,
Wm. Cullen, Agent

Chapter 17

In April, John Ross returned from Washington to his home at Head of Coosa. A stranger was sitting in the rocker on his wide verandah. As Ross dismounted, the stranger stood and touched the brim of his hat.

"Chief Ross," he began confidently, "in the lottery last month, I drew the winning ticket to this property. I didn't consider it right to make your wife leave until after you had a chance to get home and help her get your things together, so I've let her and the children live in two of the rooms. I trust you won't delay things any more than necessary, sir; living this way is kind of inconvenient."

Quatie and the children had been crowded into the two smallest rooms with much of their furniture and as many of their personal belongings as they could fit into the space. With as much will power as he could collect, Ross managed to keep his temper in check despite the injury to his pride and his concern for his family.

"They've treated us as well as we could have hoped for," Quatie said of the new owners.

Ross wrapped his arm comfortingly around his wife's shoulders. Though the front room window, he looked out at the multitude of barns and outbuildings, the large herds of cattle and sheep, that graced his land.

"We'll have to leave just about everything behind," he told Quatie as gently as he could. He thought of the library he had spent a lifetime collecting. There was room in the wagons for his private papers, but not for the books.

As principal chief, Ross had always cautioned his people that recourse to violence could do nothing but harm. And now, put to the test, Ross restrained himself. When the wagons were crammed full, he led his family and slaves from their home on horseback, giving a parting glance to the plumed peacocks that graced the wide lawns.

The procession made its way down to the lucrative ferry his family had for generations operated across the Coosa and found it in the hands of two rifle-toting strangers who had drawn it in the lottery. For the first time in his life, Ross paid the fee to ride his own ferry.

On the other side of the river at Red Clay, safe within the border of Tennessee, Ross installed his family in a one-room cabin. Here he could be near the new council grounds, which had been moved from Georgia soil nearly two years earlier. Quatie Ross, who had been accustomed to living in a mansion featuring polished hardwood floors and imported Oriental carpets as well as the braided Cherokee rugs, now found herself standing on packed dirt. In place of the neat white clapboard siding and bright red bricks she was used to, Quatie's new home, like many provided for Cherokee throughout the Nation, was constructed of rough-hewn logs. She didn't complain; Quatie Ross was no longer a young woman, but she was of the same rugged Cherokee background as her husband. And she, like he, had faith in the triumph of justice.

Rich Joe Vann and many others didn't fare so well with the holders of winning lottery tickets as Ross had. For some reason no one could understand, Vann installed his family in rooms upstairs, then invited a former sheriff to take up residence in a guest room. When Colonel Bishop of the Georgia Guard arrived with an eviction notice, a shooting spree broke out between the sheriff and the Guard. Bishop was unable to remove the former sheriff, so to smoke him out, he had his men toss burning firebrands into the vestibule. The resulting fire threatened to burn down the house along with the Vanns on the upper floor. After the sheriff had been hauled off to jail, more dead than not from the numerous wounds he had received, the Guard put out the fire.

"And what was he doing here in the first place?" Bishop demanded of Vann.

Van refused to give him an answer and Bishop later told his men, "More than likely the old coot was trying to stake out a claim of his own to this place. That's why he wormed his way in somehow. But he didn't have a chance." Bishop grinned. "The winning ticket just happens to have been drawn by my brother."

"And what's going to become of all this?" Vann asked, sweeping his arm in an arc to describe his huge estate.

"Oh, you'll receive compensation for the buildings, crops and livestock, Vann—that's thanks to the money you've spread around in places that matter. But before we can make any settlement, we'll have to determine the value of the pasturage your animals have been using. There's also the matter of rent, and . . ."

*　　*　　*

In February, Sam and Ann Worcester were turned out of their house at New Echota by Colonel William Harden.

"You want a mission, preacher man?" one of Harden's men hissed as he shoved Worcester out his own front door. "Then we're going to help you."

In time, the Worcesters were escorted to the Brainerd Mission in Tennessee. There, with their two small children and another not yet born, they awaited transportation to Arkansas lands.

Aggie Lake watched from the courthouse as Elijah Hicks was arrested and taken off to court on charges of libel. He had reported in the *Phoenix* that Georgians were raping Cherokee women.

Hicks was released from jail after posting a two-thousand-dollar bond, half of which Elias Boudinot had put up. Upon returning to the shop, he showed his defiance by removing his name from the masthead of the paper and placing it directly under the title. He used the largest, boldest type he had for the purpose.

Little Tree was loading the week's papers onto his wagon when Aggie walked over to him. He handed her a copy of the paper and she scanned it hurriedly. "Where does Hicks find all this garbage?" she demanded.

"Almanacs, mostly. Some stuff from old papers that Elias never used. There just isn't much news to report, Aggie."

"Not much news? How can the man possibly not be aware of what's happening? He bombards us with 'Cultivation of Peach Trees.' 'On the Constituent Parts of Water.' And this, 'The Benefit of Female Education,' while our homes are being stripped from us as if they were peaches ripe for the picking! Dozens of Cullen's enrollment agents are getting people drunk so they can be tricked into enrolling. Did you know Atalah Anosta, Little Tree?"

"I think so, Aggie. Why?"

"Why?" she snorted, remembering the incident. "He was one of the ones who was tricked. Two days after Atalah signed he was forced to go to the stockade. His wife and children pleaded that he be let go but the militia dragged him away anyway. Then somehow, he escaped on foot through the snow.

"Cullen sent out a recovery detail after him, and when the men failed to capture him, Atalah's wife and children were arrested and hauled to the stockade without even being allowed enough time to put on warm clothing. They were close to freezing in the raw rain, but the soldiers kept them outdoors all night and part of the next day anyway.

"When Atalah's wife finally agreed to enroll for emigration, she and her children were allowed to come inside. From what I heard, the inside of the barracks was filthy. Atalah Anosta showed up a few days later—he'd heard his family had been taken—and all of them were put aboard a boat and taken to Arkansas. Within a few days, two of the three children had died of pneumonia. Atalah and his wife made their way back here and now they're staying with me.

"So," Aggie wound up, "Hicks has heard all about that, and probably about a lot more, too! No news, indeed!"

"They're not beyond tricking the women, either," Little Tree added angrily. "Annie Spring was alone last week when they came to tell her that Going Fox had taken their children and gone to Hiwassee to enroll. She went to join them and found out that the whole thing was a lie. But they wouldn't let her leave— shoved her inside—and the next time she came through the gates she was on her way to Arkansas.

"Aggie, Hicks will never print anything about what's going on. Doing that might make a lot of people unhappy and he's not going to risk it. And look at this stack of papers; only half as many as there used to be. Elijah Hicks is no newspaper man, that's for sure, and he can't touch Elias for style or courage. Take his ineptness, add it to the money problems the *Phoenix* has been having, and I'm afraid that soon what was once the proud voice of a nation united will be no more than a whispery cry."

"Why the money problem?" Aggie asked, bundling her coat around her.

"That's easy," Little Tree replied. "John Ross no longer receives the annuities from the federal government. He can no longer funnel the Nation's funds into channels he thinks will benefit the people."

Aggie shivered and Little Tree sensed it was not entirely from the cold.

"Maybe John was right to leave," she faltered.

"Have you heard from him?" Little Tree asked. "I got a letter two days ago."

Aggie nodded, remembering every word of the note she'd received that day. She'd reread it at least ten times.

Dearest Aggie,

As I write this letter, in my mind I realize just how far from me you are, but in my
heart you're with me. I am still wrenched between my respect for your steadfastness and
my concern for your safety. In Little Rock,
rumors about Jackson and his complete lack
of concern for the Cherokee are mixed with
fear for what removal might bring. Perhaps
here, in some way, I can be of more help
than I could have been in New Echota. Near

you, I am too much the victim of my deepest emotions and am unable to function.

I know what you must think of me, what everyone must think: that I'm gutless and without principle. Each day, however, I feel more confident that I am in the right. Just now I'm working for a small printing company. I sleep, I eat and I think of the day I can be more to you again—and more to your people.

In deepest love,
John

Chapter 18

Even while hundreds of reluctant Cherokee were being rounded up to fill the numbers Cullen had promised would emigrate that year, John Ross called a meeting of the Council at Red Clay for August. Affairs of the Nation were confused and disturbing. Ross presented a copy of the treaty his brother had attempted to negotiate, not for approval of the Council, but for its official rejection by the assembled representatives. With Andrew Ross had been several other prominent citizens, all of whom were now held suspect as traitors to the Cherokee Nation. Voices were raised against them and there were vows that they would die before leaving the council grounds.

But while The Ridge himself had denounced Andrew as being a bumbling, meddling fool, the very fact that he had been in Washington when Andrew was made The Ridge also suspect in the eyes of many of the members of the Council. Because The Ridge was a man who enjoyed great stature in the Nation and in the eyes of officials in Washington, whispers circulated that he too was in danger, for his was a greater crime in consequence of his position.

John Ridge rose and eloquently defended his father. "The Ridge has seen his people on the very precipice of ruin. He has told them of the danger. Was he telling the truth or not? Let every man look at our circumstances and judge for himself. Should a man be denounced for openly speaking his opinions, particularly when those opinions are shared by so many?"

Elijah Hicks moved to have the Ridges impeached, both "for their opinions and for holding to a policy that would result in the dissolution of the Cherokee community." The Council voted to approve the motion, but John Ridge hadn't played his trump card.

As president of the National Committee, he recommended that action on the motion be postponed until the October council to provide time for a thorough study and deliberation.

Less than a generation of life under the new laws of the Cherokee Nation was unable to satisfy the passions of two of the council members, James and Thomas Foreman. John Walker, Jr., one of the Treaty Party members who had been in Washington with Andrew Ross, left the meeting early. Before he could reach his home in North Carolina, he was shot from ambush and left dead on the road as a reminder to other dissidents of the consequences of betraying the Nation.

Boudinot, David Vann and the Ridges were warned of the action and took roundabout ways to their homes. Cullen acted swiftly and soon had the Foremans under arrest and charged with murder. Unfortunately, the crime took place in Tennessee, and unlike Georgia, that state had never claimed any authority in matters that involved only Cherokee. Cullen had no choice but to let them go free.

The assassination came when the Nation was reeling from the effects of whites appearing daily to claim their new property. Agatha herself was involved in such an incident. When a man came to claim the courthouse as his, Aggie refused to budge. "This is a public school," she told him. "I won't give it up!"

"The hell you won't, squaw-woman! You think you're so fine 'cause you look like a white lady. Well, I seen the records and I been warned about you half-breeds. You're as much an Indian as anyone else around here."

The man went to his buggy and returned with a hammer and a pocketful of nails. As he proceeded to nail the door shut, Aggie ran to a local lawyer for help. He in turn ran to the scene with his wife hard on his heels. Behind them came another lawyer and a young clerk from the office.

"Stop what you're doing!" the lawyer ordered the man, who was still hammering at the door.

"Who are you to be givin' me orders, Indian?"

"My name is Buchanan. I'm a lawyer here—"

Another nail was driven home.

"Please! Think of the children?" Buchanan pleaded. The man ignored him and pulled another nail from his pocket.

"You ignorant bastard!" Buchanan shouted, attempting to shove him aside. In reply, the man took a swing at Buchanan's head with his hammer. The hammer hit home, and blood flooded the side of Buchanan's face.

During the fight that followed, Mrs. Buchanan moved in to aid her husband, while the other young lawyer waded in and the clerk threw a badly aimed rock at the intruder. Eventually the Georgian was subdued, but no one escaped the fight without injury. Even Mrs. Buchanan was cut. As she tried with a damp cloth to blot the blood that was dripping down her wrist, Aggie comforted her.

The frustrated lottery-winner blustered down the steps of the courthouse, stopping only to turn and wave his fist at Buchanan. "You just made plenty of trouble for yerself, Indian! I'm going to file charges against you!" Then he wheeled on Aggie, pointing a callused finger at her. "And you, squaw-woman! You caused it all. You're gonna see some trouble, too!"

The murder of Walker galvanized Jackson into action. He bypassed the Office of Indian Affairs and wrote to Cullen himself, telling the agent that the President had been advised of the assassination of Walker and that "Ridge, the other chiefs in favor of emigration and you yourself have been threatened with death. The Government of the United States has promised protection and it will perform its obligations. Notify John Ross and his council that we will hold him answerable for every murder committed on the emigrating party."

Whites who had settled on Cherokee land took notice too, and soon formed vigilante committees. They notified the Cherokee that for every white killed by Cherokee they would select three Cherokee males and put them to death.

Governor Lumpkin wrote harshly to War Secretary Cass: "If you cannot control these Indians through some agency, the authorities of Georgia will be under the painful necessity of exterminating the evil in the only practical way." He did not specify what "practical way" he had in mind, but no one doubted that he meant extermination.

More than the death of one Cherokee, though, the incident made it clear that there was serious division within the Cherokee Nation. Jackson as well as the State of Georgia hastened to exploit that lack of unity. All the attempts the Cherokee made themselves to patch up the differences came to nothing.

Although the Council voted in October to drop

the impeachment proceedings against the Ridges, John Ridge demanded a trial in order to clear their names. When this entreaty was refused, Ridge and his father stormed out of the council before all its business had been completed. Along with Elias Boudinot, they crossed the river and went home to Georgia.

On November 27, they met at John Ridge's home and formally established the Treaty Party. Joined with the Cherokee who comprised the anti-Ross faction was Indian Agent William Cullen, who had been invited as an observer for the War Department and who would report also to Governor Lumpkin.

"John Ridge emerged from this meeting as the president or chief of the Treaty Party," Cullen reported that day. "Elias Boudinot and Alexander McCoy were selected by the delegates to be Ridge's assistants. These three shall head a six-man delegation that will be going to Washington this winter. They plan to confer with the President and the Secretary in regard to the present condition and future prospects of the Cherokee people. They are in possession of a document that is essentially a position statement, signed by fifty-seven of those who were present at the meeting. They represent about one-fourth of the people of the Cherokee Nation. Most of those who attended are personally known to me."

Jackson was more than pleased with the prospect of meeting with Ridge and his delegation. Suddenly everything seemed to be going smoothly. Sam Houston had enrolled hundreds of his Cherokee brethren in the fight against Mexico and had promised that once Texas became a part of the United States, there would be plenty of Texas land available for the Cherokee.

There was another report on Jackson's desk that pleased him. Chief John Jolly, Sam Houston's adoptive father, had molded his people into a community that was calling itself the Cherokee Nation West. Under the provisions of a treaty enacted several years before, Jolly encouraged his old settlers to leave the Arkansas lands long before the deadline that had been provided by the treaty. He established a new capital at Talonteskee in the portion of Oklahoma Territory that had been given in exchange for the Arkansas lands. Crafty old John Jolly was going to be there and settled in before John Ross made an appearance on the scene— Jackson could see how much he wanted that. The seven million acres were to be a "permanent home" for the Cherokee people, as the treaty signed in Washington declared, ". . . one which shall, under the most solemn guarantee of the United States, be and remain theirs forever . . ."

Jackson was not laboring under any delusions about John Jolly. He could easily imagine the old man rubbing his hands and thinking about the prospects of the eastern Cherokee selling their lands and moving west. After all, they would bring with them additional money, annuities in exchange for the lands they would give up in the old country.

One bright morning, Little Tree and Going Horse watched as a six-man squad of federal troops marched a group of fourteen Cherokee to the holding pens near the river. The smaller children were skipping ahead; they might as well have been embarking on a great adventure. Two of the women were at least sixty winters old and though when independent they had been strong, now their heads hung dejectedly. The three men, two of them about the age of Little Tree and Going Horse, trudged forward, walking proudly as their tears ran.

"There's something you don't see very often," Going Horse remarked as they passed. "Cherokee men openly crying."

"It happens often now." Little Tree shook his

head. "Yesterday I went to the landing and I witnessed many men with tears staining their faces. Even Bright Star wept and wailed as he walked onto the flatboat. The soldiers wouldn't allow them to wait until his wife's brother came to join them. The boats were no more than a mile away when the rest of the family came to the pens."

"How many started the journey yesterday?"

"Eight hundred, maybe a few more." Little Tree shuddered. "I don't look forward to it, Going Horse."

"Why haven't they come for you yet? You signed up months ago, didn't you?"

Little Tree nodded. "Maybe they forgot me. Or perhaps they need me to haul these false-bottomed barrels of salt pork and flour up to the agency office every week."

Going Horse snorted with disgust. "Salt pork and flour! When did a Cherokee ever eat salt pork and flour made from wheat? Venison, beef, fresh pork, smoked pork and corn. Corn bread, corn pudding, corn—"

"We probably won't see corn again once we report for emigration. Not until we can grow more in the West." Little Tree paused for a moment, and then asked a question that had been on his mind.

"Have any of your family signed up yet?"

"Not yet. My wife's father said he's going to wait until the house is claimed. It's one of the last, I guess. At first we thought they had given the tickets for all the big houses to special people, but it's been over a year, and nobody has come forward to claim Lakehurst. Maybe its number just hasn't come up yet."

The horses shied at something in the road and Little Tree pulled them back under control. "You know what people are saying, Going Horse?"

"Oh, I know what they're saying. They think that because David Lake is still living in his big house, he's made a deal with Cullen. Just like the Ridges and Boudinot. But he hasn't, Little Tree."

Again the horses shied, and as Little Tree attempted to get them under control, Going Horse looked up at the sky. "Looks like rain's coming."

The horses whinnied nervously, shaking their heads against the background of a darkening sky. Somewhere off in the woods a dog howled mournfully.

Little Tree spoke soothingly to the horses, their whinnying now turned to constant shrill complaints. "That's not rain. There aren't any clouds to amount to anything. But it sure is getting dark!"

Going Horse squinted at the sun and shouted, "The sun is disappearing! Little Tree, the sun is being swallowed! Asgaya Galunlati has sent the Great Frog to swallow the sun!"

Little Tree turned his eyes to the heavens. His first thought was that the Great Frog had indeed taken a big bite out of the sun. He had heard of this thing happening before, but thought it was only a tale told to amuse the children. After the first shock, he recalled that when he attended the school at Brainerd he learned that it was a natural occurrence and that there was nothing to be afraid of.

The white men called what was happening an eclipse. The teachers at the school even drew diagrams to explain how the moon passed before the face of the sun to blot out its light. But Going Horse, like many of his people, had not spent so many years in the schools; he did not understand.

"It is a sign from Asgaya Galunlati," he repeated. "And I am afraid to think what it might mean."

Deep within the woods that lay on either side of

the road, restless animals could be heard sweeping back and forth among the foliage as if being chased by some unseen danger. But as the sky grew darker the life sounds of the forest dwindled and what remained was only the vague murmur of the breeze swishing mournfully through the pines and the hickories. Occasionally the horses added remnants of their own nervous sounds; here and there a dog howled, as eerie as the dark and the wind.

"Little Tree, let's go to the *anidawehi*."

Little Tree looked at Going Horse in the darkness. "The *anidawehi* will tell you only that once the frog is frightened away he will spit out the sun, and then everything will be all right again. There is no reason to fear this thing, Going Horse."

Aggie Lake looked around at the eight children who remained in her school. She had long ago moved from New Echota, the seat of the Nation that was now almost entirely in the hands of new white owners, and was conducting her classes in the room that had been used for years as the office and library of the owners of Lakehurst. David Lake had opened his home to as many of his people as wanted to share it, and the house and outbuildings now served as a temporary home for eighty-three people in addition to his family and slaves. Three of the children in Aggie's school had gone home to find that their families had disappeared, and David Lake was one of many who stepped forward to adopt them. No Cherokee child was ever without a family.

He carried another lamp into the classroom and found the children eagerly studying the pages of a book Aggie had discovered in the library. He placed the lamp on the table to give them more light.

"Your children don't appear to be afraid of the eclipse, Aggie."

"Of course not, Father," she replied happily. "But where did you ever get that geography of the heavens? I had no idea you had such books."

"Even I don't know all the books I have, Aggie," David Lake replied. "But every time I went to Savannah or Memphis, I brought back books for you children. Most of them I've never read and never had any desire to read. But I knew that you could make use of them."

It was true; the Lake children had made good use of their father's books over the years. Aggie remembered how as a child she had wanted to read every book in the world and had wished that books could somehow be written in Cherokee so everyone would be able to read without learning English. And even now, ten years after Sequoyah's invention of Cherokee writing had made that dream come true, there were still only two books printed in Cherokee. One was the Gospels, the other the first portion of the Old Testament, which Elias Boudinot and Sam Worcester had labored so hard to produce.

It was Leonard Lake who had done the most extensive reading in the library, though. Aggie looked at the children studying the chart of the heavens and remembered how her younger brother had spent hours at that same table, deeply absorbed in the printed word. If any one person had read all the books in that library, it would have to be her brother. From his earliest days, Leonard Lake had proved himself a scholar, and by the time he had completed his work at the Cornwall school, he had been admitted to Yale to take up a study of the law.

After graduating from Yale with high honors,

Leonard had been offered positions with law firms in Philadelphia, New York, Boston, Baltimore and Washington. He had declined every one of them and instead returned to the Nation. Rather than go into practice with Buchanan in New Echota, Lake went to Red Clay. There John Ross immediately hired him, paying him out of his own pocket, as his personal legal consultant. Soon, Lake found himself spending as much of his time in Washington as he did at home. On several occasions when Ross returned home, Leonard remained at the Indian Queen Hotel and worked long hours in the offices of Washington lawyers who were sympathetic to the Cherokee cause.

The last time Ross visited with the Lakes, he told them, "There isn't anybody in Washington who knows more about the involved history of treaties with the United States than Leonard. He is aware of all the legal ramifications of every clause and is familiar with every judgment ever made in the courts. I'm convinced that we'll receive justice in our fight against the Indian Removal Act now that he's working for us. I wish he could have been ready ten years ago."

Aggie's thoughts were interrupted by the impatient voice of Fierce Bear. "Miss Aggie, how long before it gets light again?"

"Just a few minutes, Fierce Bear. First it will begin to get light, and then the sun will shine as though nothing had happened. In an hour or so there will be full daylight again and you'll wonder how you could have been so foolish as to be frightened by an eclipse."

Fierce Bear stretched himself to his full height and looked up into her face. "I wasn't frightened, Miss Aggie. Only longhairs are frightened by an icleeps."

"E-clipse," she corrected him gently.

"Eclipse," he repeated. "Eclipse. Nothing frightens Fierce Bear." He glanced quickly over his shoulder at the other children. Some were still intently studying the charts and others were talking among themselves. "But I'm glad you were here when the Great Frog swallowed the sun."

Aggie gave him a quick hug and sent him back to the book, then settled into the chair by her desk to write to Parker.

Johnny dear,

I was pleased to hear from you that you are still so concerned about the Cherokee people. I have learned how you've secured food and clothing to give to those of my people who have been traveling west and how you have tried to prevent them from being taken advantage of. I hear those things and I appreciate how you are needed, but I miss you, John. Somehow, time isn't taking care of that hurt. Nor is it easing my wondering whether I will ever see you again. Be well, my beloved.

Aggie

A bitter winter followed the eclipse, and there were none among even the old people who could remember a season so severe. Mountain passes were completely blocked with snow, and the temperature dropped so low that the sap deep within the branches of the trees and bushes froze and split them open.

Huddling everywhere were groups of people talking about the eclipse, seeing in it, as Going Horse had, a sign that darkness had come upon the Cherokee Nation just when it was at its brightest period in history. To the superstitious, the harsh winter foretold nothing but disasters to follow. Perhaps President Jackson, like the Great Frog, had swallowed up the Cherokee Nation and the end was coming soon.

"Chief Ross has promised that he will make Jackson spit us out and let us live in peace again."

"That is nothing but foolish talk, Green Field. I'm surprised at you. You know that the only way to frighten the Great Frog is to make so much noise it can be heard in the heavens. We have not been making the noise. No suns, no drums, no villages of people shouting fiercely. And Chief Ross cannot make enough noise with words to frighten Jackson. I tell you, it is time we stopped listening to Ross and began listening to The Ridge."

"The Ridge! Bah! He was a warrior once, just as you were. But he no longer makes war. All he can do is make a great wind that blows in all directions at one time. We are too old to consider what they say, to begin again in a new land. I prefer to remain here, where our people have always been. No, Chief Ross is right. This is our land, and nobody will take it from us."

The others were silent. In the group, Green Field was alone in his blind faith that Chief Ross was going to make a miracle happen.

Soon after, the loyal Indian had reason to be disappointed. Even his idol, John Ross, was unable to work miracle enough to keep white Georgians from taking Green Field's house, just as he had been unable to keep them from taking his own.

Green Field was old enough that it would make little difference whether he stayed in Georgia or journeyed to new lands. But there were others who had their families to consider. And to them, the Treaty Party talked good sense when it said that the end of life in the East was inevitable. Even if the laws did make it difficult openly to advocate removal, the Ridges acquired more followers every day.

* * *

On a rise overlooking The Ridge's mansion at Spring Place, Cheowa squatted and surveyed what was happening there. Once more, the members of the Treaty Party had gathered to discuss the terms they would accept when next they went to Washington.

In recent weeks, The Ridge had begun a new line of attack against Ross, and Cheowa was not alone in his growing contempt of the man he had once admired.

"Do not allow yourselves to be deceived by Ross," The Ridge was thundering. His eloquent voice had lost none of its fire over the years. "He will do nothing but bring even more troubles down upon our already suffering heads. Now Ross would have us all become citizens of the states that would seize our lands—or should I say, which have indeed been seizing our lands and encroaching upon our liberties for many years. That might be well and good for mixed-breed Cherokee, but not for the full-bloods.

"Ross and many like him would have no difficulty passing for white, but those of us who show our heritage by our appearance would to my sense of things be mere outcasts. As a group, we will be cheated and oppressed and eventually reduced in numbers, while the 'breeds retain positions of honor."

That The Ridge should attempt to divide the Nation along bloodlines was ironic. Elias Boudinot and his brother Stand Watie were half-breeds and it was Boudinot who was standing side by side with full-blood Major Ridge and his son John.

Cheowa spat contemptuously as John Ridge and Elias Boudinot emerged from the house and rode toward Washington.

Bloods and breeds. Cheowa spat again and rose to his feet. He walked back over the rise to where he had left his horse ground-tethered. After patting it on the neck, he swung up, muttering to himself, "The Ridge wants to divide us along bloodlines? Well, we'll see where those bloodlines are drawn!"

Chapter 19

Ridge and Boudinot were not the only ones going to Washington that spring. Once more John Ross was meeting with his old commander from the Battle of Horseshoe Bend. Though both men were older, neither had changed much. And each had progressed from the status of National Warrior to National Chief Executive. Jackson had lost weight, Ross had gained. Each of them carried the scars of war as well as the scars of their battles with each other. Like poker players, both men kept their cards close to their chests, alert for the perfect opportunity to make a bet. It was Ross who began negotiations by presenting Jackson with the detailed list that Leonard Lake had prepared.

Jackson took one look at the list and snorted, "We've been over all this before, John."

"This is a complete list of treaties that the United States has made with the Cherokee people," Ross began, unruffled. "Broken treaties, broken promises, broken—"

"John, you're stalling. We're here for one purpose only and that is to discuss the terms of a treaty for—"

"Another treaty that will undoubtedly be broken."

"A final treaty that will be honored forever," Jackson contradicted. "I can't understand what's happened over the years. When we fought together and I made you my aide, we saw eye to eye. You were a great warrior then, John."

"My people believe I still am, Mr. President."

Ross' formality seemed saber-sharp to Jackson.

"When you were still known as Guwisguwi you could listen to reason."

Ross smiled coolly. "I still listen to reason, Mr. President, the rational thinking of the many thousands of my people. And many of them still know me by my Cherokee name. I happen to be very proud of it. If it will give you any satisfaction, you have my permission to address me once again as Guwisguwi, and we'll proceed—in Cherokee!"

Jackson bristled. "Cut out the jabs and let's get to the treaty, John."

"I'm prepared to offer you a counterproposal," Ross offered. "In exchange for our land in the East, twenty million dollars and equivalent lands in the West."

"You're mad! What you offer is nothing but a stalling tactic and you know it!"

"Then let the Senate decide the amount," Ross suggested calmly. He knew that the Senate would have the final say in the affair no matter what Jackson offered. "Whatever they offer, my delegates and I will give it every serious consideration."

"You'd accept what they offer?"

"What I said, Mr. President, is that we will consider what they offer."

"Please give my regards to the Reverend Mr. Schermerhorn," Ross added as Jackson walked him to the door. "He seems to be occupied with other matters."

Jackson swore under his breath as Ross left the office. Returning to his desk, he considered the impossibility of keeping anything secret from John Ross. No harm could come from it, though, Jackson decided. He was still able to work one Cherokee delegation against another.

Jackson did present Ross's twenty-million-dollar demand to the Senate, which replied with an offer of five million. Ross had another counterproposal for the President and the Senate to consider. "Find out," he told Jackson, "what it would be worth to the United States if the Cherokee were to leave the United States completely. We have already taken steps to settle in Mexico."

Jackson was stunned. Ross felt a certain satisfaction in seeing his adversary at last at a loss for words. The President had been totally unprepared for such an alternative.

Later Leonard Lake told Ross that the proposal had been forwarded to the Mexican ambassador. Ross replied, "It makes no difference now. The President wouldn't even consider it. He almost threw me out of his office."

Lake shook his head. "Is it possible he thinks we don't know what Schermerhorn has been doing?"

Vice President Martin Van Buren was the one who had located Schermerhorn. Because Schermerhorn's ancestors were, like Van Buren's, originally from Holland, the Dutch Presbyterian minister had several qualities Van Buren and Jackson thought could be of use in dealing with the Cherokee problem. His ministerial background would be helpful, since the missionaries had already established credentials. He was physically large, flamboyant in his dress and speech and able to match any of the eloquent Cherokee who delighted in rhetoric. In addition, he was wily and crafty, able to influence people of importance. To Jackson, however, Schermerhorn's most important quality was that he was not hindered by any sense of right and wrong.

Jackson knew that as President, he would have to be the one to deal with Ross but gave Schermerhorn the assignment of carrying on the real negotiations with John Ridge. Schermerhorn made certain that his first offer to Ridge was not much better than the one made to Andrew Ross a year earlier. Although those terms had long since been refused, there was no sense in making an unnecessarily large opening bid.

Ridge and Boudinot knew that Schermerhorn's offer of three and a quarter million dollars was not a true one, but tossed out only for openers. So when word reached them of the Senate's five-million-dollar offer to Ross, they were able to squeeze a little more from the negotiator.

"What would you say to four and a half million in cash?" Schermerhorn countered. "In addition, we will give you an extra eight hundred thousand acres of land in the West with enough value to bring the total figure to five million dollars."

Ridge and Boudinot considered the offer, then countered with a demand for additional money to provide for Indian education. "We consider the operation of schools to be one of the highest endeavors that can be undertaken by our people," Boudinot insisted. "As a man of the cloth, you know that what the Cherokee are today is largely the result of the untiring work of missionaries among us. We have long enjoyed the support of the churches in the East and around the world, but there are never enough contributions to keep up with demands. If the Cherokee people could have exactly what they wanted, there would be a school and teacher in every village and academies for higher learning at numerous locations. The churches alone cannot support such a vast undertaking."

Schermerhorn came back the following day with an offer of a forty-thousand-dollar annual cash payment for the "furtherance of education among the Cherokee people." Ridge and Boudinot celebrated the offer, which they considered very liberal. Triumphantly they reported the details to the Nation. Because of what they saw as their coup, they expected to be treated as heroes. After all, John Ross had achieved nothing except the promise of more trouble. The Treaty Party had been able to obtain the promise of more money than anyone had ever dreamed of, more land than they had ever been offered, as well as money to operate schools and missions. Furthermore, Ross seemed determined to transfer his people to a foreign land they knew nothing of, in order, he was accused, to build a personal empire in a place where he alone was powerful.

As soon as the details had been agreed on in Washington, Boudinot had Cullen arrange for the printing of five hundred copies of the proposed treaty. Cullen had accompanied Ridge and Boudinot to Washington and after they arrived, he had divided his time between accompanying them and visiting the Office of Indian Affairs, where he kept Madden and the Commissioner informed of every development. When the copies of the treaty were ready, the group returned to the Nation and found their homecoming tainted with hostility and disapproval.

John Ross listened patiently to the angry Cherokee meeting at Red Clay that demanded that something be done about those who had formed the Treaty Party.

"They speak for themselves, not the Nation," Cheowa complained. "The Blood Law demands their deaths."

"It would be unwise to take their lives," Ross insisted. "We must show patience in this matter. Besides, the Treaty Party has been unable to obtain the support of the majority in the Council."

"But our Council has reinstituted the death penalty for selling our land without approval of all," Going Horse protested.

"And the penalty can be administered only with the approval of the national committee," Ross reminded them. "John Ridge is still president of the committee and will veto any such action."

Cheowa and Going Horse grumbled angrily as they rode home. "Did John Ridge or Elias Boudinot show the courage Chief Ross did?" Cheowa declaimed. "No. They didn't even deal with the Secretary of War. It was Chief Ross who stood up to Chicken Snake Jackson like a true warrior. It was Ross who stood up to Secretary Cass. It was Ross who stood up to the Senate. But it was weaklings like John Ridge and Elias Boudinot who would willingly trade our birthright for the scrubby land we saw with our own eyes beyond the Arkansas. If I had my way, those traitors wouldn't live another day."

Going Horse grunted his approval. "But Chief Ross doesn't want any blood to be shed. Any more assassinations and we'll have federal troops and Georgia troops swooping down on us in numbers that will make the pine cones that fall from the trees seem like nothing. We will wait, Cheowa. Our day will come."

"That is right, Going Horse. It will come as surely as the sun will rise in the morning. And until it comes, we should let the filthy cowards know how we feel."

At dawn the next day, John Ridge looked through the windows of his house at Running Water and saw the figures standing among the trees. Had he been able to communicate with his father or Elias at that moment, he would have known that the scene was being repeated at their homes, too.

The men stood silently in watchful groups of two or three. Sometimes there was only a single figure. Blankets were draped over their heads. They said nothing, did nothing. They stood, watching. The message was clear.

When the Council met at Red Clay in May, Schermerhorn and Cullen were seated in places of honor before the assembled delegates. The Reverend Agent, as Schermerhorn's many enemies called him, introduced the agreement that had been signed in Washington and aded a message from President Jackson that urged the delegates to give every consideration to the treaty.

Cullen held no authority at the meeting except as an observer for the War Department. As Schermerhorn's bull-like voice bellowed through the council house, Cullen shifted uneasily in his seat. The snickers that greeted Schermerhorn's words were not encouraging. Some of the delegates made no attempt to lower their voices as they made disparaging remarks about the man they had given the name of Skaynooyauna.

Cullen wondered how Washington could have sent a man like Schermerhorn to deal with the Cherokee. If anyone had earned the name of Skaynooyauna or Devil Horn, it was this comic opera character. In the few weeks he had lived among the Cherokee, Schermerhorn had managed to get drunk twice and hadn't even had the decency to confine his amorous activities with Cherokee women to cover of darkness. Several times, in broad daylight, he had been seen with willing partners; he saved the unwilling ones for the sheltering night.

Schermerhorn's efforts at convincing the Council they were being presented with a fair treaty were less than spectacular. The Council rejected the treaty outright and voted to give Ross "full powers to adjust all . . . difficulties in whatever way he might think most beneficial to the people."

Schermerhorn was then forced to listen while the Council turned to consideration of other matters that affected their future. The Council read letters from former members who had moved to Oklahoma. The letters lamented that the government was still faithless in keeping its promises. There had been many deaths along the way west and terrible hardships to be endured in the underdeveloped land; people were hungry, suffering.

Schermerhorn left the meeting after hearing this and so missed the balance of the discussion, which involved the Cherokees' future plans. One subject of that discussion was the revival of the *Phoenix*.

The paper was to be published at Red Clay, and one of the council members, Richard Fields, was chosen as its new editor. Ross was authorized to send teamsters to New Echota to transfer the equipment to Red Clay.

Boudinot and John Ridge managed to get word to Boudinot's brother Stand Watie at Spring Place, and along with a detachment of the Georgia Guard under Colonel Bishop, Watie managed to spirit away the press, type, bindery and all of the equipment and supplies that had remained unused. Next they raided the home of Elijah Hicks, removing all records and papers he had stored there for safekeeping.

Ross' men arrived two hours too late to stop the confiscation, and when Ross learned of the seizure, he protested vehemently to Schermerhorn and Cullen.

"Those things belong to the entire Nation," he exploded. "I demand that John Ridge, Elias Boudinot, Stand Watie, The Ridge and every member of the Georgia Guard who participated in the thievery be held accountable and punished."

Cullen replied in a letter:

> The press was originally purchased by Elias Boudinot with voluntary contributions from citizens of the United States for the general benefit of the Cherokee people. You and your partisans compelled him to give up his position as editor by not permitting him to give both sides of the Treaty question the opportunity to express their views.
>
> Instead you put the *Phoenix* into the hands of your brother-in-law Elijah Hicks, who was never any more than a sounding board for your own opinions. What had once been the voice of a proud people became prostituted into a personal propaganda sheet for party politics that misled the people and prejudiced their minds against the reasonable course of government.

Ross smarted under the attack. There had been a certain element of truth in Cullen's charges. Still, Ross knew that he represented better than three quarters of the people of the Nation and had their full support.

Several months later, in a letter to Chief Clerk Charles Madden, Cullen expressed his impatience with the bumbling Schermerhorn:

> When John Ridge called a council of his own at his home in Running Water during July, there were all indications that many of those attending could be won to the side of the Treaty Party. The Rev. Mr. Schermer-

horn, however, foolishly used the occasion to make an attack upon Chief Ross and so infuriated the gathering that for several hours I feared that we might both lose our lives.

In answer to Schermerhorn's attack, Ross replied simply that he was not disposed to argue with any man for an honest expression of his opinions. Then John Ridge stated that any differences between himself and Chief Ross resulted only from an honest conviction as to how best to preserve the Cherokee people. Ross and Ridge then agreed to meet with the leaders of their parties, excluding the Rev. Mr. Schermerhorn and myself, of course.

Of deepest concern to me, as I know it is to you, has been the increasing number of murders of supporters of the Treaty Party. I am firmly convinced that Chief Ross is totally blameless in these atrocious deeds, for openly as well as privately, he condemns any recourse to violence. Nevertheless, two of John Ridge's supporters have been slashed to ribbons by knives, one beaten to death by clubs and sticks, another smashed about the head by heavy rocks, two have been drowned, and one stabbed sixteen times and left to die hanging by his heels from a tree at the side of a public road.

I would strongly urge you to use whatever influence you might have upon the Commissioner and the Secretary to have the President remove the Reverend Mr. Schermerhorn from his position and replace him with someone who is more acceptable to the Cherokee people.

*   *   *

Andrew Jackson reviewed the reports that crossed his desk, but ignoring them, he wrote to Schermerhorn, repeating the orders he hoped would be able to bring about the downfall of John Ross, the sorest thorn in his side. "Build a fire under them," he demanded.

Chapter 20

Upstream from Fort Smith, the Arkansas River wound tortuously through the mountains of eastern Oklahoma. Mile after mile, cliffs threatened to tumble their ponderous, overhanging rocks down into the river valley. Vast stands of hickory, oak and chestnut lined the river, and the broad valleys between the mountain ridges stretched far into the distance, showing evidence of burgeoning settlements and their accompanying cultivated fields.

Sam and Ann Worcester studied each settlement with an eye toward establishing another mission station somewhere nearby. They had many days of travel ahead of them before they'd arrive at Fort Gibson, headquarters for the administration of affairs in Indian Territory. The last letter they received from the Mission Board in Boston had ordered them to report there. Once settled into their first post at Dwight, they were to listen to the advice of the cavalry officers and the Indian agent concerning suitable locations for mission stations.

Little Tree and his family had been traveling on the same boat as Worcester but the Indian was unable to share the missionary's enthusiasm over the new lands. "Wait until you see the rest of it," he cautioned.

"Wait until *you* see the surprise the Board has sent," Worcester replied.

Fort Gibson lay within sight of the confluence of the Arkansas, Verdigris and Grand Rivers and was one of the most active outposts on the frontier. Young officers just graduating from West Point had two chances out of three of being stationed at Fort Gibson and it was there they would get their first taste of "real soldiering."

Life at the fort was grueling; hard labor, heat, flies, malaria and bad liquor took their toll. During the eleven years after the post had been established in 1824 for the protection of settlers in the area, five hundred seventy officers and men had been buried in the cemetery. Since then, the outpost had been called the Graveyard of the Army.

Fort Gibson was much like any other fort built during the expansion of the United States. The enlisted men lived in stark barracks where intemperance was the rule rather than the exception. The officers' quarters were hardly better. Within the log stockade were a mess hall, a foundry, a blacksmith shop, stables, supply warehouses and administrative offices. Prominently situated near the parade ground were the stocks. They were seldom without a soldier or two who had been caught attempting to desert the post.

As the passengers debarked from the flatboats, the conductors checked their names off the lists. Little Tree and Martha, along with their children and the others in their family who had survived the ravages of measles during the journey, followed Sam and Ann Worcester to the outer stockades that had been erected to provide shelter for the immigrants. Little Tree stiffened when he saw the pointed logs that would wall them in. Noting this, Worcester laid a comforting hand on his friend's shoulder.

"We won't be here long."

"One night is too long," Little Tree answered quietly. "When we left the stockade at Hiwassèe, I thought that it would be the last of them. Are they going to ship us from one prison to another until we all die?"

The captain sat at the table under the awning outside the confinement center. As he looked up at the Worcesters, he was pleased as well as surprised to see a white family.

"Reverend Worcester?"

"Yes, sir. And my family."

"Correct," the captain beamed, fishing under the unruly stack of papers that cluttered the table. "A man by the name of David Farmer has been waiting for you, Reverend. Just as soon as your household goods arrive, he'll take you to the settlement at Dwight. The American Board of Foreign Missions has made all the arrangements."

"We're ready to leave right away," Ann said wearily. "We have nothing left to take with us."

"Nothing?" the captain repeated, surprise in his eyes. "The manifest shows you have—"

"The steamer that was carrying our household goods sank, Captain," Worcester interrupted. "We lost nearly everything. And along the way, while awaiting transfer to another boat, we were robbed of the rest."

The captain frowned. "I trust you've reported what happened to the conductor, sir. Every effort shall be made to find those responsible."

"The robbers weren't among our people," Worcester explained, his voice reflecting the exhaustion he was feeling. "Whites came into the camp at night and loaded up the Indians with plenty of cheap whiskey. After most of the party fell asleep, the whites returned to rob us."

The captain turned to a private who had been

leaning against a doorpost some distance from them. "Private Henderson, please send for Mr. Farmer."

"Yessir," the young man replied in clipped tones. "He's camped less than a mile away, I believe, sir."

Next, the captain looked up at Little Tree. "Name, please?"

"Little Tree, and this is my—"

"They'll be coming with us, Captain—all of them," Worcester interjected. "Little Tree will be working with me at the mission station at Dwight."

The Indian looked surprised, but Worcester motioned for him to be silent.

Not noticing the exchange, the captain nodded, moving his finger down the list until he found Little Tree's name, then dipped his quill into the inkstand. He wrote Dwight Station after it. Adding ditto marks for the rest of Little Tree's family, he said, "You'll all find food and blankets waiting for you at the supply room. Then you're free to leave."

As they joined those already lined up for bowls of salt pork and beans, Little Tree asked excitedly, "Sam, do you mean we're not going to have to stay here any longer than this?"

"Of course not," Worcester replied. "Just don't ask any more questions until we get to Dwight." He and Ann exchanged smiles.

Two days later the wagon driven by David Farmer pulled up at a cluster of tents and crude shelters that was the growing community of Dwight. After Worcester led the group in a prayer of thanksgiving, he strode toward to one of the few substantial buildings that had been erected. A head appeared from the doorway and a jubilant voice shouted. "Sam! Little Tree! *O-si-yo!*"

Little Tree's face broke into a wide grin. "Michael Candy! What are you doing here?"

"Come on in and look for yourself, you old mule skinner," called another voice.

It was Henry Wheeler.

"We'll be back in business in no time," Wheeler said. "Feast your eyes on this."

There, in the middle of the building, stood a press that was larger than the one that had been lost at New Echota. It had only been partially assembled, but one look convinced Worcester that they could be ready to begin printing inside of a week.

"All we need now is Elias," Worcester rejoiced. "And he'll be coming soon, I'd imagine."

"Candy's proved pretty capable," Wheeler said, "but we're still short a couple of men. I got a letter from the Board asking me to get the whole crew together—except for Isaac of course. I'd sure love to get Parker back with us. Where is he, Little Tree?"

"Tsani wrote me one letter after he got to Little Rock. I guess he's still back there. I'll write to him again and see what he's up to."

"Good idea," Wheeler approved. "The man's a good printer and he knows your language inside out. To save my soul, I still can't make heads nor tails of those letters."

"Then maybe it's a good thing your salvation doesn't depend on reading *Tsalagi*," Worcester grinned. "I thought we might be able to make use of Little Tree's experience once we get going again."

"I can work the press," Little Tree admitted, "but that's about all. That and deliver the papers."

"And get subscribers," Michael Candy contributed.

"Well," Little Tree said sheepishly, "I guess I did pretty well at that too. Sam, what do you want to bet I can get more subscribers in a week than you can?" he asked suddenly.

Ann rolled her eyes to heaven. "God help us all," she prayed. "Here we go again!"

Chapter 21

"James Adair?"

Adair nodded, unsure of what the Guard wanted this time.

"You're under arrest. You've been accused of being an agent of John Ross," the officer announced. Two of his guardsmen took the councilman by the arms.

Adair was not the only member of the Council arrested in this way. Elijah Hicks found himself jailed with the elderly Chief White Path and no charges had been placed against either of them.

Many of the Nation's leaders found themselves the victims of the fires Schermerhorn was building under them with false arrests, detentions and endless hours of questioning. Anything was fair in Schermerhorn's book. Nothing was excluded from his repertoire, provided it would hasten the day that the reluctant Indians would sign the treaty. The harassment didn't stop and Schermerhorn and Cullen doubled the efforts of the enrollment agents.

At Lakehurst, the crowd of refugees swelled almost daily. Cherokee who had refused to sign up for removal and had found themselves beaten for resisting

a government agent swarmed there. Others seeking refuge at Lakehurst had had their cattle stolen, their
homes burned and their crops set on fire.

Agatha turned to her father in desperation.

"Isn't there anything we can do? How much longer is this going to continue?"

"Until," David Lake said calmly, "we all leave
our homes and go west."

"But, Father, with the council meeting coming
up . . ."

Lake shook his head. "I was talking with Chief
Ross the other day, Aggie. He knows there is no longer
any way to prevent the removal. All that remains now
is to get the most favorable terms we possibly can."

Agatha studied the contents of the home she had
known since she was a small child, the oil portraits and
landscapes, the familiar bric-a-brac that filled the
glass-fronted cabinet in the dining room. Some were of
ancient Cherokee handicraft and others had been gar-
nered from places as far away as Venice. There were
the porcelain figurines from Holland and England and
the medal David Lake had earned at Horseshoe Bend.
Lake's framed commission as an officer in the United
States Army, signed by Andrew Jackson, had long since
been removed from display, but Aggie knew that it was
safely hidden away somewhere in one of the many
trunks that filled the attic. The bone china, the crystal,
the silver, all of that would have to be left behind to be
sold for whatever it would bring.

She remembered the astounded look on John
Parker's face the day he first entered that vestibule.
Suddenly her eyes filled with tears. She ran to her
room, wishing that she had listened and gone with him
to Little Rock. What had seemed the only reasonable
thing to do then had proved as foolhardy as he had

said it would. Even her own father, just minutes before, had said it was no longer a matter of whether they would have to move. It was only a matter of when. And by what means.

Agatha cried as she had not cried since she was a child. She couldn't leave now. Her father needed her. Her people did too, more than ever. Maybe one day, though, if she were very lucky, she'd be with John again.

During the early days of October, while the forests were ablaze with color, more than a thousand Cherokee converged on the council grounds at Red Clay. They came in buggies, they came in wagons, they came on horseback, men and women. Mostly they came on foot, their moccasins drumming the roads and trails and scuffing the dry leaves under their feet.

There were some who talked of mundane things as they moved determinedly toward Red Clay, but for the most part the travelers walked in silence. Among their numbers were all the great chiefs of the Nation. White Path trudged silently, refusing the use of a horse. Going Snake rode, as did George Lowrey.

From Running Water, at the special invitation of Chief John Ross, came John Ridge and Elias Boudinot. From Spring Place, the Ridge rode the carriage he had built to order many years earlier in Baltimore. His black slave was resplendent in military-style livery that featured highly polished brass buttons and gleaming epaulets. The Ridge sat impassively in the carriage. His blue frock coat with its satin lapels covered a tawny-colored vest that strained against its buttons.

Once near Red Clay, small groups began settling into camps for the night. Fires flickered under the already-flaming leaves overhead. Some people slept.

Many spent the night quietly contemplating the serious work that lay ahead during the coming week.

Early the next morning, an orderly, silent procession made its way not to the open-sided council house where the work was to be undertaken, but to the modest cabin of Principal Chief John Ross. On this morning, only the very oldest of the men and a few women were on horseback. Even those who had traveled so many miles in a variety of wheeled vehicles were now on foot; and many more feet were bare now than when the long journey began.

The elaborate dress displayed during the procession rivaled even the autumn splendor. Colorful blankets and robes, some of which were of shimmering satin, trailed to the ground. A few Indians wore hats, but the majority were costumed in the turbans that had been popular since the first Cherokee were taken to London and dressed like natives of the fabled land of India. Dangling from the turbans were baubles and beads that glittered in the early morning sunlight. Some marchers wore tunics with shining copper breastplates. Nearly all were adorned with drapery of some kind to emphasize the importance of the occasion.

The procession stopped in front of the gate of the Principal Chief, who opened it solemnly and stood back to greet his countrymen. They entered his grounds, removing or loosening their blankets. Silently they formed two diagonal lines that reached across the yard to the porch of the cabin. Ross solemnly shook hands with each visitor.

Once the formal salutations had been completed, the younger men withdrew, gathering in quiet bands and squatting against trees or sitting on the ground. Later, when Ross and the old men rose, the others did too, and returned through the woods to the council house.

Within hours, the Council was in session and Schermerhorn and Cullen again had seats of honor before the assembly. Schermerhorn began, as was expected, with a denunciation of John Ross. Then he handed Ross a letter, which Ross had Leonard Lake translate and read in Cherokee while Cullen approved the translation.

Lake had scarcely gotten beyond the first paragraph when the Council heard, "Mr. Ross and his party are usurpers of power and destitute of all legal authority—"

"Objection!" interjected an angry voice.

"Let him finish," shouted another. The listeners would not be quieted.

Other voices were fighting to be heard, protesting. "We've already heard what the Reverend Agent has to say about Chief Ross! We don't need to waste our time hearing any more!"

A thunderous roar of approval highlighted that comment. Lake handed the letter back to Ross, who folded it and filed it in his briefcase.

There was a brief lull, during which a point of order was debated. Then Cullen leaned over and whispered to Schermerhorn, "If you think you're going to unseat Ross, you'd better think again, Jack. If these Indians were to hold an election right now, Ross would get all but maybe a dozen votes. Try another line of attack unless you're ready to go back to Washington tomorrow with your head in your hands."

"Don't worry about me, Cullen. The old coot's as good as washed up right now."

"You'd better not bet on that, Jack. You'd be a fool."

Next came the matter of the treaty. Schermerhorn reviewed the details, the same ones agreed upon in

Washington six months earlier. He sat down smugly when the voting began, but soon his face was ashen.

Over a thousand Indians voted against the treaty. There was not a single vote of approval.

Schermerhorn was on his feet in an instant. "I have been empowered to make an offer of more money."

"How much more?"

"Don't dicker! State your limits, Skaynooyauna!"

"The government will increase the cash settlement to five million dollars!"

"Is that your final offer?" demanded one of the younger chiefs.

"It is, and if you are wise you'll find it favorable."

Once more Schermerhorn sat down alongside Cullen and waited while the vote was taken. And once more there was not a single vote in favor, not even from Boudinot and the Ridges. It was obvious from the frozen expressions on their faces that the two were not eager to speak up against an already volatile crowd. Schermerhorn was dumbfounded. He sat numbly as the Council decided there was no further business. Within hours, most of the voters had departed from Red Clay, leaving him and Cullen pondering their next move. Clearly, Ross was going to have to be dealt with more firmly. And clearly, he would have to consult with Boudinot and Ridge to find out why they hadn't supported him.

On the evening of November 7, John Ross was at home with John Howard Payne, a northern visitor who had become quite interested in the Cherokee Nation and its future and who contemplated writing their history in order to document many of the wrongs they had suffered. Deep in conversation, the men heard hoofbeats pounding toward the cabin. Almost at once, the dogs began barking and yapping. Moments later the door burst open. Members of the Georgia Guard forced their way inside, bayonets pointed. Several had pistols drawn and aimed.

"You're under arrest!" the leader barked.

"Under arrest? What do you mean? I want to know the charges," Payne protested.

"I don't need to explain anything, Indian-lover," the militiaman answered, cuffing Payne brutally across the mouth. "Just get out the door so we can get started!"

Flanked by members of the Georgia Guard who had crossed into Tennessee to make the arrest, Ross and Payne were taken in a driving, bone-chilling rain to one of the windowless slave quarters on the Vann estate at Spring Place. Shoved into a dark cabin, they discovered one of the sons of Chief Going Snake chained to a table.

The door slammed shut. "What have you been charged with?" Ross asked.

"With being Cherokee," the young man replied—Ross could barely see his face—"and with voting against the treaty."

The stench that filled the tiny cabin was almost overpowering, and as daylight began to filter in through the chinks between the ill-fitting logs, the decomposing body of a Cherokee prisoner could be seen hanging from the rafters.

Before the sun had completely risen, there was a scuffle outside. Soon after, the door opened and standing in the doorway were Cheowa and Going Horse.

"You are a free man, Chief," Cheowa said. "Come, we have horses waiting. We also have hundreds of brothers who will wipe these scum off the face of the earth."

To the amazement of the pair who had rescued them, Ross shook his head. "I've been telling you for years," he demurred, "that violence will not serve our cause well. Now leave and lock the door. Report to the Governor of Tennessee exactly what has happened here. There's a chance that'll do more good than simply letting us out."

The door was bolted shut again. Going Horse poured the contents of a jug of corn liquor down the guards' throats, providing a logical excuse for their being unconscious.

When word reached the Governor of Tennessee, he raised an outcry that shook the Georgia Guard to its very foundations. Governor Schley, Lumpkin's successor, had Ross released immediately.

"Please believe me," he pleaded. "What has been done to Ross and Payne was the act, not of Georgia, but of a few misguided men."

On November 16, Colonel Bishop arrived to offer both his apologies and those of the governor.

"Gentlemen," he concluded, "the only thing I can say that will come close to convincing you of my horror over this incident is that as of this day, I am resigning my commission."

It was another week before Ross was able to secure the release of Payne. During that time the northerner was accused, among other things, of being an abolitionist, probably in the hopes that the neighbors would be roused enough to lynch him. Finally freed and reaching home, Payne wrote scathing denunciations of this treatment as well as of the subjugation of the Cherokee people.

Schermerhorn and the Ridges had held several secret meetings and now Schermerhorn had called for a December council. Cheowa and Going Horse sat back and watched as clusters of people gathered at New Echota. To boost attendance, Schermerhorn had offered free blankets and a cash stipend to anyone who attended.

"How many do you make out, Going Horse?" Cheowa asked.

"Seventy-five, not more than eighty. Does old Devil Horn think he's going to be able to pull off a treaty with only eighty qualified voters?"

"No telling what goes through that pile of pig dung he calls a mind," Cheowa replied. "The only voters with any standing at all are the Ridges, Elias and Stand Watie. Practically everybody else came here to get the free blankets and money. You heard what Elias told the Reverend Agent didn't you?"

"What?"

"That Chief Ross warned everyone to stay away. Then old Devil Horn announced that anyone who didn't appear in person to vote against the treaty would be assumed to be in favor of it. The man is mad. His words are worth no more than the fart of a jackass."

As the sparsely attended Council got underway, Cheowa and Going Horse listened to Schermerhorn present the tired provisions of the treaty once more. "In his usual grand style," Going Horse commented dryly as the former preacher launched bombastically into his discourse. "Only more so than ever. Damn, Cheowa, I'm tired of listening to that old crap. I can't take much more of it."

As Cheowa dozed through Schermerhorn's presentation, Going Horse slipped outside. Minutes later, Cheowa was roused from his drowsiness by shouts of "Get out! Fire! Fire!"

The council house was emptied in less than a minute. A bucket brigade reached from the spring to ladders leading to the top of the building. The flames on the roof were extinguished in minutes and the delegates returned to their seats.

Going Horse reappeared and quietly sat next to Cheowa on one of the rear benches. Cheowa grinned. "You trying to earn the name of Junaluska?"

"That's me," Going Horse replied, One Who Tried and Failed. He smirked playfully. Then, "Quiet, The Ridge is going to speak."

The Ridge appeared frailer than he had not long before, but his snow white hair still lent an air of dignity to his appearance as he faced the few listeners.

"I know we love the graves of our fathers who have gone before to the happy hunting grounds of Asgaya Galunlati, the eternal land where the deer, the turkey and the buffalo will never give out. We can never forget these homes, I know, but an unbending, iron necessity tells us we must leave them. I would willingly die to preserve what we have done here, but any forcible effort to keep our land will cost us our lives and the lives of our children. There is but one path of safety, one road to our continued existence as a nation. The path is open before you. Make a treaty of cession. Give up these lands and go over beyond the great Father of Waters." And so ended the last speech The Ridge would ever make in public.

Elias Boudinot added a final note. "Thomas Foreman has called The Ridge a traitor, but where is Thomas Foreman today? He sits in his home with the loud thunder! We know we can take our lives in our hands as our fathers have also done. We will make and sign this treaty. Our friends can then cross the great river; but Tom Foreman and his people would put us across the dread river of death! We can die, but the Cherokee Nation will be saved!"

Cheowa and Going Horse left for Red Clay. They didn't stay to hear the rest of the details worked out.

They did not see the delegates line up to sign the treaty. They did not hear the words of The Ridge as he added his name to the bottom of the list.

"I have signed my death warrant."

Chapter 22

Little Tree's letter from Dwight stirred Parker to join his friends. Restless, still missing Aggie terribly, he quit his job and headed away from Little Rock.

"You really did it!" Little Tree exclaimed, surprised and pleased to see his friend so soon.

"Yep! And from what I can see of the size of this operation, you really do need me."

"We've been printing a lot of pamphlets on removal, John," Wheeler said in a more serious tone. "We figure that the Cherokee have a right to know what to expect when they travel. They also have a right to know where to go for help if they need it; it's not easy to find. Anyway, how have you been? Have you heard from Aggie?"

Parker nodded, then looked away, letting what Aggie had told him about the situation back home pass quickly through his mind.

After the December council meeting, John Ross had done everything in his power to have the treaty nullified, but he found indifference and indignation from everyone who had any power in Washington.

"Slowly but surely, the wheel of fortune is turning against the Cherokee, John," Aggie had written. "In fact, New Echota is practically a ghost town and stockades are being constructed in preparation for the day when our people begin their move to the western land. . . . I'm afraid, John."

A year after the spurious treaty was negotiated, John Ross had headed a delegation of eight of his chiefs to the western capital at Tahlonteskee to hold a council with John Jolly. On December 8, 1836, the Council there voted unanimously that the treaty signed by the Ridges and Boudinot was objectionable to both branches of the Nation. Full cooperation between East and West resulted from that council.

Accompanying Ross back to Red Clay was a young Cherokee named James Mooney. Officially, Mooney's only duty was to study the removal situation, but Ross discerned that in time Mooney would be useful in solidifying the growing sense of unity between the two branches of the Nation.

The following month, more than six hundred Cherokee gathered at the stockade in New Echota to form the vanguard of the thousands who would follow. The Ridge himself was there. He had come from his home in a style befitting the third richest man in the Nation (behind Rich Joe Vann and Ross). He rode in his custom-built coach with his family and had with him a carriage for his servants and a huge wagon for his household belongings. His slaves traveled behind on foot, nervously driving a large herd of cattle, all that remained of The Ridge's vast holdings. For "improvements" to his land, he had received compensation to the tune of twenty-four thousand dollars.

For the most part, the others who came to New Echota were also among the moneyed class. They were a brightly dressed, happy lot, and the snow-covered ground where they met provided an appropriate background for the stunning plumes worn by many of the ladies. The children riding in the carriages alongside their mothers laughed and sang, generally behaving as if they were on a holiday excursion.

Agent Cullen, sitting in his office facing the commons, was arguing with General John Ellis Wool.

"The government's set aside four hundred thousand dollars to satisfy claims for abandoned property; that money's also got to pay for transportation. Sir, do you realize that little group out there has already been paid a hundred thousand dollars? And they aren't even three per cent of the people!"

Wool had already proved himself a troublemaker to the removal agents. He was determined to be fair with both sides and his lenient, compassionate attitude toward the Cherokee was disheartening to Cullen. Having tried to be fair himself, he knew the difficulties that attitude could spawn.

"Mr. Cullen, keep in mind that this is a very select group of people," Wool reminded the agent. As he gazed out the window, a group of small boys threw spears at a stone disc rolling across the snowy commons. "These are the wealthy families you see here, the influential people. They have received a disproportionately large amount of money because they controlled a disproportionately large amount of property. Look at them! They're delighted. They're acting as if this were the greatest thing that could ever happen to them. Just think what their attitude will mean to the thousands of people who look up to them, respect them, admire them. Mr. Cullen, every penny of the money we've paid out is worth it when you consider the large numbers of people this group will influence to follow."

Wool was correct in his reasoning. Reports coming back from the large communities through which the more privileged travelers passed on their overland route through Kentucky, Tennessee, Illinois, Missouri and Arkansas were encouraging to the average man who feared what might lie ahead. "Prosperous, civilized, well-mannered people," were words the whites along the way used to praise them. "A pleasure to do business with such fine folk," reported Henry Warburton, the cheating provisioner from Little Rock.

Cullen bided his time and saved his breath. The real test would come when the next group was sent off under government supervision. People like the ones in the first group would have been well received anywhere. But the rest of the Cherokee were common Indians, not having resources or the background to care for themselves.

At the last minute, The Ridge had returned to his home. He claimed illness but everyone knew his excuse was pretense. What he wanted was to be present at his daughter's wedding. Notwithstanding her father's attempts to split the Nation along lines of full-blood and mixed-breeds, she was marrying a lieutenant under General Wool's command.

Cullen knew his fears had not been unreasonable when he took a close look at the next group that began assembling in New Echota. The Indians had been lured there by the money paid in advance for travel expenses. As should have been expected, they promptly began spending whatever cash they had in the half-dozen taverns in town. Cullen's experienced eye could detect no joy in the whooping and hollering as the Cherokee drank themselves into oblivion. To him what they were doing seemed merely a way to ease the pain and suffering they were expecting.

After arduous weeks in the cramped confines of the stockades, the second group of emigrants left for Ross' Landing, where they were transferred to open flatboats. Included in the band was The Ridge, who, after spending most of his life living in luxury, traveled as unceremoniously as the others. He sat stoically on the deck of the flatboat, a blanket wrapped around his shoulders to ward off the chilling March rain.

Cheowa swelled with fury as the boats pulled away from the shore and headed for Gunter's Landing in Alabama. Most of the children were already suffering from coughs, colds and influenza. Such ill health was almost unknown before the *unaka* had come among the Cherokee. For weeks, the Indians had lived under the roofs of the stockade pens, jammed tightly in among others who had also lived out of doors until then. Now, because they were forced to live in squalor, the Cherokee had lost their resistance to illness. Pleurisy, measles and diarrhea ran rampant through the group. And like many young white men, young Cherokee had been introduced to the sinister effects of gonorrhea, which was spreading unstopped like fire in a dry forest.

Until the boats were out of sight, Cheowa kept his eyes focused on the back of the man he considered most responsible for the evils that had embraced his people. Before long the tall silk hat jammed down low over the silver hair disappeared from view. Cheowa mounted his horse and headed back to report to Going Horse. They would wait, just as John Ross had said. But Cheowa knew that many of his friends would not—as he would not—wait forever.

With the defeat of Andrew Jackson at the polls, Ross thought there might be a better chance of dealing with the new President, Martin Van Buren, or his Secretary of War, Joel Poinsett. It took less than two weeks in Washington to discover how wrong he had been. Van Buren had listened politely to him, then announced, "I find myself duty bound to carry into effect the stipulations of the New Echota treaty, Mr. Ross. It has been ratified according to the forms prescribed by the Constitution . . ."

Cheowa rode thundering into the tobacco fields to find Going Horse, who had been working with the slaves as they chopped weeds. Seeing Cheowa, Going Horse looked up and grinned. "Decided to come back home for a while?"

Cheowa sighed. "It's a long ride." The two men walked to the shade, then sat down crosslegged to smoke a pipe. Passing it to Cheowa, Going Horse said, "We've received reports that The Ridge died right after he got to Oklahoma."

Cheowa shook his head. "No such luck. Besides he didn't get that far. He left the group at Fort Smith, just this side of the Oklahoma line, and was in damned good health when he walked down that gangplank. I found out he had already picked out a homesite. That bastard knew just where he was going, all right. Some Indians went farther up to Dwight Mission or Fort Gibson, but almost everybody on board marched right off with him.

"He's got a place up on Honey Creek, just inside the Oklahoma line from Missouri. Got there one day, and by the next day, had gangs of slaves and hired *Tsalagi* clearing fields for crops. They were putting up a house, too. No, Going Horse, The Ridge isn't dead by any means. And he's still sly as an old fox."

"What do you mean?"

"There's practically nobody else up in that part of the territory," Cheowa explained. "The Ridge can slip across the border to Missouri in fifteen minutes, ten if he hurries. You know what I think? I think the old buzzard knows he sold us out and made sure that now that we're in Oklahoma he's got a convenient back door."

Going Horse studied the bowl of the pipe, then knocked the ashes out on the heel of his hand. "Maybe. And if he's not in Indian Territory, then he'll have the protection of the laws of the United States. Tribal law won't be able to touch him."

Cheowa snorted. "Look," he directed, drawing a crude map in the red soil. "Here's Fort Smith and here's the border up to Missouri. Good road along the line. Here's Honey Creek. I made the ride from The Ridge's place to the border in eleven minutes, and there are several other routes as good. There's no way the cavalry can watch every trail that goes through those mountains, even if they could move as well among them as we do."

Going Horse studied the map in the dirt, then wiped it out with his foot. "Eleven minutes, huh? Like a picnic!"

"Like a picnic," Cheowa agreed. "We wait."

General Wool had had his fill of removal. As ordered, he had presented Ross with a letter from Poinsett stating that the time for voluntary removal was drawing to a close. "If the Cherokee do not remove according to the terms of the treaty, tell them they will then be forced from this country by the soldiers of the United States."

Wool did take action, but what he chose to do aroused the ire of Alabama and Georgia. While he diligently urged the Cherokee to enroll for removal, he also protected them against the robbery of their lands and houses. Wherever he found white settlers had illegally driven Indians off their lands, he ousted them and reinstalled the rightful owners. He compiled a long list of cases for the courts.

Another action of his was even more drastic: he arrested anyone who was found selling whiskey to the Indians.

"Damnit, General!" an Alabama legislator complained. "That's takin' away the means of livelihood from men who got families to support. Ain't nothing wrong with makin' an' sellin' whiskey."

"There is definitely something wrong when the sole purpose of it is to befuddle the Indians and make them accomplices in their own destruction!" When news of the ruckus reached Washington, Wool found himself dismissed from his post.

In Tennessee, Brigadier General Dunlap had been in charge of the Tennessee volunteers engaged in building stockades at strategic locations around the state. The work was far behind schedule; the half-hearted Tennessee mountain men had no desire to work for the expulsion of the Cherokee, whom they generally preferred to their white supplanters. Most of their time had been spent protecting the Indians from marauding bands of Georgians.

Late during the construction operation, Dunlap made a brief visit to John Ross at Red Clay and the two were seen shaking hands as Dunlap left Ross' cabin. The following day, Dunlap marched his men home, dismissed them and retired, leaving the stockades unfinished.

In September, John Ridge and his wife, his sister Sally and her white husband, Elias Boudinot and his new wife, a missionary named Delight Sargent, assembled to begin the journey by carriage to the western lands. Harriet had died a year earlier of what some said was overwork and worry. Elias had provided first a place for Delight to run her school and then a home for her with him. The group that left in the fall comprised the last of the Cherokee who had signed or approved of the treaty.

Not far from Dwight, at a place Worcester called Park Hill, Boudinot settled down and built a house. Like his father, John Ridge also constructed a house along Honey Creek and set out to become a prosperous merchant farmer, establishing a general store as well as clearing a hundred and fifty acres of land for crops. Despite the loss of fifteen persons during the overland journey, Boudinot and the Ridges felt they had entered the promised land.

Once again Ross was in Washington, this time to present to the American people, as well as to the politicians elected to represent them, a memorial that had been signed by thousands of Cherokee. It read in part:

> What have we done to merit such severe treatment? What is our crime? Have we invaded anyone's rights? Have we violated any article of our numerous treaties? Have we, in any manner, acted in bad faith? We are not even charged with any such thing. . . . Are we to be despoiled of all we hold dear on earth? Are we to be hunted through the mountains, like wild beasts, and our women, our children, our aged, our sick, to be dragged from their homes like culprits and packed on board loathsome boats, for transportation to a sickly clime? Already we are thronged with armed men; forts, camps, and military posts of every grade already occupy our whole country. With us, it is a season of alarm and apprehension. We acknowledge the power of the United States; we acknowledge our own feebleness. . . .

With trembling anxiety, we most humbly and respectfully ask, will you hear us? Will you sustain the hopes we have rested on the public faith, the honor, the justice, of your mighty empire?

In less than a month, the memorial's title page was stamped, "Laid on Table." To John Ross and Leonard Lake, there was no mistaking the repercussions that would follow.

Chapter 23

The spring of 1838 bloomed early, bringing its warmth to the hills; after the first of March there was little snow or cold. Buds burst and the trees were filled with blossoms. Birds sang accompaniment as Cherokee cleared brush and weeds from the corners of their fences and cleaned up hedgerows in preparation for the planting of the corn.

On the day before the full moon of Planting Month, soldiers watched as towns' entire populations assembled for the Purification Ceremony. The *anida-wehi* marked off the sacred circle around the ground to keep out evil spirits and enemies. In most places, the soldiers stood their distance, awed or amused, and allowed the ceremonies to proceed.

When the entire village had lined up up on the circle, seven young virgins, one representing each clan of the Cherokee people, filled the sacred vessel with water from the spring in the center of the circle. Into the water were placed leaves and herbs collected by the men; then hot rocks were added until the mixture boiled. When everyone had sipped the bitter beverage, they all stripped and bathed in the spring's pool.

Afterward, to the rhythmic beat of drums, they danced around the fire until sunrise, the gourds and turtle shell rattles that had been collected over generations adding their special sound. As they danced, the Indians sang and chanted prayers to Asgaya Galunlati. By daybreak the Purification Ceremony was over. The participants returned to their respective homes, now feeling worthy in the sight of the Great Spirit to plant their corn.

One detachment of troops near Spring Place waited until several families had returned to their homes and planted peas, beans, corn, squashes of numerous varieties.

"It's real sweet of them Indians to work so hard," one militiaman sneered to his companion, "especially since they're never going to taste their harvest."

"Let's go, men!" the troop leader shouted with a forward wave of his hand. "We've got some roundin' up to do. Those flatboats are too darn empty!"

The Rogers family consisted of James, his wife Grace, three children under ten years of age and Grace's mother, Helen Bearclaw, who was close to eighty years old. They straightened from their labors as the soldiers advanced.

"Time to move out." The sergeant's voice was firm but friendly.

"Please, we need time to pack our things," Grace protested.

"You've had years to pack," the sergeant replied.

James Rogers hesitated a moment, then felt the prick of a bayonet on his shoulder.

"Move!" ordered a trooper.

With the children crying at their mother's heels, the family returned to the cabin and began gathering clothing and cooking utensils. Helen Bearclaw took one of the down pillows she had made years before, slit open an end, and shook out the fluffy, ancient duck feathers into the bushes outside the cabin. The ticking was then crammed with as many more of their things as it would hold.

Eight soldiers held their rifles ready. Their bayonets glistened in the sun as the six members of the Rogers family began the eight-mile walk to the stockade. Less than a mile down the road, they met Betsy Laurel, who was staggering under a huge sack that contained what was left of her life with Tom.

Rogers dropped the bundle he was carrying and put an arm around old Annie, taking her huge sack with his other hand. She weakly smiled her thanks and the marchers started off again. The two older boys, seven and nine, struggled to pick up the sack their father had dropped but couldn't lift it.

The younger boy received a kick and a curse for his trouble. Grace cried out, "You've no right to treat a child that way! Are you some kind of beast?"

"Shut up, squaw-woman," the soldier snapped. "Yer boy was holdin' things up and should have gotten worse for doin' it!"

"You wretch," Grace screamed, lunging toward the man, but Rogers held her back. The boys hurried to join their parents and the bundle lay in the road as the procession moved toward the stockade.

This scene was repeated in many parts of the Nation as troops rounded up enough Cherokee to fill the waiting boats. But not all of the Cherokee were ready to submit peacefully.

One family had been taken by surprise and marched to the Indian agency on the Hiwassee. The man Tsali, his wife, his brother, his three sons and their families were moving at bayonet point when Tsali's wife paused long enough to open her blouse and offer her breast to her crying baby. One of the guards lashed out at her with his whip, then prodded her with his bayonet to keep her moving.

"We cannot tolerate this treatment!" the enraged Tsali said, managing a brief discussion in Cherokee with his brother and the other men. "It's worth the risk to give these militia bastards what they deserve, then try to hide in the hills."

Tsali's companions nodded their agreement. In the next few moments, years of fury were unleashed against the guards. One was killed, the others overcome.

The Cherokee grapevine carried messages as efficiently as a telegraph. Soon dozens, then hundreds of Cherokee were taking to the safety of their beloved mountains. There they joined Tsali and his ever-growing number of resisters, surviving on berries, nuts and roots, preferring even starvation to the treatment they knew they'd be receiving from the soldiers.

General Wool's successor, General Winfield Scott, shook his head. "If they don't come out of the hills," he swore to an aide, "we'll—God forbid—hunt them down. I don't want to do that; I want those Indians to be moved without bloodshed. But I will if I have to."

To support this wish, Scott ordered his men to show the Indians every possible kindness and said that each man under his command was responsible for seeing to it that no fellow soldier insult or unnecessarily injure any Cherokee man, woman or child.

"But," he declared, consumed by the difficulty of recapturing Tsali and his followers, "all Cherokee must be in the stockade, ready to be moved west, inside of three weeks."

Scott knew it would be difficult for him to follow through on this promise. He didn't have the troops to track down the Indians in an area that was totally unknown and totally hostile to white men. The terrain was difficult to maneuver in. But Cherokee behavior was so warlike that he had to do something to indicate a show of strength. There was no way he could let the murder of one of his men go unpunished. What Tsali did might set an example for hundreds—maybe thousands—to scatter and hide, and then the odious job of finding them might take years instead of days. In addition, if the Indians weren't cleared out of what they called their Nation by the end of the year, there was a very good chance that Georgia and Alabama would secede from the United States and settle matters even more drastically.

Scott turned to William Thomas, a white trader who had lived for twenty years among the Cherokee of North Carolina. If anyone had their confidence, it was this man.

"Well, that's my position, Mr. Thomas," Scott concluded after a lengthy talk. "Get the message to Tsali that if he and his family surrender themselves to military justice, the rest of those who've hidden out in the mountains can go free. Let Tsali know that if he doesn't surrender, we'll be forced to track down every one of them."

"I know Tsali, General," Thomas replied. "There's no reason to doubt he'll come down. It's a question of honor."

Tsali did surrender along with his brother and sons. They were marched to the stockade and all but the youngest boy, Wasidana, were shot by a firing squad without benefit of a hearing.

From that moment, William Thomas spent the rest of his life helping Cherokee who managed to escape the roundup. Eventually he gave them a large portion of his own land and fought for them in the courts. This faction of the Nation were the last who clung to their East Cherokee homeland and remained distinctive inhabitants there.

The roundup continued, although under General Scott's direction it was more like organized warfare than a peaceful roundup. Armed troops spread out from stockades all across the nation to seize men from ambush, from their work in the fields, from their homes while they were assembled at the dinner table or on their knees in prayer. Women were torn from their spinning wheels. Children were snatched from their play.

As the momentum of the roundup increased, people were not even given the opportunity to take their belongings from their homes but instead roughly shoved to the stockades. And close behind came the vagabonds who picked through what was left, looting anything of value and frequently burning what they could not carry off.

One soldier, Private John G. Burnett, was a member of a detail that burst into a cabin to arrest the family there. The white-haired former chief who was head of the family asked, "May we have a moment for prayer before we go?"

The astounded Burnett and several other members of the detail found themselves on their knees as the old man led the group in the Lord's Prayer in Cherokee before he rose to his feet and led his people from their home.

At another home, a family had been arrested outdoors.

As they were marched off, Burnett accompanied a corporal on a final search of the buildings, only to find a beautiful rocking horse inside the cabin.

"Look at this thing, Eddie. It's something!"

"Somebody must have spent a lot of time carving it. Damned horse almost looks real, doesn't it? Look at those eyes and the mane. Hell, you can almost feel the wind blowing it."

Burnett propped his rifle against the table.

"What do you think you're gonna do, Burnett, join the Indian horse troops?"

Burnett was sitting on the little wooden horse feeling the smoothness of the rockers. "I've seen a lot of stuff these people have left behind, Eddie, but this is just about the most beautiful piece of woodworking I've seen anywhere. I'm going to take it apart and ship it home as a souvenir."

"Well, don't take too long. We ain't got our quota for the day yet."

"Hell, it'll only take a minute to knock the pegs out and—" Burnett stood back and scratched his head. "Eddie, this thing hasn't got any pegs holding it together. Look at this! It's carved out of a solid hunk of hickory!"

"Well, I'll be damned," Eddie said on closer inspection. "Never before saw a rocking horse made from a solid piece of wood. Well, now what are you going to do with it?"

Sadly Burnett stood up and reached for his rifle. "No way I can crate it and ship it home, I guess. Just have to leave it."

He gave the horse a touch, imagining the love and work that must have been poured into its creation. The little rocking horse moved to and fro on the hard-packed floor.

Half a mile down the road, Burnett turned in time to see three men riding off with sacks of plunder. By the time they had disappeared, the cabin was in flames. Burnett shivered. The rocking horse probably was already gone, he thought, just as was the Cherokee Nation.

Later Burnett noted in his diary that incidents involving scavengers were not unusual. Bands often followed troops as they hunted down the Cherokee and frequently they began to pillage cattle and pigs even before the owners had been hauled off to the stockades.

Like many others, Burnett was revolted by these acts and knew they were directly inspired by the removal. Particularly repulsive to him was the robbing of graves.

Traditionally, a Cherokee male was buried with all of his personal belongings, since custom warned that no one could tell what he might need on his journey into the western sky. Before they were placed into the grave, his war club, knife, bow and arrows were passed through a fire for purification. All other personal belongings, silver and brass ornaments, coins, trinkets of all kinds, were placed around him for his use on the journey.

It was easy for grave robbers to know when they had discovered the grave of a warrior, for a warrior was placed in his grave in a sitting position, a robe over his shoulders and a buffalo skin under him as a seat of honor. If he died on the trail, his companions would bury him in the proper manner, then add a cairn of stones over the grave. Travelers, even those of enemy tribes, never disturbed an Indian's resting place, but instead added another stone to the cairn.

The time his squad led off an old woman from her hut back in the hills, Burnett was particularly disgusted. Marauders were already at work, sifting through the pathetically few things the woman had left in the cabin.

"Please!" she wailed. "Not that!" Two young men were digging up the grave of her husband and the woman had to be restrained from attacking them with her fists. Burnett raised his rifle and cocked it, drawing a bead on one of the robbers. "I'm counting to five as fast as I can," he warned. "If you aren't smoking your boots down the road, that Indian's going to have company in that grave. Do you understand me?"

The two ditched their shovels and fled. At Burnett's insistence, the squad allowed the old woman time enough to drop a stone into the hole. Then they prodded her on toward the stockade. Behind her, Burnett and Eddie each took a moment to drop a stone into the desecrated grave.

Five families had fled from Georgia into Tennessee, hoping to escape the roundup. Their goal was to reach the mission school at Brainerd. They had no way of knowing that the school was virtually deserted, that its staff and scholars had long since left. Camping in the woods near the school, they spent nearly a week with their dogs, cats, cattle and horses, plus the household goods they had been able to salvage in their flight.

Alerted by the fires at night, a company of soldiers descended on the families as they were preparing for breakfast. "We'll gather them up, Captain," one young soldier offered ambitiously.

But a driving rain fell, making the ground slick and unstable. During the effort to round them up, children screamed for their mothers, unable to see them easily in the storm. A soldier's horse slipped in the mud, then slithered helplessly toward two women struggling to escape the flailing hooves. A sick old woman needed a litter. Her moans for help sounded eerily through the backdrop of pounding rain.

Then, finally, the troops gathered everyone together and drove their prisoners ahead of them like cattle. Across rugged terrain and through the raging waters of the Chickamauga they traveled, hardly hesitating even when a child was swept away.

The roundup of Cherokees had begun on May 26, 1838. It was completed on June 20 of the same year. The federal troops had taken less than a month to herd the proud Nation into confinement. Sixteen thousand people had been forced into the squalid pens. General Scott had missed his target date by four days.

Although he later confessed to "distress caused to the emigrants by the want of their bedding, cooking utensils, clothes and ponies," and even "the loss of the property consequent upon the hurry of capture and removal," he blamed the Cherokee themselves for having put too much faith in John Ross' ability to save them. "And where is Ross now?" Scott remarked to Cullen. "Is he here with his people? No, he's in Washington on another useless begging expedition."

Cullen was in charge of assembling the fleet of boats that would carry the vast majority of the people west. While some would be taken by overland caravans, most would go by water. A year earlier, enough boats had been readily available, so the authorities thought they could contract for them as needed. Now, with sixteen thousand men, women and children to move, more boats would have to be procured. A boat builder in Memphis wasted no time in assembling the skeleton crew of workers that would begin the project.

Cullen entered the stockades one afternoon and studied the faces he saw. The stink of so many people crowded together was overpowering, and when he found the man he'd been looking for he was close to retching.

"Cheowa, I'd like to talk to you."

"Talk, Cullen. I've got ears."

Two men staggered past, their jugs of whiskey hanging from their necks by ropes.

"Come on outside. We can talk better there."

"What's the matter?" Cheowa prodded, smiling contemptuously. "Doesn't your tender *unaka* nose like the smell in here?"

"Frankly, no."

"Well, if you have anything to say to me, Cullen, you can say it right here. Maybe a few minutes seeing what you've done to my people will be good for you. Talk or get out!"

Cullen inhaled sharply. "Cheowa, we're badly in need of carpenters to finish boat construction. Are you interested in making some extra money?"

Cheowa hesitated before answering. "Not if it means building a gallows for my people."

"What if it means you can get your family out of the stockade and camp outside until the job is finished?"

"And then come back in to live like pigs?"

"No. Once the boats are finished, I'll see that you have a team and wagon, and you'll be able to go overland rather than by water."

"And you can have us shot for trying to escape. Cullen," Cheowa said, twisting his lips grotesquely, "you're no better than a weasel who steals eggs from a chicken."

Cullen spoke harshly as Cheowa whirled to walk away. "Cheowa! Turn around and take a good look at me." Cheowa turned slowly, his dark eyes boring into Cullen's. "I know you hate me, just as you hate every *unaka*. But as sure as God made me, you know I've never lied to you or to any of your people. I've done what I've had to do, but I've never done that. And what I'm telling you now is true."

For a brief instant, Cheowa's expression lightened. "What you say is true, Cullen. I won't say you're a courageous or particularly honorable man, but you're honest. You will provide a team and wagon for my family?"

"Yes, and that's in addition to the wages you earn building the boats."

"My mother and father, my sisters?"

Cullen stifled his surprise. "That isn't what Colonel Davidson had in mind," he said in a controlled voice. "You, your wife and your children were all the family he was thinking of."

"My sister's husband is a good carpenter, too, Cullen. In fact, Going Horse is almost as good a carpenter as I am."

Cullen's thoughts raced, considering how he could face Davidson and tell him that the best carpenter in the Nation wasn't going to cooperate unless he could ransom his entire family and all their relatives. My God, half of the Indians out there were related one way or another!

"How many other carpenters do you know who might consider working on the boats?"

"Well, there's one good carpenter." Cheowa spoke grimly. "His name is Harry Jones."

"Where can I find him, Cheowa?"

"You can go up the Arkansas River, Cullen," Cheowa said in one last burst of fury, "above Little Rock. Place called Cadron Creek. Harry Jones is buried there. He was one of the hundred and ten people who died of cholera after he agreed to go west. Go to Cadron Creek, Cullen, and be damned!"

As Cheowa slipped into the crowd and disappeared, Cullen was left facing the angry looks of those who had been listening to their conversation. He shrugged his shoulders and made his way through the ankle-deep mud to the gates, where he would make his report to Colonel Davidson.

News of Cullen's offer and Cheowa's refusal ran through the stockade in a matter of minutes. David Lake made his way from the lean-to where he was staying with his family and pulled Cheowa to one side.

"You're a fool not to do it," he commented.

"A fool, Father? You would actually have me build a stinking boat that will carry you away from the land where your father is buried?"

Lake scowled at his son. "It makes no difference if you build the boats or if the whites build them. Even if the boats were made by monkeys, it would make no difference. We are destined to take them from here to Oklahoma no matter who makes them. I have seldom asked anything of you in your life, Cheowa, but think about this. I did what I could to give you what I thought was best for you and all of my children. I never complained when you turned your back on us and went back to the old ways. I've even told you that I admire you for it. The old ways were never bad ways, and if that was what you wanted, so be it. But now I am asking one thing of you."

Cheowa waited for his father to continue.

"What I'm asking is that you build the boats—for your mother and your sisters, Cheowa. I would sooner trust their lives to a boat you build than to any boat built by those riffraff they've brought down from Memphis. For your family, Cheowa, do what Cullen asks."

Before the sun went down that evening, Cheowa and Going Horse led their wives and children through the gates. In a short time they had set up a shelter where they would live until the boats were ready.

Colonel Davidson had almost vetoed having that many of Cheowa's family released for the sake of two carpenters. "Cullen, you have no way of knowing if they're going to stay here until the job is done. They're more than likely to slip away during the night. Then all hell will break loose. Scott will have my neck."

"You don't have to worry, Colonel," Cullen assured him. "Cheowa might be a throwback to an earlier time, but he's an honest man."

"But how do you know that he and his family won't take off over a hill someplace once they're on their way west? Others have done it, haven't they? Every state these Indians have traveled through has had to round up a few who managed to escape from the caravans."

"You forget, Colonel. Those people didn't want to go to Arkansas or Oklahoma in the first place. Cheowa and Going Horse do want to go."

"I'm not sure I believe that, Cullen. If they wanted to set out there that much, why did they wait until they were gathered up and forced in here?"

"I'm sure they have their reasons. Just take my word for it, Colonel. Those two want to go west."

The keelboats were built much like others that traveled the inland rivers. Without any power of their own, they were designed to carry cargoes of freight or passengers and be towed behind steamboats. Each boat was a hundred and thirty feet long with a huge cabin and two decks. On the roof above the upper deck was a railing and stairs led to the lower areas.

Each level was divided into four rooms measuring about fifty by twenty feet and the outer walls were lined with windows. The common rooms contained a stove for heating and hearths were built on the upper deck for cooking. While the boats lacked many of the comforts that were taken for granted on most river-boats, Cheowa imagined they would be adequate for the job.

Going Horse paused to sharpen the blade of the jackplane, then grinned. "I didn't know I was this good a carpenter, Cheowa."

"I didn't know it, either. I've seen you working around my father's place, though, so I figured you'd be good enough. You're doing okay; what do those *unaka* know anyway? You know, these boats are a lot better than that flat scow that carried The Ridge when he went sailing off into the sunset."

It was the first time The Ridge had been mentioned by either man in months. They exchanged a knowing glance, then returned to their work.

The fleet of boats was capable of carrying a thousand people or more on the first leg of their journey; then they would return for more. Scott had organized things so that as people were rounded up in small communities, they would be moved in a group to the larger stockades on the river. Three principal concentration camps had been erected, and it was from these that the majority of Indians would start their journey. Scott was pleased that he had succeeded in one of his main objectives: Get the Cherokee out of Georgia before they could retaliate and cut the whites to ribbons.

Now the first of the boats were about to depart. Colonel Davidson swore under his breath. Crafty old Ross had managed to foul things up even though he wasn't on the scene. In order to facilitate the movement of the masses of people, Cullen had received orders from Washington that the Cherokee were to be accounted for not only by numbers, but by names as well. Without this census, the report stated, there would be no way of knowing exactly how many people would be entitled to receive payments once they reached western lands.

At first the project proceeded smoothly, but suddenly there wasn't a single person willing to give a name. Even worse, the Indians refused to tell how many were in their families. Davidson had no proof, but he was convinced that somehow Ross had been responsible for the confusion, even though he was still in Washington. Damn the old rascal!

Chapter 24

What had begun as an early, warm spring had stretched into a hot dry and oppressive June. Wells were drying up. Leaves were curling on the trees as though in an oven, and there was only an occasional breeze. Lieutenant Randolph Reese walked from his quarters down to the river just as the sky was beginning to lighten. His mind was troubled.

The keelboats were pressed nose to stern along the riverbank, ready to transport the hordes of Indians who were only a short distance away in the stockade. Standing offshore was a hundred-ton steamboat, keeping up a head of steam. The black smoke rose nearly two hundred feet in the air before catching a lethargic westerly current.

Studying the water, Reese noted that it was lower again. Every day, it seemed, the level dropped another inch, inch and a half. Scott had better get some of these people started on their way before the river dropped so far that water passage would be impossible. The only alternative then would be to march them all overland, and in this weather, with the heat and the drought, the drive would amount to murder.

Of all his assignments in the nine years he had spent in the army, the removal effort had been the most difficult and the most puzzling, too, Reese decided. Without realizing, he fingered the scar along his ribs where an Apache arrow had come close to ending his career. Then his thoughts revolved again. How much different these people were from the Indians of the plains and Southwest. And how proud. And how stupidly they had been treated by the United States Army. But then, the army had never encountered anything quite like the Cherokee.

Just as they had with other Indians, the soldiers had brought the Cherokee into camps like this and given them food and clothing, blankets mostly, but there was always a supply of pants and shirts on hand, and skirts for the women. But these Cherokee were so damned proud! They entered the gates, some of them naked, refusing any clothing. In fact, most of them even refused food. They had brought their own. They would far rather live on dried corn than on salt pork and flour.

And those two, over there, Reese noted, the carpenters who had been working on the fleet of boats. Both of them spoke English. The big one who never wore pants, Arthur Lake, probably spoke better English than half the enlisted men in the army. But the way he—

Reese tamped down the tobacco in his pipe. Arthur Lake and the wife of the other one were walking his way.

"Lieutenant," Cheowa said, "we are leaving. The work is finished."

Reese nodded and looked again at the six keelboats. "Fine job, too, Mr. Lake."

"I would like to get Jonathan and Mildred now," Catharine Going Horse said simply.

"Jonathan and Mildred, ma'am?" Reese repeated. The tall woman before him was beautiful. If it weren't for the moccasins and buckskin dress she wore, she would have passed for white.

"My sister's slaves," Cheowa growled as if anticipating a problem.

"Well, I don't have any authority to—"

Before he could finish, Cheowa dashed off to Cullen's office as Catharine went back to the wagon. Going Horse was giving it a last-minute check.

"Cullen," Cheowa shouted through the door, "are you a man of your word or aren't you?!"

The door opened, and Cullen stood there, naked to the waist, his feet bare, and his dirty underwear sagging under his hairy potbelly.

"Now what's wrong, Cheowa?" he asked impatiently.

"We're ready to go, and we want Jonathan and Mildred."

"Who are Jonathan and Mildred?" Cullen asked, as mystified as Reese had been.

"My sister's slaves, Cullen."

"Now, we've been over this before, Cheowa," Cullen sighed wearily. "I was able to talk Davidson into letting you take Going Horse and your sister, but I can't let your whole family go."

"Your promise, Cullen, your promise, remember? For work on the boats we were to have a team and wagon. You've been generous enough to give us a team and wagon that you paid my father sixteen dollars for. But we were also to be allowed to take with us our personal property."

"That's right." Cullen could feel defeat gnawing at his guts.

"Jonathan and Mildred are my sister's personal property, Cullen. She wants them."

"Now, look Cheowa—"

The contempt in Cheowa's eyes stopped Cullen in

mid-sentence. In all the years he'd lived and worked among the Cherokee, there were only a handful of Indians who could intimidate him.

"My sister's personal property, Cullen!"

"I . . ." Cullen hitched up his long johns. "Nothing's going to happen to them, Cheowa. We're giving them food and clothing, and there are doctors to take care of them—"

"Which we paid for, Cullen! What you call the 'charitable acts' of your government have been paid for with our homes, our farms, our crops, our blood! Now you would take my sister's slaves, too? Your word, Cullen!"

Cullen swore under his breath, knowing that he'd have to do some fast talking to explain the situation to Davidson when he returned from General Scott's headquarters. But it would be worth the trouble to have Cheowa out of his hair for good.

Reese's breakfast of hominy, scrambled eggs and salt pork wasn't settling well. He and his men had been trying to take a census for nearly two hours now, but there still wasn't an accurate count of how many people had boarded the boats. None of them would give a name, and when they were told to slow down and be counted, they surged forward in a mob.

"How many do you make it, Lieutenant?" Colonel Davidson asked Reese.

"Probably about eight hundred, sir."

"That'll still leave close to two thousand. I'd like to get them off in three groups if we can."

"I don't think the boats will take that many," Reese said carefully, hesitant to offer an opinion.

"Two hundred people per boat, plus one boat to carry their belongings. More than sufficient."

Boarding the Indians was only the first of the

chores involved in the initial leg of the journey. The boarding had been accomplished easily enough, but two of the loaded boats settled so low in the water that they had grounded, and it was necessary to winch them off the bank and into the stream.

The keelboats were lashed alongside the steamer, three on each side, and by noon the flotilla was under way. Reese rode in the pilot house of the steamboat. On the decks, as special passengers, were some of the lesser chiefs and their families.

"This all the headway you'll be making, Captain?" Reese asked.

"Wait till we git t' them rapids, Lieutenant. Five miles an hour's gonna be plenty, b'lieve me."

The skipper was right. The Tennessee River presented to its travelers a series of dangerous rapids known as the Suck, the Skillet, the Frying Pan and the Boiling Pot. As the river passed through a narrow gorge in the mountains, Reese noticed that the Cherokee on the roofs of the outer barges were being pitched violently from side to side, and many were hanging precariously from the railings.

To correct the problem, the steamboat was moved toward the north bank, where two of the barges were unlashed from each side. After they were made fast to the bank, the steamer moved through the dangerous waters with only two keelboats, then returned for another two.

On the second pass, a swift change in the current pitched the steamboat at the bank, crushing one keelboat against the rocks and splitting it open. Screaming frantically, the Cherokee passengers were tossed into the swift, muddy current. By the time the skipper regained control of the steamboat, bodies, blankets and debris were being swirled downstream.

Five corpses were found later in the day and by nightfall two more had been washed up on the banks farther downriver. Reese was helpless to estimate how many passengers had been lost, and the sullen survivors were little help.

The party camped overnight on the banks of the river and Reese estimated that some fifteen or twenty escaped in the hours before dawn. By the time the group reached Decatur, where the next leg of the journey, this one by train, was supposed to begin, the numbers had visibly dwindled.

At Decatur, there were thirty-two cars behind double locomotives waiting for the Cherokee, but they were able to carry only half the group. Reese dismissed the guards, making room for as many extra Indians as possible.

During the trip through the last of the rapids, one old man had been lost overboard and one baby born. While at Decatur, there was another birth and a man died while attempting to rescue his hat from under a moving train.

Later, the train carried the Cherokee to Tuscambia, where the river journey would be resumed. But by the time the return trip had been completed, Reese estimated, another hundred of his charges had been lost in one manner or another. Three died of dysentery and most of the rest were lost to intoxication or overland escape.

When the entire party had been reassembled and loaded onto two double-decked keelboats for the trip down to the Ohio, Reese was finally able to get an accurate count. Of the approximately eight hundred Cherokee who had begun the trip at Ross' Landing, there were fewer than five hundred left.

Reese conducted the remaining Indians the rest of

the way down the Ohio and Mississippi and up the Arkansas without another death. A total of nine more escaped before the group reached Indian Territory, but he learned later than only a few ever made it as far as Fort Gibson.

Once inside Western Cherokee Territory, the passengers, hailed by former neighbors and friends, promptly began tossing their baggage overboard. Reese ordered the steamer halted and let the Cherokee go. As he wrote, "I issued a sufficient quantity of domestic cotton to the Indians for tents to protect them from the weather. I have done so in consideration of their destitute condition, as they were for the most part separated from their homes in Georgia without having the means or time to prepare for camping. It was also the opinion of the group physician that the health of these people would suffer if they were not provided with some protection."

Other groups followed Reese's. Some fared better, although most endured similar hardships. Because of the Arkansas River's extremely low water and treacherous, shifting sand bars, most were forced to make the journey overland through Arkansas and Oklahoma. In the meantime, news of the hardships ahead spread swiftly through the camps of the Cherokee who waited to go west.

Assistant Chief George Lowrey fumed. He had attempted to have Scott delay his departure until the autumn rains arrived to provide a more appropriate climate for travel, but Scott had adamantly ignored Lowrey's requests and loaded the flatboats to more than capacity each time they returned. The steamboats docked only long enough to take on wood and provisions for the crew and relieve Scott of another eight or nine hundred Indians.

"You know what I'd like, Cullen?" Scott asked.

"What's that, General?"

"I'd like to have every one of these people moving west by the time that damned Ross comes back from Washington."

But again, Scott was destined to miss his objective.

John Ross returned home on July 13 and was sickened by what he found. The once-proud Cherokee Nation had been reduced to a pile of rubble. Empty cabins had been looted and neglected, often burned to ashes. Some, in fact, were still smoking as scavengers sifted through the meager debris. Crops lay untended in the fields. Looters foraged through garden plots in hopes of finding a few ripe vegetables that had not been eaten by the pigs that ranged across the countryside.

What had once been thriving little towns were now deserted shells whose streets were cluttered with leaves and trash. Many of the larger homes still stood, tragic memorials to what had once been a proud nation.

Ross could not go to New Echota, of course. There he was subject to immediate arrest, as he was anywhere in Georgia. Had he been able to see the town, he would have wept; the former capital had been turned into an army post. The council house had become a barracks, and the courthouse, temporarily leased from its new owner, served as administrative offices for the post commander and the small army of clerks that had been hired to assist in the removal. The commons was now the site of a stockade where people waited for transfer to similar confinement at Ross' Landing. What he had seen, coupled with the reports he had received of the fate of the first of his people to be shipped west, made Ross' blood boil.

"General," he complained to Scott, "the conditions in the stockades are not only humiliating, they are endangering the health of my people!"

"You should have thought of that long ago, Ross. If you had agreed to work for the fulfillment of the conditions of the treaty, you and your people would have been safely out west five or six years ago and settled into potentially prosperous lives. What you are facing now is the result of your own delaying tactics. If you were honest with yourself, you would admit that."

"The treaty was never signed by anyone of importance," Ross scornfully replied. "It is therefore invalid, General. Besides, I cannot argue against what is already an accomplished act. What I can do is appeal to you to allow us to handle the arrangements of our own departure."

He handed Scott a resolution that had been signed by the major chiefs of the Nation and represented the authority of them all. Scott read it. "Let me make sure I understand you," he said. "What you want is to hold a council and work out your own arrangements, is that it?"

Ross nodded.

"I can't permit any council to be held."

Ross indicated the resolution. "We have held one, if you notice," he pointed out.

"Ross," Scott said, ignoring the gibe, "we've been very lenient. We have allowed all of your district chiefs to remain in their homes until it was time for them to remove. The gesture was a courtesy, not a right."

"I'm not surprised, General," Ross said, his blue eyes flashing. "I have always thought you believed my people were not entitled to any rights at all."

"Ross, that's not fair. Besides, you will have all the rights you want once you get out west."

"*If* we get to the West. And that question is what I wish to discuss with you. It is also the reason for the council I have called at Rattlesnake Springs in two weeks. I am prepared to surrender to the inevitable, General. And for the sake of my people, I am prepared to advise them that they should move—but only under certain conditions."

Scott waited.

"The major condition is that there shall be no more emigration during the hot summer months. When the weather cools in the fall, we will move under the direction of our own leaders."

"Do you speak for all your people, Ross? Will they listen to you?"

"Among our people, General, nobody commands. We advise. Whatever agreements, treaties, or anything else we do in the Cherokee name must have the consent of the people."

"Then you admit that the people might not agree to your proposal?" Scott looked skeptical. "I can't take the chance, Ross. I can't permit you to hold the meeting."

"It will be held nevertheless," Ross countered firmly. "And," he said rising, "I invite you to attend so you may witness for yourself our intentions of conducting a peaceful removal."

The Rattlesnake Springs Council was the last to be held in the Cherokee Nation East. Many chiefs spoke to give their support to Ross. Afterward, Ross made an impassioned statement describing his love for the land of his ancestors. "But it is time to move on," he urged. "It is time to turn our hearts toward the land west of the Mississippi and build for the future there."

Ross' closing appeal touched Scott almost as deeply as it affected the chiefs assembled around him. "Let us go west as a great nation," Ross concluded, "under our own leaders, traveling with the dignity that befits us as a great people."

Scott granted the request to delay further emigration until cooler weather had arrived. "But October 20 is the final date, Chief. By that date all of your people must be on their way west."

"It shall be done," Ross agreed. "Our chiefs will determine those routes most compatible with maintaining speed and health. We would be grateful if you'd be kind enough to provide us with up-to-date maps of the terrain."

Scott promised to provide Ross with as many maps as he would need. "But remember," he added convincingly, "if you can't handle the removal satisfactorily, I'll be forced to use every method at my disposal to complete it myself."

Ross gave him a steel-hard look. "And be as ruthless as you were with Tsali? Thank you, General, but we Cherokee are a strange people. We would rather die at our own hands than at yours."

As Scott rode back to his headquarters, he thought once again what a paradox this man Ross was. More Scot than Indian, Ross could have done as most mixed-breeds had for years: adopted the ways of the white man. To his credit were wealth, power, influence, yet he had chosen to cast his lot with a people who were destined to lose everything they had. Stranger still was the blind faith his people invested in him. Those who had signed for removal early and then learned that Ross had been opposed to it were not only reluctant but frequently quite stubborn in their refusal to leave when it was actually time to go. Now, after Ross had created this suffering for them, they again were ready to follow his will. Yes, Ross was a strange man, and the people that bent consistently to his beliefs were stranger still.

Chapter 25

John Ross and George Lowrey remained adamant as they listened to the excuses offered by the army physician. "I'm sorry," he commiserated unconvincingly. "There isn't much else I can do for your people. They're just not responding well to treatment."

Lowrey looked him straight in the eye. "Much more of your care and there won't be any left to treat."

"Perhaps once you get on the way—"

"Doctor, these people have been crammed together for months," Ross retorted. "They haven't had the food they need, they—"

"Hold on, Chief, they're getting the same food our men get, and our men are doing fine."

"Maybe your men thrive on this stuff, Doctor, but if our people can't eat what's available, the result is no better than starvation. We aren't used to salt pork and flour. We eat fish, lean meat, vegetables, corn."

"What about those conjurers of yours?" the doctor complained. "Do you think they're doing your people any good?"

"Your treatments aren't any better. Many Indians have died. Besides, my people trust the *anidawehi*."

For the first time, the doctor's face relaxed enough to express genuine caring. "chief, I don't like to see your people suffer any more than you do. But I'm really stumped for answers."

"Do the same thing we do, Doctor. Pray. Then just carry on the best you can."

"I'm particularly concerned about one of the white missionaries," the doctor confessed.

"Why should you bother more about her than anyone else?" Ross asked.

"She's close to dying."

"And a dead white woman," Lowrey answered, his voice tired and filled with frustration, "is of more concern to you than a dead Cherokee woman?"

The doctor threw up his hands in a gesture of helplessness. "Gentlemen, I give up," he groaned. "No matter what I do I can't please you." Ross and Lowrey watched as he moved to another lean-to and other patients. Then they listened as the *anidawehi* chanted over one rapidly failing form after another.

Later, in a nearby section of the stockade, they conferred with David Lake and several men who would be assigned as drivers.

"How did the meeting with Scott go this time, Chief?" Lake asked.

"I was officially named 'Superintendent of Cherokee Removal and Subsistence'—that's some joke, isn't it, after all that's happened? There are a few details to be worked out, but most of them are what I asked for. We'll have our own conductors and travel in thirteen groups of roughly a thousand people each. If the army sends any officers and men along, they'll act strictly as observers, nothing more than that. We will have our own light-horse cavalry again to police the people and give protection to each of the groups. One of the details still to be arranged is the price we'll pay to buy back some of our cattle to take along with us. David, I'll leave assignment of the drivers in your hands."

"What about other provisions?"

"For the most part, we'll purchase what we need along the way."

Lowrey's broad face broke into a grin. "I would have given anything to have an artist paint a picture of Scott's face when we told him the estimated total cost of the removal would come to sixty dollars a head."

Ross chuckled as he remembered the meeting. "I showed Scott the list of items we needed and had costs broken down to sixteen cents per day per person. Without even blinking, Scott advised me that the War Department considered such things as coffee and sugar luxuries. And he had nerve enough to get upset about the cost for soap. He couldn't believe we consider soap to be an absolute necessity. He probably thinks Indians never wash."

"He should get a whiff of his own men," Lake laughed. "Most of them never bathe between rainstorms, I'd bet on that! Anyway," he changed the subject, "Where's Leonard?"

Lowrey grinned again. "Locked up with the accountants, I'd imagine. They're going over every item on the lists everyone has presented for indemnities. According to the terms of the treaty, each Cherokee is to be paid a fair value for what he lost prior to the time of removal.

"The money men can understand the value of property belonging to people like the Lowreys, Rosses, Lakes and Foremans. Silver, crystal, libraries, pedigreed horses, dogs and cattle have obvious material value. But they can't seem to understand that someone like Willy Night Hawk's wife places just as much value on five ducks, a green cloak, three spoons (one large for cooking), a set of china with two cups missing handles . . ." Lowrey paused and closed his eyes as if trying to visualize the list. ". . . one blowgun, a fiddle with three strings, an umbrella, a coffee pot, one shovel, two hoes and a plow. Night Hawk's wife also said that it was only fair to deduct the dollar thirty-three cents she owes the white man at the store and pay it to him."

David Lake enjoyed another hearty laugh. "If anybody can get those claims paid, it'll be Leonard."

"*O-si-yo!*" Ross greeted Aggie, who had just walked up. "How are the children doing?"

"Not badly. Fierce Bear is just about over the measles. He's been terribly weak, but I think he'll be all right."

"Is there something troubling you, Aggie? You look upset."

"Yes, Chief Ross. One of the girls who's been helping me with the orphans was raped last night by two soldiers."

Lowrey stormed to his feet. "Does she know who they are?"

"Yes, but she's afraid to tell. They got her outside by saying they needed some help with a child who'd wandered up to the gates. Then they dragged her into the bushes and threatened that if she didn't do what they wanted, they would have her parents hanged. Now the girl's afraid that if Colonel Davidson hears about what happened, her parents will suffer."

Ross got up too. "Colonel Davidson will hear about it," he assured her, "but not until we've taken the matter directly to General Scott. Let's go, George."

The two highest-ranking men in the Nation hastened to present the girl's complaint to Scott, but David Lake was not optimistic about the results. "Scott probably won't do anything about it. Too many girls have been all too willing to sneak off at night to exchange their favors for some extra rations or even a little whiskey."

Aggie sat down on the bench next to him and leaned her head on his shoulder. "But this was different, Father. Angela is just twelve, and she wasn't willing. And don't remind me that most girls get married when they're twelve or thirteen."

"Did I say anything? You're the one who always keeps bringing it up." Lake put his arm around his daughter and gave her a tender squeeze. "It isn't good for a man to be without a wife or a woman to be without a husband." Tears welled in his eyes as he said the words. His own wife of thirty years had sickened and died soon after they were forced into the stockade.

"Well," he said clearing his throat, "here we are, two pretty sad-looking characters!" So deep in thoughts of John was she that Aggie didn't match her father's attempt at cheerfulness with her own.

"You love him very much, don't you, Aggie?"

"I didn't know if you knew, Father."

"There is little a man doesn't know about his own children, my child. Your Tsani Parker would have been a good man for you. I didn't know him well but I could tell that."

"That was long ago, Father," Agatha murmured.

"But the pain is like yesterday, isn't that true? It is cruel of me to say it now, perhaps, but I believe you would have done well to go with him."

"You are wrong, Father. I miss John, but it is as well I didn't go. I shall never leave my people. Never!" Tears spilled over and Agatha allowed her father to wipe them away as he had done many years before. "Thank you for understanding," she whispered.

"What else is a father for?"

"I've decided definitely," Parker informed Little Tree while they were distributing pamphlets one evening. "I'm not going back to Little Rock except maybe to collect the rest of my things and bring them here. I love it here. What more could a man want? Here I've got close friends, work I enjoy—even more because I am doing it with people I care about. I have plenty of wagers to make, too, if I please—" Parker winked at Little Tree.

"Then I guess you do have everything you want," Little Tree agreed, "everything, that is, but Aggie.

"I know," he went on, waving Parker's protest off, "it's a cruel thing to say. But you love the woman, so why," he asked, "why in the hell don't you write and tell her to get out here?"

"Damn it, Little Tree, how does Martha put up with you? You think you know everything!" Parker shouted, half-kidding. "I can't make Aggie do anything she doesn't want to do. That would be obvious to anyone with eyes. She loves me, though, at least I've got that."

Little Tree slowly shook his head, then turned to other work. "That may be so," he acknowledged as he walked away, "but long-distance love sure doesn't keep your body warm on cold winter nights."

Before bed, Parker wrote Aggie more about his new life. "I'm lonesome for you," he signed off. "All the causes and work in the world could never make up for what we're missing being apart."

Chapter 26

After long weeks of dry stream beds, the late September rain came rushing down. As the date appointed for removal neared, long lines of Cherokee stretched toward Rattlesnake Springs, the place from which they would start their overland journey. Thousands had camped over a ten-square-mile area, and for the first time in months, happy voices could be heard resounding through the valleys.

One group of about seven hundred kept to themselves, and seemed virtually ignored by the others. These were the members of the Treaty Party who had not yet emigrated; they'd refused to have anything to do with the supervision of John Ross. Because these few hundred had been supporters of the federal government from the beginning, they had received special consideration while in the stockades; and now they asked for and received increased allowances for their travel. Most of their baggage had been shipped in advance by riverboat. They traveled in grand style, and leaving a week ahead of the next party, they requested that Lieutenant Reese be their guide.

During the first stage of their journey, they were a haughty bunch, most riding in carriages, followed by dozens of slaves. But even these favored travelers were unable to escape the obstacles that lay ahead. In many places the roads had been washed out by the recent heavy rains and they had to make frequent halts to clear fallen timber and other obstructions. Reese considered himself lucky if they did more than ten miles a day.

At dawn on the morning of October first, the drivers began assembling a string of horses and wagons that stretched a quarter of a mile along the road. Assistant Chief George Lowrey rode up and down the line, checking every detail, making certain that this first group of non-Treaty Party travelers would set an example to all the others who would follow. When Lowrey was satisfied with what he saw, he moved to the head of the column and waited. A short distance behind him, old Chief Going Snake was astride one of his favorite ponies.

All along the line of wagons, solemn-faced people said farewell to those who would soon follow. Much time was spent reassuring the travelers about the trip ahead. Children laughed and played while their parents talked; now and again one fell out of a wagon while tossing or catching a favorite toy.

The light-horse guards, formerly the Nation's police force, gravely listened to the orders of their superiors, then took up their posts along the flanks of the column. As John Ross climbed up on a wagon, the voices hushed for a moment, then swelled again as their leader led them in the Lord's Prayer. Just as the prayer concluded, an ominous peal of thunder rolled through the valley, and then a bugle sounded to start the caravan.

Chief Ross' nephew, William Shorey Coodey, wrote, "At noon all was in readiness for moving, the teams were stretched out in a line along the road through a heavy forest, groups of persons formed about each wagon, others shaking the hand of some sick friend or relative who would be left behind. The temporary camp, built of huts covered with boards or bark, that for three summer months had been their only shelter and home, was crackling and falling under a blazing flame; the day was bright and beautiful, but a gloomy thoughtfulness was depicted in the lineaments of every face. In all the bustle of preparation there was a silence and stillness of the voice that betrayed the sadness of heart."

The twelve mounted light-horse guards kept the column moving and in order as the people marched forward. Only the aged, the sick and the crippled rode in the wagons; most were on foot, including mothers with babies in their arms and heavy bundles on their backs. The wagons were reserved for animal fodder, also for the pots, pans, blankets and cooking utensils that the column would need along the way.

The groups were scheduled to begin several days apart. Each contingent had its own conductor, in most cases a respected chief who had willingly accepted the responsibility. There was also a physician attached to each group, as well as a contractor to take care of provisions. All of these officials had been either appointed or approved by John Ross well in advance of the departure.

It was estimated that eighty days would be necessary for the trip and that the staggering of groups would provide for the natural fluctuations in the progress they made. As some moved forward, they would catch up with the ones from the previous group who fell behind, and they were close enough to keep in contact with each other by messenger.

Elijah Hicks was the conductor for the second group. He sent the first report back from Nashville and his message was anything but encouraging. "The company is suffering sorely from lack of clothing. I fear that scores of my people will perish of disease and cold before we reach our destination. When we reached Nashville, already forty or fifty were ill. We buried five on this side of the city."

Hicks reported that on the twenty-third of October they had caught up with the slower-moving party of George Lowrey. "The people," Hicks wrote, "are loath to continue and unusually slow in preparing for each morning's start. I am not surprised at this. They are moving to an unknown region where they do not desire to be."

Venerable Chief White Path had been ill prior to leaving but remained too proud to ride in a wagon. He died on the trail while leading a detachment of Indians near Hopkinsville, Kentucky. The group stopped to bury him. A box was placed over the grave and around it were set poles with streamers so that others following could recognize the spot and remember him. As it turned out, White Path's burial place became a shrine where it was customary for passing Cherokee to pause, to add another stone to his cairn and to pray for a man who exemplified to them everything a respected Cherokee should be.

Behind the Elijah Hicks detachment followed the one led by Jesse Bushyhead, who for many years had been a missionary among his own people. Behind Bushyhead came Evan Jones, a Baptist minister. Both conductors found their Christian fortitude taxed to extremes.

"There are large numbers of sick and injured," Bushyhead wrote to Ross. "So many have to be transported in the wagons that there is no room for fodder for the horses and oxen. We were delayed for two days when the animals got sick from eating poisonous weeds along the road."

Aggie and the children marched along with the missionaries, her younger brother Jimmy helping keep Fierce Bear in line. David Lake spent most of his days walking with Jones, whose preaching style he had so much admired over the years. As the group neared Nashville, they buried the first of the old people who had died, as much of the bumpy wagons as of their advanced years.

Standing by a fresh grave, Aggie asked, "How many more do you think we'll bury before this is over, Father?"

"Too many," he mourned.

Jones had just finished reciting a brief prayer of committal when the burial crew was interrupted by one of the light-horse guards racing back from the head of the column.

"We've got trouble," he panted anxiously.

"What do you mean?"

"Farmer says we're trespassing, won't let us pass till we pay a toll."

At the head of the column, Jones and Lake found four armed men blocking the road with a wagon.

"Yep, this here's my land, mister. You ain't takin' them Indians nowheres till you pays the toll."

"Your demand is outrageous, sir," Lake snapped. "We've had no reports from those ahead of us about any toll roads in this area."

A wide toothless grin was the answer. "Reckon it ain't our fault you didn't hear," the man wearing it went on. "Now you either pays the toll, or you kin turn all them Indians around an' skedaddle right back where you come from. Y'hear me?"

After a brief conference, Lake, two of the chiefs and Jones concluded that there was nothing they could do but pay. The other choice was to be faced with the charges of trespassing—or be shot at—not to mention what actions the light-horse guards might be held responsible for.

"How much?" Jones demanded.

"Fifteen cents a horse an' forty cents a wagon. We ain't gonna charge nothin' for the people, mister. That'd be sinful, wouldn't it, Rufe?"

One of his companions nodded with exaggerated solemnity. "Wouldn't hardly be Christianlike, thet's what I hold."

Jones and Lake paid the sum of forty dollars, and by the time they reached the next "toll collector" two days later, a new feature had been added. Each of the collectors was now wearing a shiny brass badge with the words Official Toll Collector deeply embossed on it. It was evident that the men were all working with each other; the badges looked freshly made and the rates seldom varied by more than a penny or two.

By the time the third party traveled through Nashville, the road had been so badly rutted by the hundreds of wagons that had passed through before that they bounced, thudded, pitched and tilted, unmercifully tossing the ailing passengers about. They had to stop more frequently to allow the doctors to care for their patients or to bury those who had failed to survive the punishment of the journey.

And then came the heavy rains. The roads melted into thick, red gumbo. One day, Jones reported that they had traveled a total distance of only two and a half miles. It was easy to measure; the rear of the column at nightfall lay at the same clump of trees that had marked its head at daylight.

Often crowds lined the roads to watch the travelers pass. As they trudged along one afternoon, an observer sitting at the side of the road suddenly jumped to his feet.

"David," he called. "Ain't you David Lake?"

Lake stopped. The two men studied each other for a moment and then warmly embraced.

"Aggie, come meet someone!" Lake called out to her.

"David, you old scoundrel," the man said with a knowing wink as Aggie approached. "What a pretty young wife you got yourself!"

"My eldest daughter, Tom, so put your eyes back in your head. Aggie, this is Tom Andrews. He was with me at Horseshoe Bend."

Aggie nodded a greeting. Afterward there was an awkward silence for a moment, then Andress said, "David, I'm sorry it's come out this way."

"Tom, I can't blame you. We fought together and respected each other once. Even though your country has turned its back on me now, I don't hold you personally responsible. I guess if I blame anyone, it's that old man over there."

Andrews turned his head and looked back toward the Hermitage. "Yep, can't blame you for hating Jackson's guts, David. Did you know he was about to cash in? He don't hear none too good, he can't see out of one eye, and some days he don't even remember the names of the slaves who bathe and dress him. He's in mighty bad shape, Old Hickory is."

David Lake sighed deeply. Two wagons were passing, the loud wailing and moaning from its occupants drowning every nearby sound. "And so are my people, Tom. Well, take care of yourself, you old buzzard! We all have to do the best we can with what we have."

*   *   *

The trail extended across Tennessee and Kentucky, then westward through the southern tip of Illinois. Some of the conductors took their people straight west across the Mississippi to Springfield, Missouri, while others cut south through Arkansas. As the days grew colder with the onset of winter, the trail became increasingly easier to follow. As the road surface froze and thawed, froze and thawed, hoofs and horseshoes, boots and moccasins, even bare feet gradually trampled flat the deep ruts and high ridges in the sucking, clinging, but now hardening mud. But even so, there would be no mistaking the line of graves strung out behind the ribbon of mournful Indians that wove its way toward Fort Gibson.

In December, President Van Buren reported to Congress, "It gives me great pleasure to be able to apprise you of the entire removal of the Cherokee Nation of Indians to their new homes west of the Mississippi. The measures authorized by the Congress have had the happiest effects, and they have emigrated without any apparent reluctance."

He then read War Secretary Poinsett's report, proudly declaring, "The generous and enlightened policy toward the Indians was ably and judiciously carried into effect with promptness and praiseworthy humanity. They have been treated with kind and grateful feelings, not only without violence, but with very proper regard for the interests of the people."

While was making his address, Evan Jones and David Lake were chipping into the frozen dirt of Illinois, where in one day they buried twenty-two members of their party. Sixteen had fallen to pneumonia, the rest frozen to death while sleeping on the ground without the blankets that were waiting for them hundreds of miles away at Fort Gibson. One old man was found that morning sitting under one of the wagons, his pipe still clenched between frozen toothless jaws. Immediately, attempts were made properly to bury the old man, who had been an admired warrior. But because the rock-solid earth resisted every effort to dig deeply, he had to be placed in a shallow grave on his side, still in a sitting position, still with his cherished pipe, facing the rising sun.

Late one afternoon as they passed through Illinois, a buggy bounced across the fields from a farmhouse a mile away. One of the light-horse guards rode to meet it, then escorted the driver back to Jones and Lake.

"My name's Williams, George Williams," the man said, his breath visible in the chilly air. "Don't know how you'd feel about it, but you folks are welcome to put them kids and oldsters in my barns tonight."

"That's mighty decent of you, Mr. Williams," Jones replied. "I'm afraid we can't pay you, though."

"Pay? Brother, them people've already paid enough. Near as I can count, I got 'bout thirty of 'em buried on my land. Least I can do is let a few more sleep awhile. I don't never want it said that Deacon George Williams turned a stranger away from his door in the middle of winter."

Two hours later Aggie and her father herded the last of the younger children into the barn. Most of the sicker members of the party had been bedded down in vacant stalls and the hayloft. Williams and his wife brought huge pots of steaming coffee from the house, and for the first time in weeks, Aggie felt warm clear through.

It didn't take the children long to start a game of beans. Williams watched as they flipped six bean halves into a flat basket. Each team had five players, and their squeals of enthusiasm filled the barn.

"What in tarnation are them kids playin'?" Williams asked.

"*Tagu*—beans," Aggie explained. "Depending on how the beans land in the basket, with flat or round sides up, they score points. The first team to score twenty-four points wins."

Fierce Bear, the oldest of the children in the group, was only half-heartedly following the game. Williams invited, "Sonny, you want to see something?"

"He doesn't speak English, Mr. Williams," Aggie apologized. She told the children that their host had a surprise for them.

Williams pulled his fur hat down over his ears and a few minutes later returned from the house with a shivering fox terrier. After the dog had received some eager petting and cuddling from the smaller children, Williams snapped his fingers. The dog at once stood on his hind legs and walked in a circle, pleased to have such a large, appreciative audience. He had also been trained to walk on his front legs and flip himself. In addition, when Williams fished a harmonica from his pocket and began playing a hymn, the dog sat and howled right along with him.

It was well after midnight before any of the children settled down for sleep. "This has been quite a diversion for the youngsters, Mr. Williams," Aggie said gratefully. "These children haven't had this much fun since they left their homes. I don't know how I can thank you."

"Don't think about it, Miss Lake. Me an' my wife just love havin' kids around the place."

"Don't you have children of your own?"

"We did." Williams paused, trying to keep control of his emotions. "Four of 'em. Typhoid fever took three from us one year, and the fourth died the year after that."

"I'm sorry to hear that," Aggie comforted. "The last one from the fever, too?"

"No, ma'am. We had us a homestead out in the Dakotas. Blackfoot raiding party burned us out. The boy died in the raid."

"I don't quite know what to say," Aggie began. "But I think it's wonderful that after your loss you can open your door to any Indian."

Williams shrugged. "For a long time I carried a lot of hatred around inside of me, Miss Lake. It was just like carrying a millstone on my shoulders. Wasn't until I got me baptized an' changed my ways of thinkin' that I started livin' again."

Suddenly, as if deliberately changing the subject, he said, "Oh, I got something else for you people."

He returned from the house with two huge baskets filled with eggs. "Reckon it ain't gonna hurt us none to give some of these up. Those fool chickens don't seem to know it's winter. They've been layin' like crazy. We boiled 'em so they'd travel."

When Jones and David Lake began assembling the people in the morning, Williams helped carry two of the litters from the barn to the wagons. " 'Bout ten miles on, you'll come to a place that's got a single oak and two maple trees at the house. Reckon you'd be wise to stop for the night when you get over the rise and see the house about half a mile down the far slope. Or if you got time enough, keep goin' till you pass the next rise."

"I gather that we'd be unwelcome there?" David Lake inquired.

"Unwelcome ain't the word for it. Old man Harrison deserves what everyone says about him. He's mean, downright mean, and afraid he's going to be robbed blind. Wouldn't be surprised if he ain't sittin' near the road with his scatter gun. That man hasn't got no more kindness in his soul than a rock's got honey."

It was another week before the travelers met a white settler who showed them any kindness, but no one along the way came close to matching the hospitality offered by the Williams family.

In January they arrived at the bank of the Mississippi. Evan Jones knew that the blizzards they had trudged through in December would seem a minor inconvenience compared to what lay ahead. A bitter cold spell had set in. The Father of Waters was plugged with ice that was too soft to cross on foot but too solid to allow boats to make the crossing. With temperatures below zero, Jones ordered a camp set up. Soon his was joined by the Bushyhead and Foreman groups.

Bands of Cherokee spread out for miles searching the countryside for firewood. Blankets and canvas were stretched between wagons to provide protection from the howling wind. By the time a ferry crossing was possible at Cape Girardeau, five thousand people had bunched up in the camp. Many of the younger men were able to keep warm each day only by digging graves. For those who never completed the final three hundred miles of travel—for those who did—the route became known to everyone as Nunna da-ul Tsunyi, the Trail of Tears.

Chapter 27

Henry Warburton's gold teeth flashed as he smiled at his visitor. "I can fix you up with with just about anything you want, Mr. Lake. How many blankets?"

"How many can you get us today?" Leonard Lake asked. "Two thousand?"

Warburton choked. "Two thousand? I don't even know if there are that many in my warehouses here. I know I can get them from New Orleans, but it'll take time."

"We need them now," Lake said determinedly.

Warburton flipped the pages of an inventory ledger. "Let's see . . . blankets . . . oh, here we are! Blankets. I can provide you with eight hundred and seventeen."

"Pants?"

"Wool or cotton?"

"Wool. It's cold, Mr. Warburton."

Again Warburton flipped through the ledger. He had some seven hundred pairs of lightweight trousers, red or green, but fewer than a hundred of warm wool.

"Color makes no difference if you're freezing," Lake snapped.

Warburton felt a surge of relief. He'd bought the cotton trousers from a wholesaler in Baton Rouge who had counted on making a huge profit selling them to insurgent bands of Mexicans fighting Santa Anna. The end of that war had left him with a warehouse filled with trousers nobody wanted. Warburton had taken them off the wholesaler's hands for less than the cost of the raw materials. Now this Cherokee lawyer with the huge letter of credit from the Arkanasas Bank and Trust was willing to pay anything to clothe almost the last of the Indians passing through. Nothing like winding up a venture like this by making a sweet profit.

"What about boots, Mr. Warburton?"

"Boots I can't help you with. Brogans, yes. Let's see here . . . five hundred twenty pairs. That's all I've got left."

While Lake and Warburton began tallying the cost of the goods one of Warburton's clerks went back into the warehouse and brought samples of everything into the office. Lake picked up a pair of the red trousers, felt the material and examined the workmanship.

"Let's say we cut the price for these trousers by a third, shall we, Mr. Warburton?"

"Why?" They're perfectly good trousers. Maybe a little light for winter wear—I'm sorry about that, really am—but I can't lower the price any more."

"Whatever you say," Lake concurred. He dipped the pen into the ink and drew a neat line through the order for cotton trousers.

"You don't want them. Mr. Lake? It's cold, as you say—"

"That's right, and it'll be a lot colder before General Cardoza needs any more dress uniforms for his ragtag army."

Warburton swallowed hard. "Well, maybe I *could* lower the price. A third off, you say?"

"Mr. Warburton, these are the last large group of Indians you'll be seeing for a while. After these go through there will be fewer than three hundred, only the ones traveling with Chief Ross. Do you understand what I'm saying? And if you do, shall we lower your asking price by half?"

"Half? But that's—" Henry Warburton paused. Considering the amount of money he had made in the few short years that the Cherokee passed through Arkansas, he could afford to be generous. Why not cut the price in half? He'd still be making a decent profit. Besides, Lake looked serious about it.

"Agreed. How soon will your men be ready to load your wagons?"

"They're in the café across the street right now, having dinner. I'll have them here in an hour."

The four Cherokee in the restaurant had been coldly received. Had it not been for the intervention of Big Jim Daniels, the owner would have refused them service. Big Jim had been a reporter for the *Arkansas Gazette*, which was next door. He, along with John Parker, had written a number of articles on the Indian removal problem. Now that there were some Cherokee in Little Rock, he wasn't about to let them slip through his fingers without getting a story.

Only one of the Indians spoke English, and Daniels had a difficult time following him, but his pencil raced across the sheaf of paper as Moon-in-Morning told him of the hardships on the trail.

"Womens cry, mans cry, everybodys cry. Many many die. Every day we make graves. One day make grave for my father, next day grave for my wife. Two more days I carry baby in my arms. Then make grave for baby. That night make grave for my mother. Maybe we all die before we get to Indian Territory. But every days we march more to setting sun. Always we keep marching. Nobody smile. People say I look like never in my life I smile, never in my life I laugh. Moon-in-Morning once could laugh loud enough to shake trees."

Unbeknownst to Daniels, John Parker had returned to Little Rock only an hour before. For a reason even Parker himself didn't know, he had been reluctant to announce his presence, to say his final hellos and good-bys before he headed back to Fort Gibson. Despite spurts of cheerfulness, he had been melancholy lately. That had to do, he knew, with his memories of leaving New Echota—and Aggie—for whatever good reason he had seemed to have at the time.

Now, as he sat in an out-of-the-way corner of the same café where Daniels had interviewed Moon-in-Morning, an old drinking friend spotted him there and joined him.

"I didn't know whether we'd see you again, John," Jake Jorgensen commented, sitting down. "You sure don't look very happy to be here."

"I've been listening to that Indian talk to Daniels," Parker confessed. "I guess the talk and the sight of those Cherokee reminded me of my life in Georgia."

Jorgensen shrugged. Parker was silent.

Jake could not possibly have understood what he was feeling. He remembered how Little Tree had feared being thought a coward for signing up to emigrate. He had fought those same feelings himself. Finally he could admit that he was ashamed of having left.

Jorgensen's voice jolted him. "You look ready to cry, John. If you loved those Indians so much, maybe you should have stayed with them! Well, buddy, I've got to go. After this sparkling conversation I'd better go and drink a little sunshine to cheer myself."

Parker barely looked up. Just talking about what he had done made him feel sick. The Cherokee were coming through Little Rock now. How could he face the people he'd turned his back on? What if Little Tree should be on board one of the boats? Even worse, what if Aggie . . .

It's their affair, he told himself. It's their affair, not mine. He half-closed his eyes as he lied to himself once again.

Not leaving the café till dawn, Parker kept his mournful mood. He looked down toward the piers. Seeing a steamer smoking, he walked over to look at it, thinking of some of the large boats that had carried the Cherokee to Little Rock or past it.

Cherokee. My people, he thought. My people who had the strength and the courage I never had. And Little Tree thought *he* was a coward.

In the midst of wishing for some of the strength Little Tree and Aggie and Going Horse had shown him, Parker stopped dead in his tracks as he approached the steamboat *Victoria*. John Ross was walking ashore. He was leading several of his slaves, who were carrying a litter with a body wrapped for burial. As the procession neared, Ross looked up at Parker, still stalled, and his blue eyes twinkled only momentarily before he smiled thinly.

"*O-si-yo*, Tsani Parker." Ross indicated the litter. "My wife Quatie. She died near midnight last night." Later, Parker found he had taken a shovel from one of the slaves and was helping bury Quatie in the frozen soil. After recovering enough to lead the group in a brief prayer, Ross and Parker headed the procession to the steamboat. Reaching it, he grasped Parker's hand. "*Wadan, wadan*. Thank you, Tsani."

"Chief," Parker blurted, "I live near Fort Gibson

now, only came here to pick up a few things. I want to be with the Cherokee again." Parker hadn't realized it but the words were pouring out in the familiar old *Tsalagi.*

Ross laid a hand on Parker's shoulder. "We'll always have room for people who want to help us grow again." He looked over his shoulder at the steamboat and added, "We'll be getting under way in about an hour. You're welcome to come with us."

Parker never had a chance to answer. A pair of lips, warm and trembling sweet on this glorious, frosty morning, were smothering his face with kisses. "John! John! I thought I'd never see you again!"

Enfolding Aggie in his arms, Parker exulted in a joy he hadn't felt in years.

"Aggie!" he said again and again as they clung together. "We'll never say good-by again."

Chapter 28

Sam Worcester performed the wedding ceremony. According to Cherokee tradition, Parker's marriage to Aggie Lake made him a full member of the Cherokee Nation. David Lake readily gave his approval to the union. In fact, everyone seemed to approve—everyone, that is, except Cheowa, who removed himself from the celebration and grimly watched his sister leave the chapel with her new husband.

Little Tree and Martha had built an adequate cabin on the banks of the Illinois River near the little town of Park Hill. Soon they found themselves helping the Parkers to get themselves settled.

Fierce Bear was now officially part of the family. His parents had disappeared before the roundup began, and Aggie had simply adopted him as her own. When she married, Parker eagerly accepted Fierce Bear as his son, in keeping with Cherokee custom. Fierce Bear was fourteen and no longer considered a child; he was an adult member of the Nation.

Because John Parker had been officially adopted by David Lake, he enjoyed all the rights and privileges of any Cherokee man. The first time he attended a meeting of the provisional council, he was entitled to vote but hesitated, uncomfortable. Fierce Bear was more than ready to cast a vote and chided Parker for keeping silent. The boy was truly a man in the eyes of his people.

One of the first things Ross did after arriving at Fort Gibson was to make an official complaint to General Arbuckle about the quality of the food that the government had provided.

"The terms of the treaty state that we are to receive provisions for a period of one year in order that we may begin building up our lands. What you have given us is unfit for consumption!"

Arbuckle had been waiting for Ross. He had been warned by the War Department that Ross was going to be a troublemaker in the West as he had been in the East. Arbuckle had also been cautioned by John Ridge and Elias Boudinot. After Ross finished his list of complaints, Arbuckle assigned Major Ethan Allen Hardesty to investigate them and submit a report.

Hardesty accompanied Ross to the distribution center at Park Hill, which was quickly developing into a good-sized community. The contractor who had agreed to furnish the War Department foodstuffs had recognized a chance to make an easy profit.

"There, Major," Ross pointed out, leading Hardesty to the cattle pens. "Are those what you would call beef cattle?"

Hardesty's eyes needed only one glance at the small herd. "It would be fair to admit they were a poorly bunch, Mr. Ross."

"A poorly bunch, Major! Some of those animals can barely stand up! There isn't five hundred pounds of meat in the entire herd!"

"Justifiable complaint, Mr. Ross. What about the meat in the warehouse?"

"See for yourself," Ross invited, taking him there

and opening the door. The stench that hit Hardesty's nostrils was overpowering.

"Putrid!" Ross exclaimed.

Hardesty backed out and pushed the door shut. "All right. I agree. It's no better than carrion."

"We've only begun," Ross carried on. "Come and inspect the flour and corn. We haven't found a barrel of it yet that isn't infested with weevils or ants. And this garbage is what you expect my people to eat!"

Hardesty's report to General Arbuckle confirmed the rumors about the provisions and recommended that the contractor be held criminally liable for defrauding the government. Arbuckle transmitted the report to the War Department and Secretary Poinsett. Poinsett, in turn, sent the report to the Treasury Department, where it was read by an assistant secretary who advised that it be shelved and never be made public. Eventually, the assistant secretary received another cash payment from his close friend Henry Warburton, whose contracts to supply the provisions to the Cherokee Nation West ran for another two years.

While all the papers were shuffling around the departments, John Ross was able to purchase food with money that was slowly being sent at General Scott's authorization to defray the costs of removal. To the money that should have been paid before the Cherokee left their old homes Ross added some of his own, vowing that the Cherokee would make it on their own, without benefit of any government aid administered by Fort Gibson.

Little Tree and Parker, assisted by Going Horse and Fierce Bear, finished putting the roof on the Parker cabin. Then they sat back to enjoy a smoke.

"Not going to be big enough, Tsani," Little Tree

said critically. "You'll be adding another room inside of a year."

"It's twice the size of the one I lived in back in New Echota."

"Yes, but you didn't have a family there. Now you've got a wife, a son and a sister."

"Not a bad cabin, I'd say," Going Horse commented. "Maybe Catharine and I will move in with you. David's house is going to be crowded."

"Come ahead," Parker grinned. "I've got all the space you'll need," he said with a wide sweep of his arm, "to sleep out of doors!"

Parker remembered the fine mansion at Lakehurst and compared it with the modest six-room house Cheowa was building for his father about twenty miles away at Takatokah, near the council grounds. There was little money left to build anything larger. David Lake had received less than four thousand dollars for the "improvements" to his land near Spring Place, and those funds had been spent for provisions along the trail. Most of the securities he'd taken with him were now in the safe at the Arkansas Bank and Trust, pledged against the loans Leonard had negotiated.

As soon as Cheowa and Going Horse had arrived in Indian Territory, they'd traveled up along Honey Creek. There, Cheowa settled on a piece of ground about four miles from the Missouri border. As soon as their cabin had been built, their wives began planting a garden while the two men returned to the Park Hill area.

Going Horse chose to settle in a well watered valley not far from Park Hill. With the help of Catharine's slaves, he and Cheowa put up a substantial cabin for himself and his family, then spent a couple of weeks searching for the right place for David Lake. Fortunately no one else claimed the spot before David and Leonard Lake arrived. It was then that Cheowa began directing the construction of his father's new home.

The different sites had been chosen for dissimilar reasons. David Lake's land was perfectly suited to his goals. Soon he would be farming hundreds of acres again. His land was well watered and well drained and had timber of sufficient variety to provide building materials. There was enough open land that his property would not all have to be cleared before crops were set out. Much of it, Catharine had decided, reminded her a bit of home in the old country.

Going Horse selected his site for its proximity to his father-in-law; he would be close to his work of supervising the slaves in the fields.

Cheowa's home was almost a hundred miles away in the northern part of the Territory. Again, he had chosen to live remote from his father.

John Parker built close to Park Hill; Parker was not much farther from this print shop than he had been from the one in New Echota. Because Aggie would teach school as soon as Sam and Ann Worcester could begin one again, the Parkers claimed only enough land to set out a kitchen garden.

Cheowa and Going Horse harbored additional reasons for settling where they did. The Ridges had settled up along Honey Creek, almost within sight of Cheowa's cabin. And down in Park Hill, just a few minutes' walk from Going Horse's cabin, Elias Boudinot's new house was being laid out close to Sam Worcester's.

At every opportunity, Cheowa reminded Parker that he still considered him a worthless *unaka*. "You're not worthy of being a *Tsalagi*, Parker."

"I know, Cheowa. I haven't done much. I've only

married your sister. Your father has merely adopted me. I've simply become a father to the boy your sister adopted on the way out here. I cravenly left Little Rock after helping Chief Ross bury his wife to live here working with your people, with his blessings. I have no intention of registering with the Indian Agency to claim one cent of the annuities, so I can't be doing this for the money. I hardly ever speak English anymore. I even was treated to a couple of sore ribs at the ball play two weeks ago—Wheeler was pissed because he thought I'd busted a finger and couldn't set type. You're looking at the garden Aggie and I planted after the Purification Ceremony, according to custom. It sure must be a deep plot I'm hatching!"

Cheowa squatted on his heels and studied the fire. "Just being here and doing those things doesn't make you *Tsalagi*. All you look like to me is a white fool playing Indian. Why didn't you stay in Arkansas, Parker? You can get free land anywhere. Why must you live on the land that has been given to us? Why not live in the Dakotas, Nebraska, Texas? Personally," Cheowa added, burning a stare into Parker, "I think you're here for a free ride."

Parker slammed his fist against the cabin wall. "Damn it, Cheowa!" he shouted, "I'm here because this is where Aggie wants to be, and wherever she is, I'm going to stay! For your information, I like it here, and I work too hard to call it a free ride."

"Now that you've made your choice, Parker, you'll be wise to see that nothing happens to my sister. Because," Cheowa said, rising to his feet, "I'll tell you what I think, *unaka*. I think you'll turn and run as soon as things get hot again. And I don't think you're much of a man!"

"What do you think, Cheowa? That because I don't wear next to nothing and ram around threatening war with the whites, I'm a coward? That I don't like the Cherokee or understand you? That I'm lazy or greedy or a spy for Van Buren? No, Cheowa, you don't think any of that. You just don't like me. And what's more, I could a sight sooner do what you do than you could do what I do, and you must know it. But the fact that I don't choose to fight with my hands doesn't mean I can't fight at all."

"The question, Parker, is whether you will fight for us or against us when the time comes."

"I'd give my life for your people if I had to."

"So you say." Cheowa mounted his horse and glared down at Parker. "But you work for Elias Boudinot, *unaka!*"

"I'm working for Sam Worcester and the American Board of Foreign Missions. Elias happens to work for them, too."

Cheowa spat on the ground, missing Parker's feet only by inches. "We have wasted too much time in talk. I wish to get the boy from the garden. He has much to learn."

"About being a warrior?"

"About being *Tsalagi*. His father cannot teach him, so someone else must."

"What can I say, Cheowa? You are Fierce Bear's uncle. How long will you be gone this time?"

"Until the boy learns a few simple things you'll never learn. *Donadagohvi.*"

"Of course, see you later, esteemed brother of my wife!"

Cheowa almost smiled. "At least you've learned something, *unaka!*"

Sam Worcester was back at work with the man he considered absolutely essential to him. Although he had an excellent command of the Cherokee language, he would not trust his own translations of the Holy Scriptures; instead he relied on the judgment of Elias Boudinot. More often than not, Boudinot's few corrections were on minor points.

"I'll never master the language, Elias."

"You don't give yourself enough credit, Sam."

"But the verbs, they're impossible. Take the root of the verb that means to know. In English we can say, 'I know he is chopping wood.' In *Tsalagi* there are so many different forms. I know he is chopping wood because I see him doing it now. I know he is chopping wood because I saw him a few minutes ago and he was chopping then and has enough more to chop that he must still be chopping. I know he is chopping wood because I hear his ax even though I cannot see him. I know he is chopping wood because someone has told me he is chopping wood. I know he is chopping wood because this is the hour when he customarily chops wood. How can anyone ever learn all that and keep it straight, Elias?"

Henry Wheeler snorted, "Easy, Sam. Start all over and be born Cherokee. Either you speak the language from the cradle or you never speak it. I'm not about to waste my time trying. I leave the Cherokee columns to Parker and Candy. Me, I like the feel of good old English."

"You know what I heard in Boston, Sam?" Elias asked. "A very learned scholar told me that most Indians will never learn to speak English because they cannot grasp abstract concepts. But you forgot something when you were listing all the possible wood-chopping situations."

"What?"

Boudinot spoke a phrase of Cherokee that Parker immediately recognized, but the particular nuances were lost to him, and everyone else too, except Michael

Candy, who leaned against a table appearing quite amused.

"What does *that* mean?" Sam asked, his pencil ready.

"It means I know he is chopping wood because his woodbox is empty and his wife will beat him if she does not have wood in time to get supper and he is afraid of being beaten again by his wife because the woodbox is empty."

Michael Candy roared with laughter while Sam scratched his forehead, seriously considering whether Elias might not be pulling his leg again. "Elias, you don't know how happy I am that Saint Paul wasn't a wood-chopper," he said finally.

"But, Sam, think! The Lord Jesus was a carpenter! Can't you see how important it is to know everything about chopping wood?"

Sam groaned. "The chopping wood part wasn't even what concerned me; I was still worrying about the verb to know."

"Here's another good verb for you to work on, Sam: to worry. Think of the possibilities there!"

Parker was already worried. Cheowa had gone off, who knew where, with Fierce Bear, and they didn't return for nine days. Aggie wasn't particularly worried while they were gone, but Parker had been. When the boy returned, there was something different about him, a new politeness in his voice, nothing exaggerated, but Fierce Bear was just a shade more aloof. And there was something about his eyes. A coldness had found its way into them and now, Parker realized grimly, they had the same blank look as Cheowa's.

General Arbuckle sat in his office at Fort Gibson, reviewing the information he had on John Ross. Many of the reports held old, familiar items, forwarded to him long before Ross had arrived in Oklahoma. There were the detailed reports from the War Department, the Office of Indian Affairs, and those from the agent who had lived so long with the Cherokee. Cullen probably had accumulated more firsthand knowledge of John Ross than anyone outside of Washington, but Cullen, he had heard, had died somewhere in Missouri while accompanying one of the groups of immigrants.

There were the reports from Arbuckle's own intelligence agents, some white, some Cherokee. Most disturbing, though, were the conferences he had held with Treaty Party members who feared that Ross was going to manipulate Indian politics for his own purposes now that he was out west. Certainly, Arbuckle thought, Ross could be a tough one. And he didn't seem to care how many people he stirred up, so long as he got what he wanted.

The growing tension spreading throughout the territory had made Arbuckle apprehensive. What the Cherokee Nation had been through in the turbulent preremoval days seemed calm as a mountain lake compared to the storm-whipped ocean that was swirling now.

The old settlers, who had come out between 1808 and 1928, and the ones who had followed in small groups over the last ten years were understandably nervous. They were vastly outnumbered by those who had come at the point of a bayonet.

After building their homes, the old settlers had established a reasonably smooth system of government. There wasn't much trouble except when government payments began falling behind; then complaints about delays began to mushroom.

When the Treaty Party bunch came west, they cooperated with the government. They were able to bring

enough with them to get a good start on life here; the
government compensated them well for what they had
to leave behind, and few had been poor to begin with.
When they moved west, there was time as well as
resources to get well established before Ross began
moving his followers.

His followers, Arbuckle thought distastefully: destitute. Most of them didn't have even simple household
utensils, much less farm implements. He had seen
some of them using rocks to shape crude wooden
spoons and fashion rough bowls from clay they had
fired over open campfires.

The valleys were filling with crude shelters of all
kinds, while Ross' people were cutting timber for
homes that would provide more protection and comfort. Because of their lack of tools, it wasn't uncom-
mon for four or five families to wait days or weeks for
the use of an ax for only one day.

The trip had been devastating. Arbuckle was
proud that he'd never hypocritically suggested it had
been anything else. Close to twenty per cent of the Nation's sixteen thousand people had died before reaching
Oklahoma, and many had been so weakened by the
trip that months after settling in, they were still dying.

People who once had worn silk and satin turbans
and cloaks were now beginning to fashion crude coverings from the hides of animals. Housewives who had
been used to bartering eggs and vegetables for bolts of
gingham and calico were now teaching their daughters
how to spin and weave. Perhaps, Arbuckle thought, the
reverend Mr. Worcester had been correct in saying that
centuries of progress had been wiped out during the removal. "The Cherokee people are back to the Stone
Age, General," Worcester had shouted.

But the old settlers and the Treaty Party faction
couldn't be blamed for feeling that the Ross people

were going to overwhelm them. They looked to those already established like invading hordes of Mongols, and the old settlers demanded that Arbuckle do something about the newcomers.

Nothing could be done, though, Arbuckle knew. His spies had reported that in record time, Ross had built a fine home in Park Hill almost directly across the creek from Reverend Worcester's house and chapel. In response to complaints from Treaty Party members that the Ross domicile was a hotbed of intrigue and drunken revelry, he had sent Major Hardesty to investigate. Hardesty had returned with a report indicating that Ross and his followers were doing nothing more than building houses, clearing land, erecting fences and planting gardens and field crops. And, Hardesty concluded, the meetings at Ross' home weren't exactly subversive. Nothing more sinister was being discussed than how to prevent the sale of whiskey to Indians.

Thank heavens the old-timers weren't fearing Ross as much as the Treaty supporters were. Oh, they were concerned about how to assimilate another twelve or fourteen thousand people in their midst, but as far as Ross himself was concerned, they would wait and see.

"Wait and see," Arbuckle said out loud. That was all he could do, too. And it wouldn't take long to find out what would happen. In June, the council that Ross had planned to hold at Takatokah would finally meet.

Elias Boudinot was waiting to see Arbuckle again. He had made an early-morning twelve-mile ride from Park Hill before the sun's heat became unbearable. But Boudinot, like Arbuckle, was unaware that two other Indians had made the ride that morning while Boudinot waited to see the general and were inquiring about an alleged missing neighbor.

"What was that name again?" the lieutenant asked.

"Beaver Tail, from Turkey Town in Alabama."

The lieutenant checked his lists. "Don't have anybody by that name. You might try again in a couple of weeks. The stragglers will be coming in for months, I suppose."

"Thank you, Lieutenant," the older Indian said, and both men returned to their horses.

When they had ridden a considerable distance from the fort, the pair pulled off the road and tethered their mounts well back in the brush.

"What do we do now, Going Horse?"

"We wait, Fierce Bear. We wait."

Chapter 29

When John Ross suggested holding a general council at the Takatokah campgrounds for the purpose of establishing friendlier ties between the two branches of the Nation, the Western chiefs readily agreed. Everyone in the Nation was invited to attend. During the first week of June, the campgrounds a few miles north of Park Hill were packed with more than six thousand Cherokee. They spent a week getting to know one another, in some cases renewing friendships with neighbors they had not seen in twenty years.

During the middle of that week, Boudinot and the Ridges showed up to greet some of the late arrivals of the Treaty Party, as well as meet with the leading chiefs of the Western Nation.

"How about that?" Cheowa observed. "They don't even have the courtesy of walking another fifty feet to to say hello to George Lowrey."

"Maybe they think they're smart," Fierce Bear said wryly.

Whatever their motives, Boudinot and the Ridges hurriedly left the grounds.

"They weren't even here fifteen minutes," Cheowa estimated. "Maybe they can tell how most of the people here feel about them."

The Takatokah council provided much opportunity for oratory. Those attending heard congratulatory speeches, welcoming speeches, encouraging speeches from some who hadn't demonstrated the eloquence of their rhetoric on strangers in many years.

Chief Brown of the Western Nation set the tone of the council when in one breath he welcomed the newcomers and in the next reminded them that western laws had already been established and leaders elected. The newcomers, however, would be welcome to vote (sometime in the future) and even to hold office (if they could get elected).

John Ross and George Lowrey took the wind out of Brown's sails by calling for a new government. According to their resolutions, equal numbers of representatives from both branches would be charged with drafting a new constitution that would be submitted to the people for their consideration and approval.

Chief Brown, Mooney and Rogers reminded Ross and Lowrey that a council had been called for the purpose of establishing unity between the branches.

"Hasn't that already been accomplished, gentlemen?" the westerners smiled. "And, if so, what is to be gained by submitting anything to the people?"

The delegates agreed to discuss the matter further. The meeting would be on the first of July, after tempers had had time to cool.

John Parker was walking home shortly after dark that same evening when Fierce Bear breathlessly ran to him. "Father, Little Tree wants to see you."

"Well then, you'll have to take me to him, Fierce Bear. I know he hasn't gone home yet."

He followed the youngster into the woods. Two miles from the campgrounds, they came to a clearing. Several hundred Cherokee men were gathered silently around a fire in the center of it. One low whistle from Fierce Bear, and Cheowa left the group and came to Parker. Little Tree and Going Horse flanked him.

"This, *unaka*, is your opportunity to prove whether you are one of us or not," Cheowa declared. "We have talked long and hard about you."

"Are you one of us?" Going Horse demanded.

"Of course I am," Parker averred, "but what do I have to do to prove it?"

"Ride with us, Tsani," Little Horse invited. "Tonight is the night Elias and the Ridges are going to pay for their treason."

"You're asking me to help you kill them?"

"Not asking you, Parker," Cheowa said coldly. "Telling you. If you are one of us, you ride with us. If not, you will die here, and the Nation will be rid of another worthless *unaka*."

Chapter 30

The only faces Parker could recognize were those of Little Tree, Cheowa, Going Horse and Fierce Bear. The rest of the Indians had either painted their faces black or wore black masks.

Someone handed Cheowa a clay pot. He dipped his fingers deeply into it before passing the pot to Going Horse. After Going Horse and Little Tree had smeared their faces and chests with the paint, Fierce Bear held the pot out for Parker. Without hesitating or speaking, Parker smeared his own face and neck as the others had smeared theirs.

If his face betrayed his stark terror, Parker was relieved that none of the others seemed to notice. Without saying a word, Cheowa handed Parker a black hatchet. Then Little Tree passed him a knife in a beaded sheath.

The knots in Parker's stomach tightened as he watched a cavalry hat passed silently around the group. Each black-clad man drew out a slip of paper bearing in dark ink the number 1, 2, 3 or 0. Those who drew zeros silently slipped out of the meeting area on foot or horseback. The threes gathered to one side, while the twos and ones crowded around Cheowa.

"You're a one, Tsani," Little Tree murmured. "We ride with Cheowa."

"But I didn't take a number."

"We voted before I came for you, Father," Fierce Bear explained. They mounted and began riding slowly northward along a trail Parker couldn't recognize in the dark.

"Before the meeting, we elected the chiefs for each team," Going Horse began. "Cheowa will take John Ridge. Someone else has The Ridge for his target, and still another of us will have the honor of killing Boudinot."

"We chose our chiefs while we were still in the old country," Little Horse added. "Since then, we have waited."

Leaving Park Hill and Takatokah well behind them, two groups numbering four men each rode east through the valleys to the Arkansas border. Parker's heart pounded as they moved closer and closer to Honey Creek and the homes of their victims.

The twos split off and headed for the home of The Ridge while dawn was still an hour away. In the dimness, Parker recognized Cheowa's cabin, and then a short distance away, the home of John Ridge. Slowing his followers to a walk, Cheowa gave them the signal to dismount. They left the horses near the trees, where one man remained behind to hold the reins and keep the mounts still.

As Parker slid to the ground, he imagined that the noise they made sounded like thunder and wondered why no one accosted them. His throat was dry. He felt his hand shake as he pulled the knife from its sheath. He didn't know whether he would have the strength to do what he'd been told he had to do.

When the group reached the yard, Cheowa raised his hand. The men stopped, pulling back as Cheowa and two others crossed the porch and laid their shoulders against the door.

The scream of Sarah Ridge split the night. Parker felt his body jerk. A moment later, Cheowa and his party dragged John Ridge into the yard, kicking and shrieking against what he knew was happening, against what he had long known must happen.

"Now!" Going Horse shouted. The second group stepped forward.

Parker's knuckles cracked as his hand clenched the tomahawk. He took a step forward.

Suddenly powerful hands clamped around his arms. He felt the hatchet being pried from his fingers. Other hands took his knife. He tried to look around to see his captors, but the hand that was clamped so hard across his mouth kept his head immobile.

Only a few feet from him, Cheowa and his band hacked and stabbed the helpless John Ridge while his wife and their half-breed children looked on. After what seemed like hours, the attack was over. Ridge's body quivered and then lay still. As his family wailed, the raiders released them to sob hysterically and fall to the ground, and each assailant solemnly stomped on Ridge's bloody chest.

The Indians showed no haste to leave. Cheowa and his men calmly returned to their horses with Parker in tow and began the trip back to Park Hill. Every few miles along the way, first one rider, then another quietly separated himself from the group.

It was well after daylight when the remainder of the attack party rode down to a creek and washed off the black paint, sweat and blood. The return trip had been silent to that point; Parker would not have trusted himself to utter a sound. But after they had finished washing, Cheowa laid a hand on Fierce Bear's shoulder.

"I congratulate you, son of my sister. You have earned the right to the proud title *Utsodihi*, Man-Killer, though it will never be spoken openly."

He turned to Parker. "It is time for you to get drunk, *unaka*."

"What are you talking about, Cheowa? I don't drink; you know that."

"You're going to be a drinker now," Going Horse contradicted. "How else would we explain to people who ask where we were all night? You see, you had a very important part to play in this operation."

Little Tree stayed behind with Parker while his relatives took seldom-used trails to their homes. "No better time to get started than now." He lifted a stone jug from its hiding place.

Parker felt the liquor burn his throat. After the second swallow, the whiskey and the terror he still hadn't shaken off made him retch until he ached all over.

"We had to have you with us, Tsani," Little Tree gloomily apologized while Parker knelt and vomited. "Going Horse and I agreed to let Cheowa test you, but only when he promised you wouldn't have to take part in what we did or risk getting hurt."

"You mean you had planned to hold me back all along?"

"That's right," Little Tree admitted sheepishly, "since the day you married Aggie. But you did well, Tsani."

"How, my tricky friend, does one 'do well' watching another man being butchered in front of his family? Somehow, I don't feel much like thanking you for the compliment. Even knowing that what you did was justice under Cherokee law, and doesn't make you an evil man, I won't hide the fact that I'm feeling that way about myself. Probably someday I'll know for sure

I'm not a monster, but right now I feel pretty dirty. Anyway"—Parker pulled himself together—"Cheowa still doesn't think much of me. That's easy to see."

"What makes you think he doesn't?"

"He called me *unaka* again back there, didn't he? And you know what Cheowa thinks of them!"

Chapter 31

The band heading toward Arkansas had correctly predicted that The Ridge would not be at home when they rode in. News of the assassinations had spread across the Nation as fast as a prairie fire.

A messenger had been dispatched to warn him, but The Ridge was already riding south, heading for Van Buren or Fort Smith—no one was sure. The courier who came upon his body sprawled across the north-south highway that ran along the Oklahoma and Arkansas border reported he had been shot five times, apparently from ambush.

It was shortly after dawn that same morning that Elias was directing the work of carpenters who were building his new home. Four men approached him.

"Excuse me. Our families are badly in need of some medical supplies. Someone told us that Sam Worcester might have what we want. Could you take us to his home?" The man asking the favor smiled broadly.

"Of course, gentlemen," Boudinot replied, excusing himself from the carpenters and turning to lead the four men the short distance. "I'll be glad to speak to Sam for you." He had taken only two steps when the stranger who'd first spoken took a quick step forward and thrust a knife deeply into his back, barely missing the spine. Boudinot staggered forward screaming. Sam Worcester and Delight Boudinot ran outdoors and across the wide yard toward him as another of the strangers chopped at his head with a tomahawk. After several blows, there was little left to mangle, and by the time Worcester got to his side, Boudinot was dead.

The four assassins fled the short distance to the woods, where they joined a small band of armed men on horseback and escaped without being recognized.

News of the carnage reached John Ross minutes later. But by the time he could send a messenger from his home to advise General Arbuckle at Fort Gibson of what had taken place, he also heard that Stand Watie was already raising a band of men to avenge the deaths of his brother and his cousin.

In his message to Arbuckle, Ross urged the general to provide him with protection. "I had no knowledge of the plan," Ross wrote. "I see no reason why I should be murdered as a consequence of it." Arbuckle felt differently.

"Go over there and tell that old curmudgeon I want to see him in this office immediately," Arbuckle ordered Major Hardesty. "Even if that Indian didn't raise a tomahawk himself, you'll never convince me he's not responsible for what happened."

Hardesty agreed to carry the message. "But I'm going alone," he told the general. "The way the Indians are feeling now, even a detail of four would arouse suspicion and might be considered aggressive. The entire fort could be taken over if some warriors got angry enough."

Hadesty found Ross' home in Park Hill surrounded by several hundred armed guards. Only after he had surrendered his saber and pistol would they permit him to approach the house.

Ross declined Arbuckle's invitation to go to Fort Gibson and discuss the violence. "What happened is a problem that concerns only the Cherokee people, Major. It is somthing we will work out ourselves without interference from Fort Gibson."

"Mr. Ross, General Arbuckle is concerned that the Eastern and Western Nations will be involved in a civil war. And may I remind you that you only recently sent a message asking for protection? Supplying that protection would also be interference, would it not?"

"Not in the same sense, Major. Besides you need me to keep the peace. Yesterday we formed the basis of an agreement by which we could sit in peace and discuss the formation of a unified Cherokee Nation. The executions were the result of pent-up hatred. Now that those responsible for our betrayal have paid the penalty prescribed by tribal custom, tempers will cool. By the time we reconvene the Council, we shall be able to work out our differences."

Two more visitors were ushered in. Hardesty knew both of them. The hulking giant was George Lowrey and the small, lame man was Sequoyah. He hadn't met them personally before, so Ross introduced them.

"Chief Lowrey is acting as president *pro tem* of the Eastern Cherokee, Major. Sequoyah is president *pro tem* of the Western Nation."

"Gentlemen," Hardesty pleaded, "I strongly urge you not to go ahead with your July 1 council meeting."

"It has already been called," Lowrey replied firmly. "It shall be held."

"I know I speak for General Arbuckle when I tell you that serious consequences could result from your decision."

A weary smile spread across Sequoyah's long, thin

face. "Nobody is more aware of the seriousness of the council than we, Major. But we will hold the meeting."

Parker made his way through the several thousand Indians still camped north of Park Hill. He stopped briefly to exchange words here and there with people who were buzzing with news of the assassinations. Opinions differed. Some Cherokee were angered by the deed, others openly pleased. And there were many—the majority, Parker felt—who stoically accepted what had happened as a fact of life as certain as the rising of the sun.

Parker was repulsed by the sight of Boudinot's blood still staining the street. Cheowa had been smart, he thought, not to involve him with Boudinot's death. Parker had worked too long with Elias to have been able to participate actively in his murder. Despite any differences between them, Elias Boudinot had been a friend.

Aggie was hanging wash on the line when he got to the cabin. "Johnny! Where have you been? I was so worried . . ."

She pulled back, reeling from a whiff of his breath. "My God! You've been drinking." Aggie almost began to laugh, the idea of it seemed so ridiculous, but the guilty look on Parker's face stopped her.

"I don't drink very often," Parker began. "Maybe once a year. But when I do start sloshing, I get stinking."

"You stink, all right. Get out of those filthy clothes and take a bath. We need to go see Sam."

While Parker was bathing in the creek, Fierce Bear walked down and balanced himself on a rock near the edge of the water. The youth's face was worried.

"Father. I . . ." He faltered. "I want to know if you will help me."

"Help you with what?"

"I need to build a pen for a pig."

"What pig? We don't have any pigs."

"We do now. I made a bet about last night. You helped me win."

Parker didn't know whether to laugh or cry. "I have to confess that while I am proud of you, we both once respected the dead men." He paused, as if not yet decided whether he wanted to say more. After a moment his lips flickered into a smile.

"Anyway, I'm surprised that Little Horse would bet his only pig on me—the bet was with Little Horse, wasn't it?"

"Yes, and Little Horse now will have three pigs, thanks to you. And we will have one."

"Who—?"

"Uncle Cheowa. He bet each of us. And since he only has two pigs, he'll bring ours in two days and owe one to Little Horse."

Parker lay back in the water and laughed. "No wonder he's still calling me *unaka!*"

Sam Worcester was still in a daze. Having buried Elias, he felt he had cut off his right hand. "And I don't know of anyone else who can give me that kind of help with my translations. Elias and I worked together so long."

"What are we going to do about the print shop?" Michael Candy asked.

"I'd like to see you carry on," Worcester replied, "that is, if you can."

"Doesn't anybody know where Wheeler's gone?" Parker asked.

"No. He was out of town less than an hour after

the attack. Someone told me he went to Fort Gibson, but I don't really know. My gut feeling is that he won't be back."

Parker and Candy sighed, looking around the print shop. Boudinot's death was going to postpone the resurrection of the newspaper, they knew that, but on the positive side there were all the religious tracts to be printed, also the almanac pages that had already been set and readied for the press. So even though there was no leadership, there was plenty of work.

"It's my opinion," Worcester concluded, "that you men should stay with the operation, at least until the Mission Board decides what the next step should be."

Two days later, an army lieutenant came to the print shop and asked for John Parker.

"I'm John Parker."

"We'd like you to come with us, Mr. Parker. General Arbuckle would like to ask you a few questions about the murders."

Chapter 32

Major Hardesty and General Arbuckle maintained that the assassinations were not strictly a Cherokee affair. "The fact of the matter is," Arbuckle argued, "it became a concern for the United States the moment the murderers crossed the border and left Indian Territory. Major Ridge may have been Cherokee, but he was murdered on United States soil. That makes it our business."

"Why bring me here to tell me that, General?"

"Mr. Parker," Hardesty began guardedly, little beads of perspiration gathering on his forehead, "you're a white man. You—"

"You're mistaken, Major. I'm a member of the Cherokee Nation."

"You're still white," Arbuckle snapped.

"That's only my complexion, General. I left the United States willingly, and this is my home. My allegiance lies here."

And of which political affiliation are you a member?"

"Why should that make any difference?"

"It will surely make a difference if tribal warfare breaks out, Mr. Parker. I'm afraid you don't realize the gravity of your situation. The obvious assumption would be that you support Mr. Ross; after all, you arrived with him. But you used to work for Mr. Boudinot. Do you realize where that leaves you? You could be held suspect by both groups."

"Perhaps, General, but I doubt very much that I am."

"You seem quite sure of yourself," Hardesty commented. "I wonder why. Perhaps you are privy to information unknown to us."

"Do you suspect that I have any idea who made the attacks? Is that why you brought me here?"

"No, Mr. Parker. But it's true that you could be of some use to us."

"How, General?"

"Mr. Parker, there are problems everywhere. We need many eyes and ears. You could well be in a position to help us."

"You want me to be a spy?"

"That's a rather harsh term, Mr. Parker," Arbuckle frowned. "But we would be grateful for any knowledge you could pick up and pass on to us."

"I'm in no position to gather anything of value. I'm a printer. And right now I don't have any idea how much longer I'll have a job. We don't have a newspaper now, so about the only information that finds its way into the shop is about the leaflets, all of which I'm sure you've seen. And if you think there's anything clandestine going on, I'm sure Dr. Worcester will be more than happy to have you drop in and see for yourself what we do."

"Mr. Parker," Hardesty asked, sounding quite official, "where were you the night the murders took place? You were absent from your home until the following afternoon." Hardesty's face betrayed nothing, but Parker knew they had finally gotten down to the reason why he had been brought in.

"I was sleeping off a hangover out in the woods."

"You've been known as a man of very temperate habits, Mr. Parker. In New Echota, during all the years you worked there, you were never known to overindulge. It's difficult to believe that you would begin doing it now."

"Do you keep records on everybody, Major?" Parker asked, taking the offensive.

"Only in sensitive situations. You remember Mr. Cullen, the Indian agent?"

"Very well. He was a good man. I suppose he sent the War Department a notice every time I took a drink of whiskey and every time I pissed on a rock. What was he, an Indian agent or a War Department spy?"

"No need to get upset, Mr. Parker," Arbuckle said. "Mr. Cullen's reports on the situation in New Echota contained a great deal of praise for you. All we're trying to do here is help you establish an alibi for a crime and an explanation for an act that is so unlike what we know of you. Another fact that confuses matters even more is that there was no evidence of drunkenness anywhere else on the council grounds either that day or the following evening."

"I think you do need better spies, General."

"What do you mean by that?"

"It's obvious that your observers were stationed near the council meeting. And certainly, spies were circulating among the onlookers, too. That's why I'm astounded that you're not aware how much drinking there really was at the close of the council."

Hardesty and Arbuckle exchanged a quizzical glance.

"There was plenty of it," Parker went on, inwardly amazed at his ability to lie. "For a while it looked as though there was no chance that the old settlers and the late arrivals would sit down to work things out. Then at the last minute, Sequoyah and Lowrey saved the day. Everyone was in a celebrating mood, so as might be expected, the jugs started getting passed around. I don't drink very much, General, or very often—you're right about that—so by the time I had a couple I was sort of feeling it, and I wandered into the woods, where a couple of us finished off what was left. When I woke up the next afternoon, there were two men and a woman with me. They were still out cold when I came back into town and heard about the killings."

"From what you say, there was much more whiskey on the campgrounds than we had imagined."

"Not so, Major Hardesty. Only that there was too much for a couple of us to handle. I have to be honest with you, though," Parker added. "Liquor is always available if you know where to look for it."

"You know where it's coming from?" Hardesty asked gravely.

"Sure. Everybody knows. The Indians buy it from your soldiers."

The July council lasted nearly two weeks and helped heal the split between the two branches of the Nation. It was agreed that the new Cherokee land would be known as the Western Nation and the official Act of Union was signed by Sequoyah and Lowrey along with fifteen eastern and sixteen western delegates. The centrally located council grounds north of Park Hill were to become the capital. The name New Echota carried so many unhappy memories that the new capital was to be called Tahlequah, the Cherokee spelling of Tellico, where the first Indian agency in the Nation had been opened by Benjamin Hawkins in Tennessee.

A council was called for September sixth for the purpose of working out the details of a new constitution and electing leaders. On September first, Arbuckle filed a message he had received from Charles Madden, Chief Clerk in the Office of Indian Affairs at the War Department. "In the event John Ross should return to power," Madden had written at the conclusion of the letter, "we are prepared to send an agent who is perhaps more capable of dealing with the charlatan. While it is not within the jurisdiction of the commissioner to approve or disapprove of internal affairs of the various tribes, he felt you should be apprised of the cunning of Mr. Ross."

As he dropped the letter into the wooden file and shoved the drawer closed, Arbuckle allowed himself a weary sigh. "And he thinks I need to be 'apprised' of the cunning of Mr. Ross? He doesn't have to deal with the old scoundrel on a daily basis."

During the Tahlequah council, which ran for over a month, John Ross was overwhelmingly elected principal chief, and David Vann of the Western Nation was elected assistant chief. Arbuckle was no more surprised than anyone else. But he was being pressured by the War Department to bring to justice the murderers who had invaded United States territory to kill Major Ridge.

Chapter 33

Parker left the shop and walked the few blocks to the school. It was a building any community could be proud of. As far as that went, Park Hill itself was a community any nation could be proud of. Like Tahlequah, it had grown in the six years since the reunion of the Nation.

New homes were going up, most of them substantial houses, not the shanties and wooden-chimneyed cabins that had once clustered together where roads and trails crossed. Now there were stores whose shelves were filled with goods from St. Louis and New Orleans. Well tended fields bore healthy crops.

Parker looked across the creek to John Ross' home. It was smaller than his old home at Head of Coosa, but just as splendid in its own way, with fruit trees and flower beds meticulously tended by his slaves.

The last six years had been turbulent, but now the Cherokee, his people, seemed ready to carry the Nation forward and regain the momentum it had lost. Even thirty-odd more political assassinations hadn't stopped negotiations, nor President James Polk's threat permanently to divide the territory and to set border guards between the sections to prevent raids.

Parker thought back. It had been only the year before that Ross and Lowrey had been able to negotiate a treaty in Washington that brought the old settlers, the Treaty Party and the late emigrants solidly together for the first time.

Ross had pulled off another of his magic feats for that treaty, Parker remembered with a chuckle. In exchange for all three parties' settling their differences and agreeing that all the land belonged to all the Cherokee, Ross had been able to squeeze the Senate for money that had not been paid for land surrendered in the East. When the delegation came back from Washington, the Cherokee Nation was five million dollars richer, and after years of struggle and distrust, Ross and Stand Watie were at last able to shake hands.

"*O-si-yo*, Tsani!" Little Tree hailed. "You going to be in the game tomorrow?"

"Wouldn't miss it!"

"You'll be playing against Cheowa and Fierce Bear. Did you know that?"

"And they'll be playing against us. What about Going Horse?"

"Haven't seen him. Since David died, he's been pretty busy around the place."

Aggie came out of the schoolhouse behind the mob of screaming children. She looked tired, Parker thought, but who wouldn't after being with eighteen kids all day?

He gave her a kiss on the cheek. "I suppose you're getting your bets lined up for tomorrow," she said wryly.

"Haven't considered any bets, Aggie," Little Tree said straight-faced.

"Who would want to bet against us?" Parker joked. "Would you bet against your own husband?"

"Only if he was playing against my brother. The pig again, Little Tree?" she asked.

"What about some chickens?"

"Not a chance. Just the pig. And if some miracle happens and you win, you won't get it for another month."

"No fair," Little Tree argued. "I get the pig and everything in her." He tossed his head back, laughing. "Last time she had a litter you owned her, Aggie. If I win, this time the litter is mine. Besides, the pig we're talking about is the one I lost originally to Fierce Bear." He hesitated. "At least I think so. Oh, I don't know. That pig's traveled back and forth so much, who knows who she belongs to?"

"Right now," Parker asserted, "she's Aggie's pig. And if Fierce Bear sees you win her again—"

"Why didn't you tell me our son is going to be playing, too? Little Tree, is Fierce Bear going to be playing with Cheowa?"

"That's what he said."

"Fine. Then I've changed my mind. Make that bet the pig with the litter and five chickens."

Little Tree gulped. "You think they can really beat us?"

"The pig, the litter and five chickens!"

"Tsani, you married a loose woman," Little Tree kidded. "She gambles her worldly goods with her neighbors." Then to Aggie, "You've got a bet."

Little Tree took the path to his cabin and Aggie and Parker walked up the hill to the cemetery, as they did every afternoon. They stood first at David Lake's grave, then at Sam Worcester's.

"It was almost like a prophecy, Johnny, the way Sam went so fast."

"I know. Sam said after Elias died that he wanted nothing more in life than to see the newspaper started up again. And that's what he saw."

William Ross, the chief's son who had been at

Princeton during removal, returned to the Nation and took over Elias Boudinot's chore of helping Worcester with his translations of the Bible. After the Nation had received the money for eastern lands, Ross was appointed editor. Two days after the *Cherokee Advocate* published its first edition, Sam Worcester died.

"There aren't many New Englanders left, are there, Johnny?"

He shook his head. "But schools are opening up everywhere. The big difference is that now almost all of them are staffed with Cherokee teachers."

"Well, we're growing again, aren't we? At least, we're beginning to . . ."

"Yup, we sure are," he said, placing his hand on Aggie's swollen belly.

"Aggie," he said, changing the subject, "do you really think that was a wise bet you made with Little Tree?"

"A very wise bet, my love. I've watched you play before. Besides, Fierce Bear in in tiptop shape and everything he knows about ball play he learned from Cheowa."

He's learned a lot more besides, Parker thought.

The game didn't last an hour. Park Hill scored its ten points before Honey Creek made five. Little Tree gloated at the thought of acquiring a pregnant sow, even if it did cost him a broken nose in the process. Cheowa limped across the muddy playing field.

"You don't play too well with a broken leg, do you, *unaka*?" he asked, looking down on Parker at the sidelines.

"You tripped me on purpose!" Parker accused him.

"Am I supposed to think you gouged me by accident?" the Indian snarled in return, wiping blood from a gash behind his ear.

"I thought that's where the ball was."

"One of these days, *unaka*—"

"Oh, will you two stop!" Aggie snapped. "I'm tired of hearing you at each other all the time."

"Mother," Fierce Bear implored, "you go home and get supper. We'll take care of Father's leg."

"Nobody's going to take care of his leg but me."

"Go home," Cheowa said gently. "I don't want you to hear the coward scream when we set the bone."

Reluctantly, Aggie cut across the soggy field; it was futile to argue with all four of them. When she was out of sight, Little Tree and Fierce Bear lifted Parker and carried him through the woods to the edge of the stream where they had gathered with hundreds of others six years earlier. It was a place they had returned to often in the years since then. Now only Going Horse was absent.

"Ready?" Cheowa asked.

"Ready." Parker clenched his teeth.

Little Horse and Fierce Bear took hold of Parker by the waist, and Cheowa held the ankle with one hand as he felt along the shin with the other.

"Same place," he muttered, then gave a deft twist and sharp yank. The broken bone made a loud snapping sound as it slipped back into place. In only a few minutes a splint was in place on it and Parker was propped up against a tree.

"How'd I do?"

"Better, *unaka*," Cheowa grunted. "But you look like you hurt."

"Of course I hurt!"

Cheowa looked disappointed and Little Tree taunted, "You'll never be a real *Tsalagi* if you can't learn to keep a straight face when we set that leg."

"How many times is it now, Father?" Fierce Bear asked. "Three times or four?"

"Four."

"Why don't you give up?" Cheowa grunted. "One of these days your leg isn't going to heal if you keep breaking it in the same place. Why don't you try breaking the other leg once in a while?"

"I happen to like the feel of this one being broken," Parker joked grimacing. "It reminds me of old times!"

Little Tree reached inside the hollow log and brought out the jug of whiskey. One by one they passed it around, each man taking one swallow. When Parker passed the whiskey to Cheowa, the Indian asked, "You sure one slug is enough for you?"

"It'll do," Parker replied. He stuck the jug back into the log and lit the pipe that was always shared among them when they came together at this spot. After taking a couple of puffs, he passed it to Cheowa.

"Thanks, Brother," Cheowa said, then puffed.

"Uncle Cheowa, are you and Father going to keep deceiving Mother forever?" Fierce Bear questioned. "Shouldn't she know that you don't hate each other any more—since that night?"

"Do you want to explain it to her?" Little Tree asked.

Fierce Bear played with that idea for a moment, then shook his head. "That wouldn't be very smart, would it?"

"No, Man-Killer, it wouldn't," Little Tree agreed.

Cheowa playfully slapped Fierce Bear on the shoulder. "Some days, young man, you're as dumb as that *unaka* father of yours."

"Shut up, Cheowa. Pass me the pipe."

A written response to the Indian Removal Act that was sent to United States President Andrew Jackson in 1830 by Speckled Snake of the Cherokee Nation.

Brothers! We have heard the talk of our great father; it is very kind. He says he loves his red children. Brothers! When the white man first came to these shores, the Muscogees gave him land, and kindled him a fire to make him comfortable; and when the pale faces of the south made war on him, their young men drew the tomahawk, and protected his head from the scalping knife. But when the white man had warmed himself before the Indian's fire, and filled himself with the Indian's hominy, he became very large; he stopped not for the mountain tops, and his feet covered the plains and the valleys. His hands grasped the eastern and western sea. Then he became our greater father. He loved his red children; but he said, "You must move a little farther, lest I should, by accident, tread on you." With one foot he pushed the red man over the Oconee, and with the other he trampled down the graves of his fathers. But our great father still loved his red children, and soon made them another talk. He said much; but it all meant nothing, but "move a little farther; you are too near me." I have heard a great many talks from our great father, and they all began and ended the same. Brothers! When he made us a talk on a former occasion, he said, "Get a little farther; go beyond the Oconee and the Oakmulgee; there is a pleasant country." He also said, "It shall be yours forever." Now he says, "The land you live on is not yours; go beyond the Mississippi; there is game; there you may remain while the grass grows or the water runs." Brothers! Will not our great father come there also? He loves the red children, and his tongue is not forked.